T0097781

MEN WITH BROOMS

Paul Gross Molly Parker and Leslie Nielsen

MEN WITH BROOMS

A Sweeping Epic

DIANE BAKER MASON
Based on the sreenplay by Paul Gross and John Krizanc

McArthur & Company
Toronto

Published in Canada in 2002 by
McArthur & Company
322 King Street West, Suite 402
Toronto, ON M5V 1J2

National Library of Canada Cataloguing in Publication Data

Mason, Diane Baker
  Men with brooms : a sweeping epic

Based on original screenplay by Paul Gross and John Krizanc.

ISBN 1-55278-263-8

  I. Gross, Paul II. Krizanc, John III. Title.

PS8576.A79537M44 2002   C813'.6   C2002-900443-8
PR9199.4.M38M44 2002

Design & Composition: *Mad Dog Design Connection Inc.*
Cover Art: *Mad Dog Design Connection Inc.*
Cover Photo: *Michael Gibson*
Printed in Canada by *Transcontinental Printing Inc.*

The publisher would like to acknowledge the financial support of the
Government of Canada through the Book Publishing Industry
Development Program (BPIDP) and the Canada Council for our publishing activities. The publisher further wishes to acknowledge the financial
support of the Ontario Arts Council for our publishing program.

10 9 8 7 6 5 4 3 2 1

A BRIEF HISTORY OF CURLING WHICH IS NOT OBLIGATORY READING BUT WHICH MAY SERVE AS A BACKGROUND FOR THE BEHAVIOR OF OUR HEROES AND FOR THE EVENTS THAT UNFOLD IN THE COURSE OF THEIR STORY

Once upon a time, there was a very cold country full of rocks. One particular province of this country, known as the Province of Ontario in the Dominion of Canada, was simply chock full of cold and rocks. The rocks, being rocks, didn't mind the cold. They just carried on, being rocks, until someone (an immigrant from a not-quite-so-cold but just as full of rocks place called Scotland) disturbed their peace.

Canada has never been quite the same.

The aforementioned peace of the poor rocks was disturbed by the importation of a game. This game involved three elements one would not normally find in the same field of reference: a frozen lake, a spherical rock sliding across said lake, and brooms. The object of the game is to throw the rock and see if it will hit a target painted on the ice in red and blue. To encourage the rock, which no doubt would have preferred to be left alone enjoying being a rock, men with brooms run in front of the wildly spinning and possibly nauseous rock, sweeping the path of its progress clean. They sweep like deranged housewives, encouraging an inanimate object to go in a direction it was never meant to go, and in which direction it never would have gone had it not been thrown. They do this in the hopes of getting the rock to stop "on the button" (which is not in fact a button but a big white dot in a red circle), and to whack other unsuspecting rocks out of the way. This is curling, and it is very serious stuff.

But what would one expect, in Canada? To survive in Canada, one must get serious. Frivolous people might not survive our climate, our mountain ranges, our reversing tides, our carnivorous but deceptively cute-looking fauna, and our debates between the honorable members in the House of Parliament. This is a country where it can be thirty degrees above [centigrade] in August and three months later be thirty degrees below. (For American readers, that's "very very hot" versus "very very cold.") We realize that what a toque can do to a coiffure is worth the embarrassment, seeing that the alternative is losing one's ears to frostbite. We'd rather keep our ears, and risk looking a little silly.

Which is not to say that the story of what unfolded in the lives of a particular group of men with brooms is silly. It most certainly was not. Indeed, there was death, there was drunkenness, there was space travel, and there was unrequited love. And, there was curling. Our heroes *curled*.

Our heroes would probably roll their eyes and snort

at the idea of being called heroes, and propose that I have another Moosehead brewski because I sure did need one. But nevertheless they *were* heroes. They had a lot to overcome. They worked hard. And despite the losses that they suffered, they came out of it better men, with some dreams fulfilled and others finished forever. They could have quit. They could have let it all slide, missed the button, said it was too hard. Claimed it was impossible: that four has-been ne'er-do-wells from a town that had seen better days might reassemble their old curling team in a quest to win the treasured Golden Broom, and to settle the restless ghost of an old man whose last wish involved the mighty Copernicus stone and its somewhat macabre contents. They might have turned their backs, and said such things couldn't be done.

But they did them, these men with brooms. And this is their story.

PART ONE

1

From his vantage point on the hill overlooking Long Bay's main street, on the day of Coach Donald Foley's funeral, Chris Cutter could see it all. The whole town, such as it was. Long Bay. Population twenty-three thousand, and falling. It had taken him three days to drive here, from where he labored on the Alberta oil fields – nonstop driving in his black car through blacker nights. The distance he had to travel could be no barrier. Donald Foley was dead, and Chris Cutter had missed his chance. The least he could do was not miss the funeral.

He drove like a madman, cutting as straight as he could through the very center of his Home and Native Land, breaking speed limits if not the sound barrier. Compelled by time, impeded by the sheer size of his country. The biggest country on the planet. He cut through the Prairies, feeling the highway begin to incline upward as he reached the westernmost lip of the Canadian Shield – that vast bed of semi-exposed igneous rock against which crashed the pseudo-tides of

Lake Superior – and felt his ears pop as the road sank again. And rose. And sank. Watched the forests spring up on either side, looming packs of conifers as dark as his mood, and his determination. Watched those same forests thin and break like an old man's hair, giving way to the bursting rock beneath – rock fertile as prairie soil, but with copper and zinc and nickel and even gold. Looked to his right, and saw the oceanlike expanse of Lake Superior, and knew he was coming close. Crossed a river a half-a-kilometer wide, its rapids seething and bouncing with deadly mayhem. Saw the mining roads creeping off from the highway, angling away into the curving mounds of rock. Saw the sign that said LONG BAY, and felt his breath catch (with guilt, perhaps?) at the add-on plaque, *Birthplace of Julie Foley.*

Not so very long ago, he'd sworn he'd never cross paths with the place again, this backwater armpit of a burg. But as he drove by the smelter and the mine, he saw the slagbuckets overturning one by one, pouring incandescent lava down the man-made mountains of gravelly waste copper, and felt for a moment that he'd been welcomed with a salute – one filled with a bereft and lonely beauty.

And now, leaning up against his beloved '66 Impala (the only beloved he had nowadays), he could indeed see the whole town: the main drag with its two- and three-storey shops and its two or three stoplights, the secondary strip (where the funeral home stood, as well as the gas station, the Tim Hortons, and the public school), and then the patches of frame houses and turn-of-the-century mansions lining the twenty or so residential streets, each with a stately maple in its front yard. He could even see at the town's edge the raw earth where some entrepreneur had dug and bulldozed a stretch of land, but in the torn mud there was only one house standing. He retrieved a beer from the trunk of the car, as well as his good (well, *better*) clothes, and his mood began to lift. He had made it. He'd met the challenge. Donald would have been pleased.

So he relaxed somewhat, and took to watching the funeral procession roll along behind one of Long Bay's triad of police cruisers. He found himself thinking of the people in those cars, wondered what they looked like now, what they'd been doing these past few years. If they'd remember him. If they'd ever forgive.

The cop car, with its lights flashing, was followed by every car in town, it looked like. Frances Darte – *Officer Darte* – would be in the cruiser, with her hat off out of respect for the dead (*put your darn hat back on, Frances, you got hat-head*, Coach would have told her). She'd be pleased by being able to turn the flashing lights on, and by being in the lead. In the limo behind Frances, Eva – Coach Foley's widow now, and not his wife – with their younger daughter Amy, the one who'd actually stayed in town, and who'd been there when her father died. Eva would be solidly smiling to herself, content with having been Coach's wife for so long, but Amy – well, Amy had a sensitive personality, far too loving really. She was a *giver* – she gave and gave; gave until it hurt. Of all the people in town (even more than Julie), Chris longed to see her, for she had been his great friend, and he was worried about how she was coping with it all. Seeing her father fall to the deck of that boat, clutching his heart, as his ticker ticked its last…a hellish moment for her, and not one Cutter couldn't be sure wouldn't make her fold like a bad poker hand.

He knew that he had come here – driven both himself and his Impala to exhaustion – not only because of his need to make amends, but because of concern for poor, sweet, fucked-up Amy, who was the one person in town who had never felt there was anything to forgive him for. Who had sent him the telegram: DAD DIED SUDDENLY YESTERDAY STOP HE FOUND THE STONES STOP THOUGHT YOU SHOULD KNOW.

And as for Coach's other daughter, Julie? The woman whose name endorsed the town as her birthplace? Cutter couldn't begin to imagine if she'd be there. Certainly not if she thought *he'd* be there. But his own hubris made him smile. It wouldn't be his presence that would keep her away: nothing intimidated Julie Foley. No, it would be her job that would trap her in Houston, and keep her from boarding a plane to come home. The Yanks who run the American Space Agency don't excuse their astronauts for the deaths by apoplexy of old men the small foreign towns, even if those old men are the astronaut's father. *Get back in the program, sister, this is America.*

Cutter sighed and scanned the cortege to its end. He could see Eddie Strombeck's AMC Pacer, which he'd had since high school, just like he'd had his wife, Lily. They must have kids by now; surely they'd managed to do *that*. It had been, even all those years ago, a crucial goal for them both – to have a houseful of rug rats and curtain climbers, the girls looking like Lily and the boys like Eddie. Chubby, blond, angelic girls; dark-haired boys with irascible good natures and low-average IQs. But when Cutter last saw them, they were still childless, and Eddie was still working in the copper mine. Nevertheless they were both mindlessly hopeful. To them, every roll in the hay was the one that was going to start the family circus.

Maybe if Eddie was still driving a Pacer, it was because he had so many kids he couldn't afford decent wheels. Or maybe it was because his business dealings continued to be a catalogue of one embarrassment after another. It was a drag to think that the only success Eddie'd had in his life was as one of Coach Foley's curlers. Was that really *it* for Eddie Strombeck?

And then there was the hearse itself, driven by Neil Bucyk. Good ol' long-bodied, sad-faced Neil, gainfully employed pumping dead people full of preservatives, painting their cheeks with rouge, and setting the finished product out on display for a few days, missing only a "best-before" date. Not a job Cutter would have done for all the beer in Bavaria, but Neil earned a solid income and that was saying something in Long Bay. He owned a five-bedroom backsplit with main floor laundry, family room, island kitchen with ceramic backsplash, two five-piece baths, powder room, and three-car attached garage. Often, Neil's pride could convince him he even *wanted* to own such a thing, and that it wasn't just because he was following the magazine-inspired dream of his social-climbing wife that he lived in an immaculate white-walled palace, where fresh flower arrangements were brought in every week on her standing order. The flowers, in fact, were the only thing Neil truly loved in his own home…that and his two kids, his boys, with their charmingly endless questions, and incongruous red hair.

And then there was the fourth card of that long-folded hand: Jim Lennox. Now that was a lost cause if there ever was one. Cutter wasn't averse to a toke or two, or a game of poker, but Lennox never did have any sense of self-control. Still, he'd been Cutter's friend since they were boys in Grade 3, knocking the bark off the maples with stones fired from their slingshots – even then, obsessed with the idea of *aim* and *targets*. There'd been a bond among them all – between Cutter and Lennox, and Eddie, and Neil. Cutter had loved the misbegotten lot of them.

Enough was enough. He had a funeral to go to. It occurred to him again that he might not be entirely welcome (Julie's face came to mind, and then his own father's). Wearing the shirt he had on would make matters worse. Although Coach Foley wouldn't have cared if Cutter had sallied into the church buck naked with the little soldier saluting, the minister might have a thing or two to say on the matter.

Cutter reached into the car, pulled out a clean white shirt, and began to dress for the funeral of the man who – a long time ago – had made so much possible for four young men who had nothing in their lives that mattered.

Except curling.

2

The surviving Foleys climbed out of their car, three generations of Coach's legacy, to greet the mourners who gathered like a flock of grackles, murmuring and chirring their sympathies. The whole town was there – the shopkeepers, the street sweepers, the cops who worked with Frances. It seemed not a soul had stayed away.

Eva Foley, who at past seventy was still a stunner in her own small-town way, took her grandson Brandon's hand, while her daughters gathered around her in support. Amy and Julie (for Julie had insisted on – and received – a week-long compassionate leave) were in simple black suits, their skirts a respectful length. Amy had tied her long brown hair back, but stray bits fell in copious curls around her still-shocked face, like a Pre-Raphaelite nymph's. Julie's hair was tidier – more directed, somehow. But then again, so was Julie.

Cars kept pulling up, discharging the many friends of Coach Foley. Eddie Strombeck's battered Pacer rolled to a smoky stop at the curb. He and Lily climbed out, and Eddie managed to keep himself together for a full two seconds before falling apart like a spilt bag of marbles. Cooing, dabbing at her eyes with a pink hankie, Lily tended to her husband.

A screech of tires, and up pulled a cab, its tires mounting the curb and sending a few mourners scuttling. Every head turned, including the Foley women's. Brandon was particularly impressed by the screeching tires, and grinned in approval. Amy gave him a clandestine poke.

"Jim Lennox," someone said.

Lennox and his escort emerged, a suspicious-looking cigarette dangling from Lennox's lips. The woman, a tall thin blond whose barely appropriate outfit (as in barely there and a little heavy on the marabou fringe) was only funereal in that it was black, immediately began to fuss with Lennox's tie, even while Lennox headed toward the crowd.

"Hey," he told her, not unkindly, disengaging her long-nailed fingers from his neck, "you're my rent-a-girlfriend, not my fashion consultant."

"I'm just fixing your tie," she trilled.

"C'mon baby, leave it."

He squirmed free and headed up the steps to the funeral home, but not before those lacquered fingers nipped the joint from his lips and tossed it aside.

Shaking their heads, Amy and Julie gathered up their mother and Brandon, nodded hello toward the still-recovering Eddie, and led the whole town into the funeral home, to say a last goodbye to Coach Donald Foley.

The sun didn't seem to know it was a sad day, or perhaps it hadn't wanted to miss the funeral. It smiled inanely down as the doors to the home opened and out poured the friends and mourners, who were already turning their minds to the next step of the long farewell: the wake at McTeague's tavern.

Hoser Dave, the town's self-appointed piper, fired up his bagpipes to signal the way. Eva Foley and her daughters and grandson remained inside, for the final ceremonies and cremation. By the time they got to the wake, everybody would be three sheets to the wind, as Coach would have wanted it. "Enough caterwauling," he'd have said. "It's time to break out the beer."

Jim Lennox lit a cigarette, scanning the crowd with Eddie by his side. They were missing Neil, who was still tending to the final disposal of the mortal remains – heating the crematory oven. Neil's wife Linda hung by them, with Lily Strombeck, who offered Lennox's rent-a-date a warm smile of greeting.

"I'm sorry, we didn't properly meet," she said. "I'm Lily Strombeck."

"Shit," said Lennox, realizing he'd forgotten his date's name. "Lily, this is Jeannie."

"Joanne," said Joanne.

Lennox groaned. "Joanne. Sorry. Jesus, I don't know what's wrong with me. Must have Namesheimers or something."

The women ignored him. "Beautiful service, wasn't it?" said Linda.

Joanne launched into a mindless burble. "*Totally*

beautifully and *totally* moving and I didn't even know the guy. But then I'm *super* sensitive, especially at high attitudes. Are we at a high attitude? It feels like it. Anything over 25,000 feet and I get kinda dizzy. Not that I'm not kinda dizzy anyway sometimes. Hey, am I talking too much? Because I do sometimes do that just to break up the monogamy."

Linda absorbed this speech long enough to determine that Joanne was not going to help her collect any social climber points, whereupon she turned on her heel and went off to scout for better prospects.

Joanne looked crestfallen. Lily, who was no more than a year or two older than Joanne, was nevertheless the quintessential mother. She patted Joanne on the arm, and tried to make up for Linda's rebuff.

"What is it you do, Jenny?"

"Joanne," Joanne said, brightening at the kindness. Then, with pride (and a quick flex of her admirably decorated pecs): "I'm in the fitness industry."

Lennox smothered a snort of laughter, but Lily lit up. "You're kidding! My husband and I have just taken an interest in that very industry. Isn't it weird how all over the world the same idea can surface at the same time?"

Lennox gave Eddie a meaningful look as the women launched into an exclusively female discussion of leotards and cellulite. Without a word, on a mutual signal, they started toward McTeague's, with the magpie women right behind.

"Any sign of Cutter?" Eddie asked.

Lennox snorted. "You think he'd have the nerve?"

They all failed to notice the figure in a clean but very-travel-rumpled white shirt, sitting on the hood of a black Impala, discreetly watching as an entire town followed Hoser Dave into a low-rent bar in a nowhere town called Long Bay. Not until every man, woman and child had cleared the street, did Cutter hop down from his automobile and amble off into the funeral home.

3

Eva Foley sat with lips tightly set, watching Neil Bucyk and his young, russet-haired assistant Ronnie perform a few final gestures for the six feet of cold meat that was once her husband, Donald Foley. She waited until Neil lay a single rose across the corpse's chest in its Sunday suit, and until he whispered a private goodbye into the unhearing ears. Only then did she give the ultimate, solemn nod – the authority to start the cremation.

Neil was every inch the professional funeral director, as lanky as Ichabod Crane, and with his finest poker face in place, in keeping with the situation. He stood by the casket, which lay on a conveyor belt, like the grocery-rolling ramp at the Safeway, but much shorter. His hands were folded before him. A solemn bell struck a dirge (a pre-recorded dirge) and Neil gave the signal to Ronnie to activate the belt. It started humming, and began to drag the casket toward the crematorium chamber.

The chamber door slid open with a hiss, revealing a mouthful of flames. The bell rang on. Eva and the girls and Brandon sat in the front pew, holding hands, while Neil and his assistant remained beside the conveyor belt, like an honor guard, professionally solemn.

Suddenly the belt made a noise like a lawnmower hitting heavy gravel, and the family frowned and exchanged glances. The smell of burning rubber wafted from the conveyer's motor. Gears ground painfully. The coffin stopped dead in its tracks.

Neil felt prickly sweat rise on his neck as he sprang to attention. "Ronald – the conveyance, please," he said, keeping the concern from his voice.

Ronnie began thumping buttons on the control panel, but the belt didn't respond, at least not at first. Neil didn't dare look at the women. You never knew with mourners – they were emotional, on edge, and often got hysterical. There was very little room for screw-ups. Neil had to get that coffin moving again. If word spread that things had gone badly – if people took their dead to the next town, he could lose a lot of business, and he'd never get into Linda's country club – he'd lose Linda – he'd lose her father's business – his *kids*…

Something Ronnie pushed convinced the conveyor to restart. Unfortunately, it had misunderstood the instructions and it proceeded in reverse, and at a good clip too, nearly catapulting Coach Foley's coffin away from the broiling chamber. Ronnie made a panicked little gurgle and thumped the control panel with both fists. This really offended the conveyor belt. The engine whined like a struck dog and hit overdrive. Neil saw there was about one second before the box containing

Donald Foley's mortal remains would go shooting off the conveyor's free end like a spat watermelon seed. This situation needed a boss, and that was him – Neil Bucyk, man in charge. Maker of decisions.

Neil threw himself into the path of the oncoming casket.

This turned out to be a less than optimum strategy. The coffin, objecting to the interference with its journey away from the nasty hot burning place, decided to throw caution to the wind and its contents onto the floor. The coffin tumbled off the belt, hitting Neil soundly in the foot. Neil shrieked like a man not in charge. The coffin burst open. Coach Foley, who was all soft and pliable again now that the rigor mortis phase had passed, flopped out in a slump, his neatly folded arms unfolding, the farewell rose poking him right up the nose.

Ronnie and Neil didn't dare look at the family as they both pounced on the escaping Coach Foley, abandoning all pretense of solemnity as they tried to stuff him back into his coffin. The family stared in fishlike amazement.

"Did we pay *money* for this?" Julie Foley declared.

But Neil and Ronnie succeeded in jamming the reluctant body back into its box, and slapped shut the lid. Neil, breathing hard with exertion and standing on his uninjured foot, leaned over the coffin as Ronnie gave the conveyor motor a solid kick. At the same time he pressed the *forward* button on the panel one last, desperate time. The motor coughed, stalled, and then apparently regained its senses, recommencing the transport of the coffin as if nothing had happened at all.

Except, unfortunately, Neil had slammed the coffin shut on his tie. He had a brief thought of *what's this about?* before realizing that he was about to be pulled into a blazing furnace, tied like a street corner mutt to a dead man's casket.

Ronnie grabbed him around the waist. Neil grabbed the coffin, embracing it and pulling it back away from the flames, hopping along on his good foot while Ronnie heaved backward.

"Good God and all His angels," Eva said.

Julie was about to step forward and put an end to the farce by pulling the circuit breaker by the exit doors, when something stopped her dead in her tracks, deader even than Coach Foley. The belt stopped, and Neil and Ronnie and Coach Foley's chariot all stopped too. They looked up at the man who stood in the doorway, the tall, dark-haired, good-looking son-of-a-bitch who'd left town in a mighty rush those years ago, leaving Julie Foley standing at the altar. Who'd broken his oddball father's heart. But who still made Julie and Amy gasp, and Eva and Neil and even Ronnie break into irrepressible smiles of recognition, which they all quickly smothered. No doubt Coach Foley was smiling, too.

"Sorry I'm late," said Cutter.

"Late!" said Eva. "Hell, Cutter. Things were just starting to get interesting."

4

Nug, the bartender at McTeague's, was a man who knew his way around a bar. A hefty guy, twice as broad as your average Joe, he had a sweet face and an unflappable ability to run a tavern full of inebriates. Being such a pro, he had things in order long before Hoser Dave crossed his threshold squeezing "Amazing Grace" out of his tartan bagful of cats. Nug had slipped in at dawn, making sure every table was wiped, every glass available and every keg tapped, so that he would have plenty of time to get to the funeral service, and still time to get back and open for the wake. The jukebox was dusted, and there were new 60-watt bulbs in the low-hanging, stained-glass lamps over the shuffleboard and billiards tables. He'd even put fresh scent-cakes in all the urinals.

It would be some strange doings – having a party of that size and decibel level, without Coach Foley standing on a table or two, holding forth about the days when *his boys* whupped the lily ass of every curler that dared come near their town. There would have to be a lot of liquor downed and glasses raised, to cover the ringing absence.

In accordance with a Long Bay wake tradition that had started when McTeague's was just a shack in the wilderness, Nug rang the bar's handbell, to summon everyone's attention. The assembled crowd – every Long Bay man and woman of the age of majority, and a few   not-quite-drinking-age-but-who's-counting   – turned to meet his somber gaze.

"Ladies and gentlemen," he intoned. "To Donald Foley."

Up went the glasses, lifted in the silent air. "To Donald Foley," the town replied, and then glasses met lips. Ladylike shots and entire pints were downed. Nug's pint of Moosehead was gone in two gulps.

Almost in one voice, the assembled mass of mourners sighed with what was part sorrow and part relief. Conversation started: stories about Coach, of course, but also the touching-base of old friends and neighbors who'd been brought together by his death. His *bizarre* death. Just how Donald Foley had died was a major topic of discussion.

"It's not every day a man croaks retrieving curling stones from a lake bottom," someone remarked.

"It wasn't him did the diving, ya know," said another. "His daughter – that Amy, not the astronaut of course – took the scuba lessons at the night school. She was the one lugged it up to the surface. It was the sight of the thing – the excitement and all – what did his ticker in."

"Nevertheless, he gave his life for the sport," another added. "Died for curling."

"He died for stubbornness." This from a woman on the leeward side of middle age, a contemporary of Coach Foley. "Mule-minded old fart could never let things go. Now his poor girl Amy's gonna drink herself bat-blind, thinking she had a hand in him dying."

"Aw, cork it up, woman. You just don't understand what's important. Nug, pour the wife another rye and ginger – stop her speaking ill of the dead."

Nug never had another quiet moment that day. He pulled beer and poured shots until well into the night, glad to do it, for it kept him from hearing the absence of Donald Foley's voice.

Amy Foley stood aside in the funeral home's tiny lobby, helping her mother and son with their coats. Julie was on a bit of a tear, obviously shook up by Cutter's unannounced appearance, on top of the rather unorthodox ending to Coach Foley's final journey. Julie was not a person who cared much for disorder, incompetence or surprises. One did not achieve status as second alternate astronaut in the space shuttle program by tolerating a lot of coffin-toppling.

So when Cutter slipped into the lobby and stepped up beside the seething Julie, asking for a private word, Amy thought for a moment that he must have lost his mind, putting his head in the lion's mouth like that. But Julie stayed cool – *ice* cool – pausing long enough to let him offer a few low-toned words, beneath the range of Amy's hearing.

Amy tried not to look at the two of them, how they leaned in close as if they were still in love and altar-bound. Cutter's appearance had made Amy's jaw drop, true, but it had also made her heart rate triple. She'd hardly dared hope to see him again. But there he'd been, cutting short the circus act of Neil and his minion wrestling a casket. Cutter, as lean and good-looking as ever. Leaning up against the circuit-breaker panel; almost smiling. And watching – of course – only Julie.

But why wouldn't he watch her, Amy? she asked her-self. *They were the couple. You were the single-mom sister, the buddy, the neutral corner to retreat to when he needed someone to pal with. And don't forget, Julie has the brains. You have the bottle…*

She corrected herself: *had* the bottle! *Had it!* This time, she'd had it with drinking; she had Brandon to think about, and now her mother. Who was alone, widowed because of Amy's playing along with her father's bone-headed stunt to retrieve the Copernicus stones. Why had-n't she just told the silly old goat that she'd have nothing to do with it? Why hadn't she told him *forget it, Dad, for-get the whole thing. What is it with you men and that curling tourney? Forget it already – it was ten years ago!*

Eva Foley whispered to Amy that she was going to take Brandon to a neighbor's, and that she'd see Amy at the wake. Amy didn't respond, watching instead as Julie wheeled around, giving Cutter her back, and marched toward the front doors, her flustered hands struggling with her coat buttons.

"C'mon, Mom, Brandon, let's go," Julie snapped, still playing the one in charge. "Amy, come *on*."

Amy shook her head. Julie could be one bossy brat – having a double doctorate (one of 'em from *Hah*-vard) sure could give a girl a fat head.

"I'll catch up to you," Amy said.

"Suit yourself," said Julie, herding Eva and Brandon out the door.

Cutter shrugged sheepishly at Amy as the doors whooshed shut behind Julie. Amy shrugged back.

"That went well, don't you think?" he said.

"Oh yeah, looks like all's forgiven." Amy looked at her shoes, which were pinching a little after the long day on her feet.

"Walk you to the wake?" Cutter asked.

Suddenly the day seemed too short. "Oh yeah," she said, desperately casual. "Yeah, sure."

Cutter ushered her out into the fading afternoon sun.

5

By the time Neil arrived at McTeague's, after tidying up the flowers and putting away the chairs at the home, the shoulder-to-shoulder throng had thinned somewhat. Eddie and Lennox were already well lubricated, and Neil wasted no time catching up. He kept having flashbacks of the slow drag into the crematorium. It reminded him of his whole life. An inexorable drag toward an ignominious end.

Nor had he been able to convince Eddie and Lennox of just how serious that had been. In fact, when Neil got to the part about the coffin closing on his tie, Lennox laughed so hard he sucked a beer nut up into his sinuses, and had to be slapped around a little until it dislodged.

"It wasn't funny, you jerkoffs." Neil sulked for at least another twenty-five seconds before he got over himself.

Linda Bucyk, however, was on a roll: she hadn't seen so many schmoozing opportunities since Mona Lafferty's bridal shower, which she'd either crashed or been "unofficially invited to through a mutual friend," which is the version she'd told the surprised hostess. She was striking out with getting Neil onside, though. He was too hammered to be of much use socially, and even when she tried to corral his drinking, those idiot friends of his kept him topped up on the sly. He was up one shit creek when she got him home – at the very least for failing to say a proper *hello-how-are-you-darling* to Muriel Thatcher (who was on the country club's board of directors yet!). But aside from that, he had been socially inept enough to report at full volume the fiasco that had marked the cremation of Coach Foley.

Sheila Bannerman moved into Linda's sights, and Linda stiffened like a sleek hound catching the scent of a prey animal. She patted her *chignon* and checked for stray hairs, then sunk her nails into Neil's arm. "I'm going to say hello first," she whispered. "You come over in twenty seconds – no more than that – and say hello as well. Is that clear?"

Off she sailed. The men exchanged dismayed glances. Poor Neil.

"S'okay, guys," he said quietly. "In twenty seconds and more, I'll still be right here."

Just then, the bar doors opened unobtrusively. It would have gone unnoticed, but the boys had – to some extent – been waiting for this. They'd had certain expectations, of a particular person's arrival.

But it wasn't Cutter. It was Julie and Eva Foley. The boys all watched them silently, keeping an eye particularly on Julie. Other than her being a bit of an object of fascination, owing to the astronaut thing and all, she was also one damn fine-looking woman.

Lily Strombeck took her husband Eddie's arm. Joanne, seeing this, copied her and took Lennox's. Lennox gave her a look of brief confusion, then went along with the game.

Eddie gestured toward Julie. "Looks like Spacewoman is alone," he said.

Lily pinched him softly. "Honey, don't call her that."

"Alone?" said Joanne, confused. For Julie and Eva had been swept up in a throng of sympathizers and well-wishers, who blocked them almost entirely from view. "She's got *lots* of friends."

"I mean the *man* is not in evidence," said Lennox, as if that explained it all. When Joanne still frowned, he added, "Chris Cutter."

"Maybe she dumped *him* this time," said Eddie.

"She dumped that Cutter guy?" Joanne shrilled.

"No," said Neil. "*He* dumped *her*."

"Originally," added Eddie.

Joanne's head spun. "Who dumped who?" she squeaked.

Lennox took a long drag of his cigarette, and raised one cynical eyebrow. "It's like this, Jessica. Cutter didn't exactly *dump* her. He just forgot to show up at the altar. Happens all the time, ya know. A year's planning, tuxes, dresses, stag parties, rehearsals and shit – real easy for a guy to overlook. No more important than a dentist appointment or an oil change. Jesus."

"Ohhh," said Joanne, not entirely absorbing the sarcasm. She looked over at Julie, who for a moment was clearly visible. Julie was a beautiful woman, tall and somehow obviously intelligent. Lennox had told her Julie Foley was actually, for real, an *astronaut*. Joanne couldn't imagine what sort of dirtbucket Cutter must be to walk away from such a woman. The whole story unfolded in her head: Julie crying at the altar, the minister comforting her, the guests all muttering in shock as the clock kept ticking past the appointed hour. What a jerk. Whoever this Cutter guy was, he was sure No. 1 on Joanne's Shit List.

She cuddled up to her ersatz boyfriend, enjoying the warmth of the others' friendship, wondering if she could ever be part of such a wonderful thing, or how this guy Cutter could ever have let it go.

Nug, in due course, could spare a second to stand back and have a smoke and a handful of beer nuts – Nug's version of a well-balanced meal. Seeing that no one, for the time being, was pounding on the bar looking for a shot, Nug picked up the bar TV's remote and switched on the sports channel.

The sound wasn't on, but it didn't need to be. Nug knew at once who he was looking at, as the camera peered right into the athlete's pompously handsome, solemnly concentrating face. Every fair hair on the man's head was strategically organized, including the boyish curl that swept down over his frowning brow. He wore the spangled colors of The Juggernaut – the curling team that had, for the past several years, owned the game of curling, rock, stock and barrel, and which was named after its skip. He was Alexander Yount, the original Juggernaut, and the finest curler in the country. By his estimation, anyway.

Yount knew what he looked like as he aimed his rock and moved leopardlike into his approach. His powerful arm swung like John Henry's hammer, and Yount dropped into his crouch, his one leg sliding out lithely behind him, his other supporting his weight in a strength move worthy of Baryshnikov. The rock bulleted forward. But the camera didn't follow it. Instead, it stayed on Yount, tracking his slide along the ice, zooming in on his expression as he began his shouts to the sweepers.

Camera operator's a dame for damn sure, Nug thought.

"YAH!" Alexander Yount hollered to his team. "Hard! Hard! Hurry hard!"

The rock sailed into the house, covering the hundred-odd feet between it and the stone it was aimed for in a trajectory so straight it might have been an arrow. It looked as if it were going to keep right on till morning. But then, magically, it started to curve toward its target.

The camera only watched the rock for the end of its journey: the culmination of Yount's takeout shot. A success, of course. Then the camera switched straight back to Yount, who was upright now, waving to the cheering crowd with choreographed motions and heavily forced humility.

"Hey, Nug!" Lennox suddenly hollered. "You mind turning that shit *off*?"

Nug pressed the remote button again, fading Alexander Yount to black.

Out in the dusk, in the twilight, Amy and Cutter strolled up one side of the main street drag and down the other. After his aborted attempt to approach Julie, Chris's vaguely hopeful mood had flapped away, squawking like a scared seagull. But thank God for Amy, who knew how he was feeling and was happy just to hang out with him, helping him work up his nerve. Wonderful no-pressure Amy, as comfortable and familiar to him – even after ten years – as his favorite shoes. Except better-looking, of course. Chris wondered how her love life had been going, since her divorce, but decided not to ask. She often got a little sniffy with him when he asked her about her romantic life. He couldn't figure out why, so he just kept off the topic.

They chatted off and on, peering into the shop windows. Every third store was boarded up with sheets of plywood and criss-crossed two-by-fours. Still others were just empty, their dark, unwiped windows displaying a few forgotten scraps or dust kittens. They passed McTeague's again and again, but Cutter couldn't bring himself to go inside.

Amy understood. She patted him on the back, and they started another circuit. She told Cutter about Coach's death. About how she'd gone along with his scheme, because it was so important to him.

"Ever since you threw those rocks in the lake, he's had it in his mind to get them back. And me knowing how to dive…how could I say no? He just kept after me and after me, begging really. To tell you the truth, it was sort of an adventure – subterfuge scuba – and such a challenge finding them down there. It was dark, really bad visibility, and the water kept seeping into my wetsuit. You can't imagine how cold that water is, eighty feet down. It was exciting. But it was the excitement that killed him, Cutter. He never stopped thinking of those stones, and what happened that they ended up there..."

Cutter nodded. "I had thought of the stones too, from time to time." More than just from time to time, actually, but he wasn't about to admit that. He glanced down at her, and saw she was crying, the way Amy always cried – to herself, with one neat tear sliding down her cheek.

"Thinking about your dad, Amy?" he asked, sliding a comforting arm around her.

"Oh, Cutter!" she wailed, surprising him, for Amy Foley was no wailer. "This thing with Dad – Cutter, I blame myself." But she pulled herself together – Amy didn't like to make people sad or uncomfortable – and slipped out from under his arm. "It's okay," she said, waving him off as she sat down on the curb. "I'll be fine, Chris. Don't fuss."

"I won't fuss, if you'll stop beating yourself up," he said quietly, lowering himself to sit beside her. He glanced away from her for a moment, saw that they were right outside McTeague's, and quickly returned his attention to her. She had wiped her nose and eyes, and now sat guilelessly cross-legged, despite her dignified funeral skirt, with her chin supported in her hands.

"Do you feel better now?" Chris asked, leaning in toward her.

"No!" she said. "I feel *responsible*."

"He had a heart attack, Amy."

"Yeah, but I'm the one that took him out on the lake. Got him all excited. He took one look at that stone, hanging off the winch – and he dropped. Like a stone himself. I saw him die, Cutter!"

"And if he saw that stone, he died happy. The stones were...*crucial*." He put his hand on her shoulder and gave it a light squeeze. "Besides, I'm the one who threw those things there in the first place. So if you want to blame someone, blame me."

Amy regained some of her humor, raking it together like a pile of autumn leaves. She gave him a big wise-ass smile.

"Cutter, I do blame you," she said. "I'm just trying to spread it around."

"That's better," he said. "That's my girl."

The sound of tortured animals began to seep from McTeague's, bursting into full volume as the door opened and out stepped Hoser Dave and his bagpipes. Dave didn't see Amy and Cutter as he walked up the center of the half-deserted street, playing a dirge of his own composition, into the setting sun.

"Kind of have to go in, don't we?" Cutter said to Amy.

"*You* should, yeah. But my little boy's at my neighbor's, so I better go back."

"Why don't I walk you? I'd like to meet Brandon."

Amy tightened her lips like a schoolteacher. "Cutter, you don't fool me. I can recognize when you're stalling.

Don't you be a chicken shit. Go in there. Face them. You'll be fine. And I'll see you around."

"Not if I see you first."

"Hardy-har-har. Smart ass." She rose to her feet. Pertly she brushed the street dust off her black skirt, ruffled Cutter's hair, and was gone.

Cutter looked at the foreboding doors of McTeague's. Much worse than the funeral home. He stood up very slowly and crossed the now-very-wide, very-empty Main Street of Long Bay.

It's funny how some things just don't get forgotten that easily. Desertion, for instance. In wartime, deserters are shot. The entire battle – hell, even the war itself – can be lost if there are deserters.

But it doesn't even have to be a matter of abandoning a war. It can be a town that's abandoned, or a woman. Or a team of men who had something very special on the go. The ones left behind – well, they don't just grin and carry on. They remember what it was like, in the days after the quitter walked away, how the air felt hollow and the beer tasted like tap water. They remember how long it took to forget the betrayal. A betrayal like Cutter's.

Into McTeague's Cutter walked, weighed by it all, weighed by the stares of those who saw him arrive. Struck by how quickly Julie excused herself from the people she was talking to, and disappeared into the Ladies'.

Neil and Eddie had just finished playing catch-up with Jim Lennox, who – since he left town – had invested in commodities. Unlike Cutter, Jim Lennox had *merely left town* – he didn't vanish like some skulking malingerer – and he came back constantly, drifted in, drifted out, like a sailboat tacking with the wind. Lennox also didn't break a generous heart in passing, either. Now here he was, with a fluff-haired hardbody girlfriend on his arm, talking about the stock market like the others had a notion of what he was jawing about.

"Holy moly," said Eddie. "Commodities? One second we're down in the mine together, and the next second it's nine years later. And *he's* Master of the Universe."

Lennox looked pleased with himself. "I'm just another working stiff."

"Stiffs," said Neil, "are *my* line of work."

"How are things underground?" Lennox asked Eddie.

"I don't go *underground* with 'em," Neil said. "Even undertakers have limits."

"I meant Eddie and the mine, you buttwipe."

Eddie shrugged and sipped his beer. "I can't tell you. I was one of the first of the layoffs. As far as I know, all they got down there now is a skeleton crew, keeping the lights on."

"Would the last one to leave the mine, please turn out the lights?" Neil offered, but no one laughed. He tried to make up for it, muttering that there was talk about starting it up again.

"Well, I'm not holding my breath," said Eddie. "Personally, I don't think there's any more copper in that hole."

"You got more irons in the fire, though, right?"

"What, there's *iron* in the mine?" said Eddie.

"No, Eddie," said Neil patiently. "You have business ideas, right?"

Eddie perked right up. "Oh yeah, I got lots on the go. Couple hundred. In fact, I'm sitting on what you might call a *many-tentacled conglomeration* of irons. Try to visualize– "

Eddie was spreading his hands out in front of him, as if conducting an orchestra, when he stopped in mid-sentence and snapped his mouth shut. He thrust both his hands into his trouser pockets and turned away from the bar. For there, across from the men, stood Cutter.

"Nug," said Cutter, "I want you to send over there a rum and Pepsi, a pilsner and a JW Black."

Nug didn't move. Eddie shuffled his feet and addressed Neil, who had also turned his back to the bar.

"I find the pilsner's a bit gassy nowadays," he said.

Neil nodded agreement. "Yeah, and the rum doesn't agree with my stomach lining."

Nug didn't budge. Cutter took awhile before he moved, and before he did, he slid his hands over the bartop as if remembering its feel.

"It's like that then, is it, guys?"

They did not answer. Nug picked up a tumbler and began to wipe it with a now-dirty barcloth. The cloth squealed against the glass, and Cutter sighed.

"I'll see you at the reading," he said.

The night he walked into was particularly black.

Marvin Fleiger, barrister and solicitor, had tended the town of Long Bay like a country doctor since the days after he'd been called to the bar. He was an older man now, with fashionable frames on his bifocals, and people whose wills he'd drawn after they'd had their first baby – well, he was now helping wrap up their estates. Things changed for him so quickly – from typewriters and carbon paper to computers and laser copiers. Still, he couldn't imagine being in a big city, where everything would have to be done to the letter, and by the book. If he were in Montreal or Toronto or Vancouver, some higher-up would have told him that letting a man do a videotape of himself reading his will was *bad practice*. It was bound to inflame the beneficiaries. It was asking for trouble. Fleiger would have been told to exercise some client control. And as for the client's hare-brained scheme about the disposal of the ashes – well, that was a borderline contravention of the health regulations. Marvin could be in hot water for participating in it.

But he wasn't in Montreal and he was Marvin Fleiger and if Donald Foley wanted to read his own will in his own voice to his wife and kids and the others, then Marvin Fleiger wasn't going to shake his finger at him and tell him he advised against it. Donald Foley obviously wanted this Copernicus stone thing very badly. Marvin could understand that. The profession he was in was supposed to be about helping people get justice – helping them achieve a balance. Donald Foley had felt an unbalance. And Marvin now had a hand in righting it.

Eva Foley and the girls, Julie and Amy, sat together

on one side of Marvin's boardroom table, which was the biggest ordinary dining-room table he could get at the local furniture barn. The boardroom was the converted second-storey sunporch to the storefront office Marvin had rented for twenty-six years. Marvin didn't believe in spending clients' money on mahogany bookshelves.

Across from the Foley women sat Eddie and Lennox and Neil in a threesome. Cutter stood apart from them, keeping his eyes fixed on one thing: the television monitor at the table's end. Marvin held up a videotape with a label clearly marked DONALD FOLEY – LAST WILL READING, and inserted it into the VCR.

Everyone, without meaning to, took a quick breath as Donald Foley's image came up on the screen. Amy actually whimpered a little, and her sister took her hand and squeezed it.

Together they listened as Donald Foley revealed his last will and testament. He read it from the typewritten sheet that Marvin had prepared and had him properly execute in front of himself and his perpetually frazzled half-blind secretary, in order to make it legitimate. All in all the main reading took no more than a minute. Foley seemed largely himself – he wore no fancy suit, just his black-and-red checkered shirt and down vest, and his khaki trousers – and he didn't seem to be making a fuss about things. There was nothing unusual, at first. He left a knickknack here and a geegaw there, then appeared to wrap up.

"The rest of my estate," he said, "if any, is to be divided equally between the loves of my life: my wife

Eva, and my two daughters, Amy and Julie. And that concludes the reading of the last will and testament of me, Donald Foley."

He paused and set the papers down, looking intently at the camera. Eva and the girls shifted in their seats, looking at each other. The only surprise in this was that there were no surprises. It wasn't like Donald to go out with such an organized little whimper.

"He's up to something," muttered Cutter.

Donald Foley just sat there, leering angelically out at them, until they all decided he truly had finished and rose to their feet (all except Cutter, who not only was still suspicious, but was already standing). No sooner had they pushed their chairs back and stood like a church choir than Donald Foley's voice barked, "Not so fast."

They all sat down again. Cutter shook his lowered head, smiling.

"There's a codicil, I guess you'd call it. Although Marvin tells me that's not quite the word. Doesn't matter. This is my wish: my biggest wish. It's the heart of me, boys and girls. My wish is that my cremated remains be placed under the handle of this – Copernicus stone."

Marvin, right on cue, produced and dropped onto the table forty-two pounds of metal-handled granite curling rock. He grimaced a little as he realized that he'd just put a big dent in his table. Oh, well, it'd make a good story – *that dent came from the time a client wanted to be buried in a curling stone.*

Marvin recovered himself enough to speak his part in the play Donald Foley had orchestrated ante-mortem. "Mr. Foley died recovering this stone from the bottom of Trout Lake. How the stones came to be at the bottom of the lake remains one of Long Bay's enduring mysteries."

Amy looked over at Cutter. He raised his eyebrows at her, and she looked away quickly.

Donald Foley continued. "There is an award, known as the Golden Broom, which you all know well. Since it was established in 1937 as the most prestigious prize in local curling, this local rink – you boys – are the closest contenders. You came the closest to winning it: you, Neil. You, Lennox. You, Eddie." He paused. "You, Cutter."

Foley stopped again, collecting himself, before he went on. "Those days were the proudest of Long Bay's long history. You were the heart of them then. You were pure spirit. It was all about heart and spirit then, boys. I died never seeing that heart and spirit again, but knowing it lay at the bottom of a lake. Therefore, my last wish is that you reunite as a rink and that you place this rock – this Copernicus stone – containing me, Donald Foley, on the button. Finish the job. Remember: the purity of the heart is to will one thing. Will this."

The image buzzed to blue, and Marvin quickly switched it off, leaving a dark screen where Donald Foley's face had been.

"That," Marvin intoned, "concludes the full reading of the Last Will and Testament of Donald Foley."

Everyone, at first, was too stunned to speak. What

was this, a monumental joke? Reunite? They weren't even speaking to each other. And win the Golden Broom, with Donald Foley's cinders set out in a curling rock, like a headstone, on the button? Neil snorted. He'd done some funny services for folks before, but this was daft even for Donald. Linda would have a conniption fit. Curling – particularly the way it was played in Long Bay – was far from country club behavior.

Eddie and Lennox also had hefty doubts. They weren't worried about a harridan wife, but the deterioration of their anatomies. They were ten years older and damn out of shape. Curling might look like a bunch of overgrown kids playing slipsies, but it takes muscles and an eagle eye. They didn't have a snowball's chance in Hades, and Donald Foley…well…he must have been losing his marbles some–

Just then Eva Foley's rich laugh broke the confused silence. "Good God in His high chair," she roared. "That man was *so* unsteady." She put her hand on the rock and gave it a little push, sliding it on the table as it might down the curling sheet. Everyone shuddered, considering its contents.

"Mom," said Julie.

"Aw, lighten up, girl. He's where he wants to be."

"He's really in there now?" asked an awestruck Lennox.

Marvin nodded.

"You put him in there?"

"No," said Marvin. "I had my secretary do it. She didn't know ashes had chunky bits in them, Neil – I wish you'd warned me. The woman nearly quit on me."

Julie looked horrified. "Marvin, really. This can't be legally binding."

"Disposal of the remains has to be dignified and in accordance with local health laws. And the disposal must not be an indignity to the remains. If the executrix – that's you, Eva – approves, and the container is sealed, well…I can't say for sure, but I think the stone may be a legitimate final resting place for Coach Foley. Whether one can actually curl with it, though, I would question. I would say that's not exactly dignified. It's like playing football with an urn. But boys, the question isn't legal. It's moral. You know what he wants you to do, and why. You're not bound by that request in any way, except by what you owe that man and this town."

Marvin picked up the stone, straining a little under its weight, and tried to hand it to Eddie, who looked away. Neil, too, turned away. And Lennox just pretended he didn't see.

Cutter, however, stepped forward. He took the stone from Marvin and spoke to the other men in the voice he used to use to shout them into sweeping.

"C'mon!" he said.

Instinctively, they all rose and followed.

The Foley women and their lawyer watched from the boardroom window as Cutter, Lennox, Neil and Eddie made it as far as the street outside. No sooner had the four of them hit the sidewalk than Cutter plunked the stone down and stopped, apparently signaling a powwow.

"What are they saying?" said Julie.

"Shhh!"

Only snatches of shouted conversation made it through the window, although Marvin struggled to raise the sash so they could eavesdrop more effectively. Cutter and Lennox were the loudest, and waved their arms and even their fists, while Eddie and Neil stood back a pace but didn't neglect to throw in their two bits. It seemed to the girls and to Marvin that Cutter was the odd man out. They heard Neil yell, "Well, maybe I *want* this!" in a half-choked squawk that carried loudest of all.

"There's no way Chris is going to do this," said Julie. "Is there?"

Amy shook her head briefly. "Doesn't look like it."

The men kept yelling. Eddie kneeled down and ran his hands over the stone while the argument raged around him. He stood up, tugged Neil on the sleeve, and the two of them headed off briskly down the street. This caused Cutter to let loose with a string of salty epithets, before he too stomped off in the opposite direction. Lennox remained behind, shoulders sagging, staring down at the ashes-stuffed curling rock at his feet.

Eva was about to remark that *that* appeared to be *that*, when suddenly Cutter reappeared, snatched up the rock, and marched off again like a furious five-year-old. Lennox didn't move. He just stayed put, staring at the spot where the stone had been.

"Of course, with those four," said Eva at this, "you just never know, do you?"

7

Outside the town of Long Bay, a few miles down a tree-lined dirt lane, lived Gordon Cutter: cultivator of mushrooms, and desirer of absolute privacy. Being private, he forgot to do things like wash his longish, white-grey hair, or shave more than once a fortnight. Since he rarely entertained, his personal habits were never subject to question.

It had not always been this way for Gordon Cutter. Once, long ago, he had been a Brier champion. He had been married to a fine woman who put up with a lot of neglect as he went off night after night, practicing and playing. She lived in a ramshackle house that he failed to keep up (he was busy polishing rocks), that had a barn and a greenhouse that she also tended to, alone. But he was a good-looking son-of-a-seacook, a curling genius with a razor-sharp wit, and he was the father of her son, Chris Cutter.

Chris Cutter was there when she died. Her husband was not.

Gordon Cutter, as his wife lay dying in a hospital

bed, was off playing in the championship round of the National Brier. He was the town's sweetheart, as big in his way as Julie Foley became in hers: a local star who gave everyone there someone to look at and dream about. So while the whole town followed Gordon Cutter's ascent to stardom, young Chris Cutter combed his mother's hair and changed her diapers and checked all the tubes in her arms, day after day of those last hard days. His father cavorted across barroom TV screens, devilishly handsome and winning everything in sight.

Chris's mother didn't get to see her husband as he made shot after shot. Her hospital room had no TV, and she was too frail to wheel into the common room downstairs. So she didn't see the TV interviewers poking microphones into his triumphant face. But she asked her son about every detail, and made him recount every nuance of every thrown stone, of every takeout shot, of every word Gordon spoke. Chris Cutter did what he was told, and every few days his father would phone in and report on how great things were going.

"And how's your mom?" he'd ask.

Chris's mother had begged him not to let on how bad things were. She'd said the curling was too important to Gordon, and Chris had to promise her not to tell.

So Chris said, "She's okay, Dad. Holding her own. She says not to worry."

"You look after her, Chris, and I'll see her the moment I get back."

Of course, the moment he got back was *after* she'd died. She died in Chris's arms, without a TV in the room, without any idea of what it looked like when her husband's rink won the Brier. Gordon came home to an empty house. An empty bed. It didn't take long for that emptiness to fill. His guilt filled it: pushed itself into every nook and cranny, stuffed every room with its burgeoning self. It moved into the space that Peggy Cutter had occupied, and squatted there, staring Gordon Cutter down.

It wasn't too long after Gordon Cutter came back to Long Bay – after he buried his wife, and after his star fell and after his bitter son skipped out – that he discovered that a particular fungus-y little mushroom that grew along the edges of the family cow's shit channel happened to have (shall we say) *special* properties. How Gordon Cutter came to know this involves a drinking bender he went on after his wife's death and his son's desertion, coupled with a semi-suicidal curiosity à la Alice in Wonderland. *I wonder what this will do? I wonder if this'll kill me?*

Only Gordon's wife and son knew what an odd duck he truly was, even before the Brier. He had, growing beneath his silver hair, a bit of a God complex. Neither his wife nor son would have been surprised to find he'd been experimenting with fungus. Besides, without his wife and son, he had crumbled like an old Saltine.

But goodness, didn't that little mushroom have an interesting side effect or two, and without the gut-roiling hangover of the morning after. Lovely colors and no hurling: that's what Gordon's magic mushrooms provided.

Gordon felt the mushrooms were the best thing that ever happened to him, after, of course, marrying his wife (and look what he'd done to her, he told himself). It wasn't easy walking around with that shame. As if that was the only shame, too – on top of it, and not long after, his only son had waltzed away from the Golden Broom championship, dumping the town's pet astronaut at the altar at just about the same time. Gordon Cutter was a bad husband and an embarrassed father and a has-been curler. He might as well get stoned on hallucinogenic cowshit-eating fungus, because that sure beat reality.

In fact, Gordon Cutter thought he was hallucinating when he saw the black '66 Impala cruising up his lane. He had been in his barn, happily massaging the rectum of his favorite cow (he now had three, to keep up a steady supply of rich, life-giving manure). The cow had been about to oblige – arching its back and lifting its tail gracefully, like a ballerina raising her hand – when Gordon heard the rumble of tires and saw the unmistakable long, black, hood.

A stream of shit spat into the bucket Gordon was holding. Gordon spoke to the cow.

"That's the way I feel about him, too," he said.

Checking the barn door to make sure it was locked against invaders, Gordon Cutter went to feed his mushrooms. He didn't see the Impala drive away again. But he felt it.

8

At the Mr. and Mrs. Neil Bucyks, dinner was served. If there is one business that keeps going no matter what happens to the economy – no matter how many people lose their jobs – it's gravedigging. Undertaking. Funeral directing. It doesn't matter what title the job is given, because somebody still has to bury the dead.

Neil Bucyk made his living with the dead. It wasn't his chosen profession – he'd inherited it from his father-in-law, a rat-thin man with a face like a bloodhound and the disposition of a simpering poodle. The man had spoiled his only daughter (now Mrs. Linda Bucyk) so badly that she *smelled* spoiled. All the *L'Air du Temps* in the world wouldn't drown out the whiff of greed that seeped out from Linda Bucyk's pampered skin.

Because he didn't have to go working in a mine or repairing asphalt on the highways bypassing town, and because he didn't have to worry about layoffs or strikes or plant closures, Neil was able to buy the model home that now sat in a wasteland of dug-up mud beside a long-gone developer's COMING SOON – NEW HOMES billboard. The developer had bought a forest, razed it, built a single model home, and then gone bankrupt. There wasn't even enough money to take down the billboard, or pay the men who'd run the dozers and landmovers their last week's wages. Neil's idea of having a backyard garden was lost, since only hard-packed, rain-drenched mud surrounded that "model" home.

But Linda Bucyk considered her model home to be truly *model*, something to set an example for the lower-class ladies of the town. It was also beautifully decorated, using lots of juicy tips from *Architectural Digest* and Martha Stewart's *Living*, as well as generous applications of Neil's income. The window treatments matched the upholstery, which coordinated with the carpet, which set off the wainscoting, which was geared to the overall faux-New-York-contemporary decorative theme. She had French doors, beveled glass, wool carpeting, exposed brick in the foyer. Linda called it her *personal motif*.

Now, it had for a long time also been part of Linda's *personal motif* to carry on an affair with Neil's undertaking assistant, Ronnie, with trysts scheduled at least once a week. They trysted in the bedroom, on the Laura Ashley bedspread, and in the laundry room, while the washer ran on spin cycle (also known as vibrate). They had been trysting since she was a teenager and he was barely of the age of consent, but Ronnie – even though he was quite the stunner, with a thatch of bright red hair – didn't have the business acumen to get Linda where she wanted to go. He would never be more than any-one's assistant, so Linda chose instead to *marry* the guy who had potential to run a business and accumulate an income and status. In Long Bay, the pickings were slim in that regard. Neil Bucyk, president of the botany club and the camera club, who played chess competitively, was the only one naive enough to marry someone who practically had the word AVARICE tattooed across her brow.

Neil's business leanings were toward greenhouses and flowers – he had a way with roses and had even bred his own brightly hued peach blossom that he called the Bucyk Beauty – but in a town built on solid rock, there wasn't much hope that a plant nursery would ever bring in enough dough to keep Linda in a model home and in model's clothes. Neil was an honor-able man, who believed in the sanctity of marriage, so when Linda cracked the whip (a sound that could be heard clear across town), Neil leaped to attention. "Be an undertaker!" Linda ordered. And Neil stopped tend-ing the soil, and began putting people under it.

In time Neil got to like dead people. They didn't lec-ture. They didn't even talk. He could palpate their faces into big smiles. None of them asked for anything. In fact, he'd never seen a dead person look anything but peaceful. Neil tried to look at the dead in his morgue as a kind of garden. He'd clip and tend them, just like they were plants. There were parallels, if he stretched his mind. He even got to plant them in the ground.

Mind you, then they didn't grow – they rotted. Neil

couldn't quite figure out how to make himself feel better about the rotting part. Looking at a dead person – whom he'd put makeup on and formaldehyde into – he could almost believe they weren't rotting. But he knew in his heart that they were decaying even as he watched.

He knew what it was like to look like you were calm, but to be festering inside.

So there he sat at the table with his two much-loved red-haired sons, Andrew and Philip, who picked at their pork cutlets while Linda marched in and out of the kitchen, bringing the beets and salad, thumping them down in front of Neil.

She was hectoring away, on the subject of Neil's latest misadventure with one of the country club's directors: the omnipotent Muriel Thatcher, who looked soaked in formaldehyde herself, but who smelled of fine cologne. Muriel Thatcher scared Neil shitless.

"'Have Neil talk to me,'" Linda hissed, in a dead-on imitation of Muriel, which she thought was complimentary. She plunked down in her chair at the far end of the long, polished, dining-room table, and crossed her legs neatly at the ankles. "And I say that of *course* Neil will talk to you. It was a perfect opportunity."

Neil sighed and looked at his boys, whose downcast faces displayed no signs of appetite.

"An opportunity you don't even see," Linda went on. "You ignore it. You *ignore* it. You *ignore* my wishes. Sometimes I'm not even sure we're on the same page. Pass the beets, please."

Neil looked at the bowl of beets before him. It was

round-based, spinnable. Between Neil and Linda was a long expanse of smooth, gleaming tabletop. On the tabletop were several bowls and a platter. A vase. A peppermill.

Linda continued her harangue. On she went, like a soundtrack, while Andrew and Philip began once again to pick at their food.

"Because," said Linda, gearing up to say something philosophical and deep, "if there is an absolute truth, it is this: you cannot snub the treasurer of the country club and expect to be looked upon favorably. The beets, please."

"Dad?" said Andrew.

"Hmm?" Neil could spy a pathway through the bowls. It would involve a certain weight, a particular line. Aim and experience.

Linda's voice continued, but Neil was immersed in the calculus of his shot. He heard only a droning sound, countryclubthis, countryclubthat, Murielthis, Murielthat, and *pass the beets*, Neil.

"Dad!"

"Yes, Andrew?" Neil's hands caressed the bowl of beets.

"When you die, what happens to your body?"

"Neil!" Linda bayed. "Neil, pass the *beets!*"

"To answer your question, Andrew," Neil said, pulling the bowl of beets toward himself, but keeping his eye on the tabletop pathway, "sometimes you get buried in the ground. Sometimes, but rarely, you get put inside a curling rock. And sometimes, you just get *married*."

With an elegant release, Neil sent the bowl off on its predestined journey – between the flower vase and the wooden peppermill, around the salad, and – with a glance off the potatoes – it came to rest gently before Linda's plate.

"There you go, dear," he said, digging into his dinner.

Lily Strombeck really, really wanted children. She didn't want to work in an office or as a greeter at the Wal-Mart. She didn't want to be a rich housewife like Linda or an astronaut like Julie. All she wanted to be was Eddie's life partner, and mom to his children. She'd done the life partner thing okay, even though Eddie never had really got any of his business "visualizations" up and running. That was okay, because one day, Lily was sure, Eddie's ship was going to come in with flags flying and guns blazing.

But the mom thing was a problem. The way the doctor explained it, Eddie had very few sperms. The sperms he had weren't very strong, either. Their little tails were broken off or deformed, and the poor things would just swim in confused circles instead of heading upstream like happy little spermy salmons. Lily had eggs, the doctor said – it was Eddie who had the problem. His sperms had low *motility*.

"But he *comes* just fine," Lily said, and Eddie nodded in agreement. He'd had to come a lot, on command, to run all the tests on his…er…on *him* that the doctor wanted-ed. The doctor had run a lot of tests on Eddie. Eddie was getting used to being handed a vial and directed toward a bathroom to produce another "sample." Eddie even took a special bare-naked Polaroid photo of Lily to use for his tests, instead of the *Hustler* magazines, which all had girls in them who looked kind of skinny-skuzzy, instead of softly happy-humpy like Lily.

It was not *impossible* that Eddie's damaged little sperms might make him a daddy some day. The doctor prescribed some sperm medicine and recommended lots and lots of sex. Eddie liked this idea. The doctor told him he would have to be always ready to accommodate Lily's "schedule." And then he told Lily Strombeck to take her *basal temperature* with a special thermometer, which she could get at the drugstore on special order. It would tell them when she was in the best condition for Eddie's low-motility sperms to achieve their goal. The thermometer would cost a fair bit more than a regular thermometer, but it was specially made for the purpose.

"Can't I just use my mouth thermometer?" Lily asked.

"It's not your *mouth* we take the temperature of," said the doctor, explaining the specifics of the process. "Don't give up. We'll make you parents yet."

"Is there anything else we should do?" said Lily.

"Make sure that you time the sex act so that you meet the rise in your basal temperature," said the doctor.

"Anything else?"

"Well," said the doctor, "it wouldn't help to pray."

And so Lily and Eddie went off to drug and boink his specially challenged sperms into action. There were some technical difficulties. The thermometer Lily bought (and *man* was it expensive) got sucked up her patootie the first time she used it. She had to fish it out (scary to have a three-inch fragile glass tube stuck up one's patootie), and by the time she'd done that, Eddie had lost his interest (something about the whole process had made him shrivel like an old cuke). Lily decided, right then and there, that the thin little drugstore thermometer was never going anywhere near her again. What was needed was something with a plug on its end – a stopper of some kind.

And so, Eddie Strombeck found himself naked and sitting in his bedroom armchair (and his bedroom was less *Architectural Digest* and more *Field & Stream/Popular Mechanics* with more than one page of *Sears* catalogue, *Canadian Teddy Bear Collector* and *Country Wife* thrown in). In among the strewn clothes and the train set, and their big mixed-collie mutt Tweetybird, crouched on the hot pink shag throw rug, was Lily Strombeck, also naked, with a meat thermometer up her back end. She listened to Eddie talk, as she timed with a stopwatch how long the thermometer had been inside her.

Eddie was talking about Coach Foley's request, while absent-mindedly massaging himself into action. He'd talked of nothing else since he'd got home, and Lily had listened patiently and with interest. Truth be told, she didn't see what the problem was. Of *course* Eddie should do it. He loved curling. He should do what he loved. Why would anyone do anything else?

"Lily, fun's fun and all, but I can't take up curling again. What about you and me? We've got plans."

"Three, two, one," said Lily, as the stopwatch ticked off the time. She pulled out the thermometer and checked her temperature. "Now, honey."

She crawled over to the chair and Eddie climbed down off the chair and lay on his back on the fuzzy rug, beside the bed. Tweetybird barked and ran out of the room. Lily climbed on top of Eddie.

"Oh," said Eddie. "Oh!"

She began to move around. Eddie almost lost his train of thought, but not completely.

"One of these days, honey," he said, his voice rising with excitement, "one of these days this is gonna work, and we're gonna find ourselves with a whole brood of kids . . ."

"Hmm-hmm," she agreed. "Eddie, *concentrate.*"

"I am concentrating."

She moved a little faster. Her face grew pink.

"I tell you we can't just drop everything for curling," Eddie whispered.

"Sure we can," she said. And then, remembering what the doctor said about praying, she prayed:

I pray the Lord this sperm will float
And make my egg a good zygote.

"Jesus!" cried Eddie, "Sweet Jesus!"

Lily was gratified that her husband would pray with her like that. She wiggled and prayed and, in the same way that Eddie *visualized* his entrepreneurial dealings, she visualized healthy little sperms with wildly lashing tails, on a crash course with a plumply ready egg.

Go, little spermies! she thought.

Meanwhile, Eddie briefly pictured sperms on a trajectory – but they didn't have tails. They were round, like curling rocks. One of them picked a path between other curling-rock-sperms, which were stopped in his way. The tailless, rock-shaped sperm headed right for the button of Lily's egg, where it slid to an impressive and manly halt, bang-on target.

The crowd went wild!

9

O nly in Long Bay would one find such a thing as
a teakettle shaped like a curling rock, but Eva
Foley's kitchen was not the only place in town
that had one. However, Eva Foley's kitchen was probably the only place in town where one would find an
astronaut, a recovering drunk, and a grieving widow
involved in as mean a catfight as a body might wish to
avoid.

"How hard do you think they're laughing in
Houston right now?" Julie Foley hissed at her sister. "I
had to tell them I need an extension on my compassionate leave because my father is in a curling rock."

"You didn't have to get that detailed," Amy spat
back. "For once, Princess Spacewoman, this isn't about
you and the Yankee space program."

"Don't call me Spacewoman," said Julie, who'd been
called that ever since kindergarten, when she'd first
announced that she'd be flying spaceships some day (it
was an announcement she'd always regretted making).
"And why isn't it about the space program?"

"Because it's about our *father!*"

"Who art in a curling rock," said Julie bitterly. The kettle began a shrill whistle, and Julie waved her hand at her mother in a request to shut it up.

"Julie," said Eva, rising to turn off the kettle. "I know you never liked the game of curling, but your father loved it. And he was a great man."

"Mom, he was a *janitor.*"

Eva looked crestfallen, and Julie instantly regretted saying it. She was about to apologize when Amy jumped in.

"Oh, so you got to be an astronaut with a loser for a father? Tell me how that works!"

"I didn't say he was a *loser.*" Julie's face was hot.

"Julie– " Eva began, but Julie interrupted.

"What? What now! You always take her side. A heart like his and she takes him out onto the lake, miles from help, when she *knows* how excited he gets. Got. Shit!"

Amy could hardly breathe the words out. "*At least I was there for him,*" she said.

"'There for him'!" cried Julie, before she could stop herself. "You *killed* him!"

Amy's jaw dropped. Shaken, she stormed from the house, practically ripping the door from its hinges. Eva put her head in her hands. Behind her, the silenced kettle poured steam into the room.

"Mom, I'm sorry," said Julie, genuinely shocked at herself.

Eva reached over and patted Julie's hands, which were gripped together on the tabletop. "Honey, we're all going to say things we regret. It's part of grieving. But you have to remember this was your father's idea, not Amy's. Like it or not, it's his last wish."

"Exactly, Mom. His last wish is…it's selfish. It does-n't involve you or me or Amy. It's about a stupid game."

"That stupid game was often the only thing that gave us all the heart to go on. This town has been through so much. But going to the arena, and watching the boys rule those sheets…hearing the crowd, and seeing the finesse of it all. They were expert, those boys were. And your dad, he was their coach. Did you know, he promised people that we'd win again? That his boys would finish the job? He was a man who kept promises, Julie."

Eva stood up and went to rinse out the teapot. The tap sputtered before shooting out a thin stream of low-pressure water. She began to cry.

"Mom, what's wrong!" Julie said, coming to her aid. "What is it?"

"Your father," said Eva, "promised to fix that. …Oh, Julie, you have to understand how much your father wants to be in that rock. And on that button. Okay, so it's not about me or you girls. But it's not about a 'stu-pid game.' It's about this town, Julie Foley. And curling is as important to us as going to a space station is to you. He wants to be in that rock as much as you want to be in that space station of yours."

Julie put her arms around her mother, and hugged her. "Mom," she said, "I'm not going to the space sta-tion. I'm second alternate. I watch mission after mission go, knowing that there are two people ahead of me in line. I might as well be on extended leave – even if Dad weren't in a curling rock that we're all bound and determined to actually *curl* with. They won't even notice my absence."

The phone rang, an intrusive yelling bell that made both women jump. Eva picked it up. "Hello?" she said, paused to listen, and then handed the receiver to Julie.

"Someone with an American accent," she said. "Calling for *Astronaut* Foley."

Joanne had struggled hard enough intellectually with the trickier nuances of the Cutter/Julie soap opera. But her mental abilities were truly taxed by Jim Lennox's attempts to explain the rules of curling to her.

They sat up in bed in the motel room, engaging in a postcoital chat. They'd been holed up there all day, and except for a half-hour when Lennox popped out for coffee and smokes, they'd basically been at it like bunnies since the night before. Now, somewhat worn out, Lennox had turned his mind to the Coach's rock-encased remains, and curling.

"As Eddie Strombeck says, let's visualize," said Lennox. "Lie down."

"Ohhh," said Joanne hungrily, but to her disappointment, Lennox did not recommence activities. Instead, he took a lipstick from her bag and drew a long rectangle on her naked tummy.

"This is what a curling sheet looks like," he said. "A curling sheet is what you play curling on. It's made of ice."

"I know *that*," said Joanne. "I'm not *totally* stupid."

Lennox doubted that, but didn't want to argue semantics. "There are two teams. The teams are called rinks."

"Why isn't the ice called a rink?"

"Because it isn't."

"I would call the rink a rink and the team a team."

"Just stay quiet, sugar, and listen." Lennox drew a bulls-eye target at each end of the rectangle. "These are the houses," he explained.

"They look like targets. Why aren't they called targets?"

"They're called houses. Just *because*. Now, there are four men on a rink– "

"Don't women play?"

"What?"

"Is it only four men? Because I think that's against the law, if women aren't allowed to play."

"Women *do* play, okay? Jesus. Try and stop a woman from doing something she wants to do. Like, interrupting all the time."

Joanne pouted, but then turned her attention back to the illustration on her belly. "How do you score points? How many points win a game?"

"Just keep your pants on."

"Aww," she cooed.

"Okay," said Lennox, grinning at her pantlessness. "Keep 'em off. But in the meantime, listen. The rink has four members: the Skip, who's the captain, and the Lead, Second and Third. All four members, beginning with the Lead and ending with the Skip, throw two stones each end."

"End?"

"It's like an inning. There are usually eight ends in a game. But in cashspiels – like the Golden Broom – there are ten ends. It takes a couple of hours to play a whole game."

"There are other things I'd like to spend two hours doing," said Joanne.

Lennox shrugged. "Jennie, baby, under certain conditions, curling is more important than sex. Now. Each player delivers his stones, alternating with their counterpart on the other team. Two of the other team members sweep the ice clean in front of the rock, so that it goes at just the right speed and with just the right curl. Sometimes all three sweep, but that's pretty unusual. Kind of only for emergencies, you dig?"

She nodded, trying to picture what kind of emergency could arise in curling. But Lennox was still talking, so she dropped that train of thought and went back to listening.

"So, the sweeping creates friction – you know, *heat* – and it makes a little puddle in front of the stone, so that it can aquaplane. If you throw it properly, the stone can curl right around – hell, even right around on itself, like a fishhook almost."

"Like, in a circle almost? That's not possible."

"I heard that it's been done. I couldn't do it myself, but I can get one hell of a curl going. Anyway, once all the stones are thrown, the team with stones closest to the button scores the points."

"How many points?"

"It's basic arithmetic, Jessie. The team with the stone closest to the button gets all the points."

"So whoever's closer, the other team gets nothing? Like shuttleboard?"

"Shuffleboard. And no. It's more like a mix of poker, snooker and free-face rock climbing." He leaned over her, in a pretense of a threat. "It's dangerous," he said. "If your rock's a hard one, it'll slide right through the house, and wind up in the hack."

He moved his hand down her lipstick-smeared tummy and into her crotch. She squealed and seized him with enthusiasm.

"Shit," he said. "I gotta urinate."

Something in this statement made Joanne hesitate – she had forgotten something, something important that had happened when Lennox went out to get the coffee. Something she had forgotten to tell him. Oh, yeah! Now she remembered.

"Jimmy, there's a friend of yours in the bathroom."

She said this, just as he opened the bathroom door, to discover it occupied by Lloyd Stuckmore, a man (so to speak) of proportions so high and broad that the entire pissoir was consumed by his bulk. To Lennox's disgust, Stuckmore was on the crapper, his pants around his ankles, his face mildly pink from the effort of moving his bowels.

"Jimbo!" he cried, with false bonhomie, setting aside his newspaper. "Good to see you! Where's my money?"

Lennox choked and slammed the door shut, wheeling to press his back against it. Joanne grinned sheepishly.

"I'm sorry I forgot about your friend coming by, but he said he had to use the toidy and then you came back and you kinda distracted me, so I forgot– "

"Forgot!" Lennox roared. "How do you forget about four hundred pounds of defecating *menace!*"

"But – but – he was *nice* – he didn't seem too bad at all, mood-wise," Joanne replied helplessly, as Stuckmore's body began to impact against the door's opposite side. "He said he was blocked, and I gave him a bran muffin to loosen him up – *oh!*"

The door burst clear of its hinges and Lennox at once lay flattened beneath it. Holding it down was an ogre-sized being, bald but bearded, wearing leather and denim and boots that had a suspicious substance on their toes – toes that stood holding the door down on Lennox.

"Where's my MONEY!" Stuckmore hollered.

"Hi, Lloyd," Lennox managed, his face crushed into the carpet. Stuckmore pulled the door off him, and Lennox (who was a wiry type) leaped up and tried to escape. But Stuckmore had the advantage of being upright. He cuffed Lennox, backhanding him like a Kodiak bear, and Lennox landed on his back, on the bed. But he trampolined to his feet, sheer terror acting as his impetus.

Standing on his bed, his feet barely sinking into the mattress, Lennox still had to look up to see Stuckmore. And he didn't like what he saw.

Stuckmore glanced at Lennox's naked crotch and smiled. "Scared of something, Jimbo?"

Lennox glanced down at the peanut-sized knob that was once his dick. "That's as big as it gets in circumstances like this," he said.

"I want my money," said Stuckmore.

Jim Lennox didn't have time to reply. Instead, he found himself flying gracefully through the air, one arm and one leg in the grip of a monster. He saw the drywall heading toward his skull, and had time to think dimly *I hope I miss the studs* before he made contact. The drywall gave way, cracking and then crumbling. Stuckmore used Lennox as a battering ram, striking two more blows, the second of which pushed Lennox's head right through the sheeting in his room, and through the sheeting of the next, into the unit next door.

As the white dust of the shattered drywall cleared, and before Stuckmore had managed to drag his prey back into his own territory, Lennox saw the occupant of the adjoining room looking at him in puzzlement. It was Chris Cutter.

"Lennox...?" said Cutter.

"Hi," said Lennox, his head promptly disappearing. There were two more ominous bangs – full body slams against the opposite wall – and a split appeared in Cutter's drywall. Lennox's head appeared once more through the now-enlarged hole, spluttering the crumbled bits of plaster dust from its mouth.

Cutter was not that surprised. It appeared Lennox had not changed his line of business after all.

"Lovers' quarrel?" Cutter asked Lennox's white-frosted head.

"Uh, business dispute."

Suddenly Lennox's shoulders and then his whole body was shoved from behind into Cutter's room, followed by the complete collapse of an entire section of drywall sheeting. Into the room surged the meaty and leering Stuckmore himself, his knuckles bloody (with Lennox's blood) and his grin victorious.

Lennox scrambled along the floor, the white dust on his face now growing pink from the blood from his temple and lip. Stuckmore kept coming, reaching for the cowering Lennox.

"Okay, okay, listen – listen! I said the money was here. I wasn't lying. This guy's got the money."

Stuckmore glowered suspiciously at Cutter. "You've got the money?" he said.

Cutter nearly wet himself. "I don't know what he's talking about."

"Come on, Cutter," said Lennox, with careful emphasis. "Don't play *games*. This guy wants to *rock and roll*. Just *skip* the bullshit before we both end up under a *sheet*."

Cutter had only a moment's thought of *what the hell is he on about?* Then the penny dropped.

"Okay, okay, I give up," he told Stuckmore. "I got the money. It's in my duffel. Here."

The duffel, fortunately, was at Cutter's feet. Cutter kneeled down beside it and unzipped it slowly. "It's kind of heavy. Gimme a hand."

"Heavy?" said Stuckmore, who essentially was in the drugs and enforcement business because he wasn't exactly college material. He bent over just enough to get into range. Cutter seized the duffel's contents – a forty-two-pound granite curling stone – and swung it upward by the handle, hard as he could, right into Stuckmore's forehead.

Stuckmore's forehead made a squooshy sound, and he lurched back. Cutter didn't pause to absorb sound effects. He swung the rock sideways and hit Stuckmore one more time. Stuckmore swayed, his hands to his head, and then he went down – backward, onto the bed. His hands flopped to his side. Blood poured from a split eyebrow.

Joanne, wearing panties now in an honest but mis-guided attempt at decorum, stepped through the hole in the wall.

"Is he dead?"

"I hope not. I hit him in the side of the head. That's a thin part of the skull, so it's possible. Shit. Lennox, you dumb-ass shit-for-brains *idiot*. A decade goes by and I'm still picking up for you."

"You call this picking up? *I* didn't kill him."

"Like I had a choice? You get into a set-to with a giant. A fucking giant walks the earth, and you get into a fight with him."

Lennox frowned. "I don't follow you."

"What! Am I speaking English? This is your problem and I'm the one saving your ass!"

"Whoa right there, my friend. This is not my prob-lem. This is your problem."

"How is it his problem?" asked Joanne, who found this the most difficult thing to understand yet – even worse than the curling rules.

"It's not *my* problem!" snarled Cutter.

"Whoa, ho, ho!" said Lennox, spreading his hands out. "Hold it right there, my bon vivant. All I did was cap some bulk mescaline for this man, for street sale, and I didn't quite get the money to him on time. An ordinary payment-plan problem. You, on the other hand, caved his head in with a curling rock. You gotta understand the difference. We're talking a minor credit delinquency versus getting physically violent. For this type of guy, collection is basically a hobby. Violence, on the other hand, is a vocation. They will not be outdone."

"Excuse me, but who suggested that I hit him with a curling rock? Was that not *you*, Lennox? I could have sworn it was you."

"Does this have anything to do with your commodities trading?" said Joanne. "Because it looks really brutal to me."

"Every business has its food chain," said Lennox seriously.

"Christ, we'll never get this guy out of here on our own," said Cutter, picking up the phone. "He's still breathing. We better get Eddie and Neil. Joanne, is that a *curling sheet* on your stomach?"

Joanne glanced down at herself and giggled. "Yeah," she said. "Do you like it?"

Cutter rolled his eyes and turned away as Eddie answered the phone.

"Eddie?" said Cutter. "Don't hang up on me. I'm with Lennox. Something's come up, and we need your help."

10

J oanne was one happy little rent-a-girlfriend. There were reasons she'd gone into the rent-a-girlfriend business. Besides the money, the low educational requirements, and the legitimate reason to wear practically no clothes at all, Joanne really really liked men. She liked their muscled arms and their scratchy beards. She liked the way their Adam's apples went up and down when they talked. She liked the way they couldn't help but look at her breasts when they were trying so hard to keep their eyes on her face. Men were just great big fun doofuses who always had some adventure going, and who didn't expect her to do algebra.

So she was very happy to be squished into Cutter's car between Eddie and Neil, watching Eddie unwrap the sandwiches his wife had packed for him. In the front seat of the Impala were Cutter and Lennox, who were mostly finished with their discussion of how Lennox was still an irresponsible jerkoff who always left Cutter holding the bag. Eddie and Neil were in the back seat, staying out of it. They'd heard it a hundred times before.

In the trunk of the Impala was the still-unconscious Stuckmore.

"You packed a lunch?" Neil asked, as Eddie offered Joanne half of his sandwich. Joanne, despite having to watch her diet, took it gratefully. All this excitement had her good and hungry.

"Lily packed it, just in case," said Eddie.

"Just in case what?"

"Just in case I get hungry. I dunno. Just in case."

"Wait a minute. Every time you step out of the house, she packs you a lunch?"

"Not every time."

"Wow. If Linda ever packed anything for me, it'd be dynamite. And she'd pack it up my ass, then light the fuse."

Joanne spoke up, her mouth full of sandwich. "Mff," she said. "If I was married to a guy, I'd make him something to eat every day. Every day I'd do it. It'd be like a privilege to make him a sandwich. Hey, did you hear that? I made a poem! Priv-lidge! San-widge! You guys hear it? Didja hear my poem, guys?"

Lennox stiffened, as if anticipating another motor-mouth session that he'd have to live down to the guys. They'd only brought her along so they could drop her off at Lily Strombeck's, so she wouldn't be hanging around the hotel room among the blood and fractured drywall should the owner of the establishment decide to call the police. Even though the police in this neck of the woods amounted to no more than a handful of good ol' boys led by the amiable and malleable Frances Darte,

Joanne did have the ability to talk the hind legs off a herd of donkeys. Even Frances Darte might be obliged to make an arrest in the face of Joanne's good-natured gutspilling.

When no one replied, Joanne's spirits sank a little. She liked her poem. Up until then she'd felt part of the game. She dropped her hands into her vastly exposed lap, below the hem of her little red skirt, and regarded the crust of her sandwich with embarrassment.

"You're a poet and your feet show it, they're Longfellow's!" said Neil, lightly elbowing her in the ribs.

She brightened and gave him a big smile. "They're only size sevens, seven-and-a-half if they're not quality shoes. It makes a lot of difference to buy quality. Take these boots. They are real leather. They go all the way up to my knee. Here, feel the leather– "

Honored, Neil happily felt Joanne's leather all the way to Eddie's place, where they dropped her off safely before proceeding with their quest.

And in the Impala's trunk, the giant began to stir.

Frances Darte, alone behind the wheel of her cruiser, couldn't help but notice Chris Cutter's black Impala as it pulled up to one of Long Bay's half-a-dozen stop-lights. It was a noticeable car under any circumstances. Besides the car itself, there was also its driver, who was the subject of much speculation lately. For instance, Frances Darte had heard that he was the holdout man when it came to the potential of the Foley Rink's reunit-ing. Frances, who was a betting woman, liked the idea of having something challenging to bet on. But she had also liked Coach Foley, and respected him. For Frances Darte was a woman who embraced the ways of Sappho and Lesbos, and from time to time had felt a certain censorious tension from certain people respecting her – as she put it – natural proclivities. But Coach Foley had always treated her with genuine respect. He'd put an end to some of the nastier insults that had started to circulate. Frances Darte had reasons for wanting the man's wishes fulfilled.

On the top of Chris Cutter's Impala, sliding around in the roof rack, was a curling stone. Because Marvin Fleiger's practice was not airtight when it came to client confidentiality (his secretary took exactly two minutes after funneling Coach's ashes into the small carved-out receptacle beneath the stone's cap to call every woman she knew about it), Frances knew that Coach was in the stone. She knew that Coach belonged on the button. And she knew that the man driving that Impala was standing in the way of Coach's wishes, and the town's greatest need.

She popped the cruiser's cherry lights on, and whooped at Cutter with the siren.

"Shit," said Cutter, and he meant it. For what was not obvious to Frances Darte (as yet) was that Stuckmore was now fully awake and kicking the living hell out of the Impala's trunk. The men in the back seat were jarred hard by the blows from the draft-horse-sized steel-toed boots that struck it from the other side.

"Everybody out of the car," said Lennox, as Cutter

pulled over and Frances tucked the cruiser up behind. By the time Frances was within four feet of the car, the Foley Rink had lined up like a Roman squadron, blocking her way. This, of course, only served to make Frances Darte more curious. She leaned to the left and right, trying to see around the boys.

"Is there a problem, Frances?" asked Neil.

Frances stood back and crossed her arms across her formidable bosom. "You know, Neil," she said, "sometimes keeping the peace involves having a certain limited vision. For instance, I don't see that questionable cigarette Lennox happens to be smoking."

"Jesus Murphy," said Lennox, promptly swallowing the joint.

Frances nodded in appreciation of Lennox's party trick. "Effective," she said. "Unfortunately, what I do still see is that your car is bouncing up and down like hell."

"Shocks are gone," said Cutter. "It needs weight. I'll just take a quick look at her, Frances. Excuse me."

He grabbed the curling rock off the roof rack.

"So life's good, Frances?" Lennox asked, dripping with nonchalance.

"Good and spicy." Frances chose to limit her vision to the three men in front of her, even as Cutter opened the trunk of the Impala and dropped the curling rock onto its contents. She also chose to disregard that the Impala promptly stopped hopping up and down.

"It's particularly good," Frances continued, "now that you boys are *all* going to take a run at the Golden Broom."

"Who said we're going to take a run at it?" said Cutter, slamming the trunk and returning to line up with the others, the Coach-in-a-curling-rock in his hands.

"Ah," said Frances. "In law enforcement, we call this deduction. To wit: I have four delinquents with a very long history of mayhem, and they're driving around with their coach on the roof. I deduce that the only reason these four men would be together at this hour, driving around with their coach on the roof, would be that they would be looking for a place to throw their coach, being as he's in a curling rock and all. Therefore, they must be looking for practice ice."

The men all grinned foolishly and agreed. "Yeah, that's it, all right," said Eddie.

"Now if they *weren't* looking for practice ice," said Frances, "I would be inclined to think that perhaps I should take a better look at their vehicle, in case they were involved in something that maybe someone like Jim Lennox got them caught up in, since Jim Lennox has sometimes been seen – not by me, of course – consuming controlled substances. And I would think that maybe they weren't looking for practice ice. I would think instead that maybe they were trying to dump someone they were carrying around in their trunk."

"What, us!?" cried Lennox. "Frances, come on now!"

"I know, I know," said Frances, shrugging broadly. "It's a crazy thought. But I would think it if I weren't sure they were going to go on together to win the Golden Broom. I would think things like, *jumpin' Jehosophat, Officer Darte, didn't Chris Cutter just clout someone with a curling rock – someone in his car trunk?* I would be obliged to take notice of the fact that even if whoever is in Chris Cutter's trunk is a mean sumbitch who's probably better dealt with by private means, if you catch my drift, that I can't be letting people move outside the law. Unless, of course, those people were just private citizens, local heroes really, going about their law-abiding business and finding practice ice so they can win this town the Golden Broom."

This was about as much verbiage as the men had ever heard from Frances Darte. They all stood very quietly, while the red beam from the cruiser's cherry light flashed across them again and again.

Finally, Cutter spoke.

"We're gonna go find that ice time now, Frances. Got a big job ahead of us."

Frances nodded and smiled, then tipped her hat to them. "Don't forget to get those shocks fixed, Chris," she said.

She swung her nightstick like a horse's tail behind her as she ambled back to the cruiser, already lining up the wagers she'd make in the donut shop, and imagining the buses arriving full of teams for the bonspiel, the girls jumping up and down, the pretty girls…

"Come on, guys," said Cutter, slapping Coach Foley back onto the roof of the Impala. "Before the Friendly Giant wakes up again."

They rolled on into the night, heading for the pier, where the Great Lakes freighters loomed nose-to-tail, ready to take on cargo.

11

The giant screws of an 800-foot-long Great Lakes freighter turned slowly in the moonlight as the black '66 Impala pulled into the gravel lot of the docking yard. The plan was to lug Stuckmore up the gangplank and dump him onto the ship's deck, where he probably wouldn't be noticed until dawn. By then the freighter would be on its way. Cutter could see some flaws with this plan, as they all could, but the train station was way out of town, and as for the bus – well, the next Greyhound wouldn't be leaving until noon. Purolator would be way too expensive, even if they could find a big enough box. A Great Lakes freighter on its way out onto Lake Superior seemed a really solid option.

Besides, the train station and the bus depot were much more heavily guarded than the freighters. In fact, the freighters weren't guarded at all. A single crew of two longshoremen loaded a pallet with canvas bags, not far from the gangplank. An automated crane dragged the pallets aboard the ship's deck, the equivalent height of a three-storey building. One solitary merchant sea-man peered over the rail. Then he wandered away.

The men in the Impala watched, waiting in the dark for the longshoremen to finish. Stunted trees murmured in the night wind. In the denser forest beyond the main road, an owl hooted at its prey. From afar came a coyote's yelping. And Neil started pumping Lennox for details about his love life.

"So how long you been dating your girlfriend?" Neil asked.

"Who, Janice?"

"Is that her name? I thought it was Joanne."

"Yeah. Joanne. I think that's it. It's probably not her real name anyway."

"Why wouldn't it be?"

"The nature of the business she's in. Anyway, Neil, what about her?"

"You been with her long?"

Lennox frosted over. "Why do you ask?"

"Just curious. But– "

"I hate to interrupt the kaffeeklatsch," said Cutter, leaning over the back seat to retrieve a coil of rope that lay on the floor between them, "but when you girls have finished gossiping, we have a troll to ship."

The longshoremen had moved off to the control shack for a beer and a smoke, giving the boys their chance. They had to move fast. However, apparently not understanding the concept of "fast," Neil paused to put his hand on the seat where Joanne had sat. He thought he could still feel the warmth of her body.

"Neil!" barked Lennox. "Quit sniffing the upholstery and come give us a hand!"

Neil jumped out and followed. "I wasn't sniffing it," he said. "I was looking for a quarter."

"We've got a body to dispose of, five minutes to do it, and he's looking for pocket change," said Lennox. "You're the only one with a job, Neil, leave me the friggin' coinage."

Cutter took a deep breath and slipped the key into the trunk's lock. "Hear anything?"

Eddie and Neil shook their heads. Lennox took a long drag of his joint.

"Maybe he's dead," breathed Eddie.

"Then he'll clear customs as freight," said Lennox sourly. "Come on, Chris, just open the trunk." He raised the Coach-in-a-curling-rock above his head in preparation.

"Don't *do* that," growled Cutter. "You're making me nervous."

He turned the key and popped the trunk an inch, and then two. They could see nothing from inside. But a low growl – deep and intermittent – did emerge.

Eddie leaned over and slammed the trunk shut. "What'd you do that for!" Chris yelled.

"He's *snarling* at us!"

"Jesus," said Chris. "He's snoring, Eddie."

By the kind of choreographed mutual effort one only finds in a semi-professional curling team, the four men effortlessly lifted the addle-pated behemoth from the car, a process that involved a great deal of moaning and straining and various indignities to Stuckmore's limply massive body. Stuckmore's head accidentally whacked the trailer hitch, a fortuitous occurrence since this latest blow knocked him out even more effectively. It left him dozy enough for long enough for the Foley Rink to carry-slash-drag-slash-drop-slash-lug-slash-heave the one-eighth-of-a-ton freelance bill collector more than halfway up the gangplank.

At that point, Stuckmore began to stir.

"Whuh?" said Stuckmore, wriggling in their grip, in a move not unlike a newborn baby's.

"Aww," said Eddie, who had babies on the brain. "That's cute."

"Fuck cute," said Lennox. *"Hurry."*

Normally when the boys heard the word *hurry*, they would all start sweeping the ice to create that special aquaplaning effect so integral to the sport of curling. So, for a split second, they all frowned in puzzlement, thinking *is he nuts? We're not curling.*

"Me," bellowed Stuckmore, "down. NOW."

"Hang on, hang on," Cutter urged, as they each grasped a wriggling limb tighter, crabwalking up the steeply angled gangplank. The gangplank was no broader than a sidewalk, with only a rope-mesh webbing for a rail, and there wasn't much room for error.

So, of course, Eddie made an error.

"I can't hold on," he cried.

"Eddie, hold on!" they all replied.

"Let go!" squalled Stuckmore, regaining control of one of his limbs – the one Eddie had.

"Arrgh!" yelled Eddie, dropping the beefy arm as it swung at him (and in passing, the other three men). Stuckmore's head, still groggy, hit the gangplank's boards. The gangplank shuddered. Stuckmore's upper body rolled enough to be hanging off the free side of the gangplank, over the shipping pallet that now dangled twenty feet below from the guy-ropes of the freighter's crane, swinging gently as it slowly ascended.

Cutter and Lennox had Stuckmore by the feet. Neil had lost his hold on his piece of the giant when Stuckmore's upper body slid over the edge of the gangplank. Eddie was standing back bawling, "I'm weak, I'm weak!"

"Let GO!" Stuckmore bellowed, swinging his fists wildly in the open air.

The bewildering stupidity of this, and the golden opportunity it afforded, were not lost on Lennox and Cutter. They glanced at each other, and raised their eyebrows in accordance.

Lennox said, "Okay."

It was a toss-up as to whether Stuckmore would hit the rising loading pallet or the water. Water was a lot farther down, but it was a pretty narrow gap between the ship's rusty steel flank and the pier edge. But there wasn't enough time to feel tense about what sort of predicament would unfold in the aftermath of Stuckmore braining himself on the concrete wall of the pier. Because, thanks to the gods of curling and drunken Canadians on foolish errands, Stuckmore landed on the pallet.

It was only a twenty-foot fall, and he landed among a load of bags and boxes, flat on his back. His eyes rolled up beneath their lids, and he slipped once more into a coma.

"Man, what a thick skull," said Eddie. "Sorry guys, I couldn't hold on."

"Forget it, man, it's working out okay. This is our lucky day. That pallet will go straight into the hold. Much better than the deck. They might not even find him until they're halfway out to sea."

Eddie's eyes glazed over with awe. Imagine traveling the world. Imagine seeing faraway cities, huge places with big buildings and busy streets. Capitals of commerce. He could just...*visualize.*

"Say hello to Port Huron for us," he told the ship, as they all headed back to the Impala.

The curling-rock-cum-funeral-urn sat where Lennox had left it on the gravel, by the car's back tire. Lennox hefted it onto the roof rack. Then, they all got back into the car.

And so, four reprobates and a dead man's leftovers headed off into the night, to find a place to curl.

12

T he Long Bay Memorial Arena was closed tight for the night, and the parking lot chained off. But the Foley Rink had its priorities. Cutter gunned the Impala and drove it into the lot via an alternative route – over the lot's retaining wall. The car landed with a whomp of protesting suspension, and spun neatly to a halt in the lot's center.

"How much do you owe Stuckmore?" said Cutter to Lennox, as Lennox picked the door lock and let them all into the vestibule of the darkened building.

"A thousand."

Cutter looked at the others, and they all in one motion reached for their wallets. "We'll cover that," said Neil. Eddie looked a little pale – that was just about all the money he had to his name – but he couldn't let the others down.

"No way," said Lennox, waving them off. He switched on the banks of overhead lights, which flashed on in order, revealing the sheets of ice, 146 feet long. Four sheets, so four games could be played at once.

"Lennox," said Cutter. "Stuckmore will be back some day. Let's just get the money together– "

"Forget it. I'm not taking money from two broke guys and a henpecked undertaker. I got a chance to do this right." He gestured at the banner for the Golden Broom, which announced first prize as twenty thousand dollars. "And it isn't about the money. I can get the money. What I need is the chance to do something with honor."

"Honor?" said Cutter. "Since when does a drug dealer care about his honor?"

"*Our* honor, " said Lennox. He waved his arm across the arena's interior, as if exposing a vista in a national park. "Beautiful, isn't it?"

The arena was plain, small-town, with a heated second-storey "spectators' lounge" that was really no more than a glassed-off, plywood-paneled barroom. The arena walls were cream-painted cinderblock, and industrial-sized ceiling fans spun slowly in the cool air. Ordinary wooden benches served as the players' areas. The men's breath frosted into the refrigerated air.

Come the Golden Broom, and there would be satin banners and beer and flowers and bleachers and TV crews and crowds. The parking lot would be full. Tour buses and team buses would block each other on the narrow streets. It would be three days of carnival.

Eddie and Neil pulled sliders onto their feet, and grabbed brooms from the rack. Within moments they were out on the sheet, gliding along its length, limbering and bending, throwing imaginary rocks, sweeping the ice surface. Lennox followed them, hotdogging belly-down just for the hell of it. The three of them stood together at one end of the sheet. Cutter remained alone at the other.

Cutter shook his head sadly. "Guys, come on. When's the last time any one of us threw a rock?"

Neil was the one to reply. "Ten years, Cutter. May 13th."

"The day you walked out on us." This from Eddie.

Lennox, lighting an ordinary cigarette for once, continued. "Which mystified the hell out of all of us," he said. "The three of us scratched our heads, saying: what the hell could have happened in that last game, to make Chris Cutter walk out on his rink?"

Cutter turned his face away. Lennox took a drag of his smoke before continuing.

"He walked out on his rink, he walked out on his fiancée, he walked away from the Golden Broom."

Lennox reached into his jacket and took a fifth of brandy out of his pocket. At his feet, among the other stones (which he nudged aside), was the Coach-in-a-curling rock. Uncorking the brandy, he drenched the stone in the liquor, and tossed away his smoke.

"Then one day, not too long ago, the answer came to me. Like a vision. It looked something like this."

He popped a wooden match alight on his thumbnail, and with the burning stick held in his teeth, slid out of the hack, throwing the Coach's stone. As he released its handle he spit the match onto the stone, glancing it off the puddle of brandy that had gathered in the cap. The brandy whuffed alight, and the blazing stone roared the length of the ice, landing in the house, not far from Cutter's feet.

"Wow," said Eddie. "A vision, like a burning bush kinda thing?"

"I don't think so, Eddie," said Neil. "I think Lennox is telling us that Cutter burned a rock. And didn't call it."

Eddie blinked with the shock of this, and looked up at Lennox. Lennox nodded. It was indeed what he meant. Cutter's foot had brushed against a crucial stone, affecting its trajectory, and he hadn't called the foul. The whole game was based on the honesty and honor of its players. It wasn't a matter of sticking by the rules, or being polite. It was the guts of the game. It was its nobility.

"Goddamnit, Cutter. We got into the finals because you cheated?" Eddie sagged to the ice. "He touched a rock and didn't call it."

"Well, it explains why he threw the stones in the lake," said Lennox.

"He couldn't face us." Neil folded his arms across his chest, feeling the chill of the arena. "And he couldn't face himself."

Cutter, unable to bear it anymore, got up and walked to the still-burning Copernicus stone. Lennox didn't let up. He called out to the downcast Cutter.

"And now here's Chris Cutter, and Coach Donald Foley – God rest his soul! – has asked us to put his ashes on the button. Coach Foley, whom he let down more than anyone. Gentlemen, will Chris Cutter do the honorable thing now, and pick up that stone?"

Cutter looked back at him, and then back at the stone. "It's on fire, Lennox."

"I meant metaphorically, Chris."

Chris regarded the stone where it sat in the puddle of water its heat had created in the ice. Then he looked up at his teammates.

"Guys, if you want me to apologize, I apologize. I'm truly sorry. But Coach Foley always told us that the lifeblood of the game is its honor. I don't deserve to pick up that stone."

Neil and Eddie turned on their heels, dropped their brooms, and walked off. Lennox paused only long enough to say one more thing to Cutter, before he too left him alone in the ringing arena.

"One way or another, Chris," he said, "you've been carrying it for ten years."

Cutter sat down on the ice with the Coach's stone in front of him, watching the flames on its glossy granite surface flicker out and die.

Amy Foley's Saturday night AA meeting had dispersed with the usual event, which Amy now looked on as a tradition. On the way out of the church basement, Grover "Groper" Whitlaw gave her ass a good palpating as she ascended the stairs.

"Groper, for Chrissake," she said. "Couldn't just for once you come to a meeting *sober*?"

Things like that made her lose hope. She'd stood up and given her "sharing" to all the people she knew from meetings before, and all the while she could hear herself crying inside. Crying for her father, for her fear for her job (they'd laid off half the staff at the physio clinic where she ran the therapy pool), for her impossible love for Cutter, who couldn't be trusted to stick around. And who, in any event, was in love with Julie "I'm An Astronaut Ain't I Great" Foley.

But sharing all that had only made her want to drink more. Groper's gratuitous fondling, which she was usually a good sport about, just served to piss her off.

She should have gone home, but she thought of Julie and couldn't face the notion. So she started walking, leaving her car behind. She walked all the way to one end of town, down close to the road that went to the docks, and then back up through Neil Bucyk's solitary model home in the-subdivision-that-never-happened (where Neil Bucyk's cuckolding wife was propped up on the counter, while Neil Bucyk's assistant, Ronnie, serviced her with mindless lust). Amy felt the snake that was the urge to drink coiling and uncoiling in its nest inside her. As long as she kept walking, it never fully awakened.

At one point, when it was no longer night and was now heading toward morning, she saw Jim Lennox, Neil Bucyk and Eddie Strombeck walking shoulder-to-shoulder, with lowered heads, like disappointed twelve-year-olds. She almost called out to them, but then realized they were coming out of the laneway that led to the Long Bay Memorial Arena. And she knew at once that Cutter would be needing a friend.

She found him on the sheet, still sitting in front of the

curling stone, although he had got up for long enough to get himself a bottle of Scotch from the club bar. He was now about a quarter of the way through it, and hardly felt how freezing his ass was. But at the sight of Amy, he couldn't help but brighten inside. After the drubbing he'd just taken from his dear friends – after all the unforgiven *stuff* had surfaced like a U-boat – what he needed most was Amy.

He felt he should say something meaningful to her, to tell her how happy he was that she'd come, his saving angel. But when he opened his mouth, the wrong words came out.

"It's a free bar," he called, gesturing with the bottle.

She shook her head, smiling softly. "Every drink has its price, if you're a drunk."

"Amy," he said, "don't put it like that. You always are so hard on yourself."

"I'm AA, Cutter – the whole twelve steps. It's not a matter of being hard on myself. It's a matter of not messing up my life…and Brandon's." She took the bottle from him, then located the bottletop where it sat on the ice, and capped the bottle closed. Cutter sighed.

"So," he said, "what are you doing out at three o'clock in the morning?"

"Trying not to drink. And you?"

"Just hanging out with your dad. Which in the circumstances is kind of creepy. Pull up a chair."

She took one from the players' area and slid it onto the ice in front of him. Cutter had unscrewed the cap of the stone so that the dusty contents were revealed, looking much like cigarette ashes except lumpier. There was no more than a teacupful in the drilled-out receptacle in the stone. The stone itself bore scorch marks, from the burning brandy.

"He was pretty wigged out, to will this," said Amy.

Cutter agreed, and she went on, peering into the stone.

"I thought I would just humor him, you know. Take scuba lessons, get him the boat….I thought he'd get over it when he realized we'd never find those rocks in that dark deep ol' lake. Which I never thought we'd actually succeed in doing. And in the meantime it was a great way to hang out with him. I had no idea that it was more elaborate than just getting the rocks. I didn't think he'd wrapped his immortal soul up in the idea of winning a curling game – a curling game that isn't going to go on. So I look at this thing now– " she gestured at the stone "–and I think, *it's just a rock.*"

Cutter startled, almost as if he'd been slapped. "It's not just a rock," he said.

"What?"

"It's forty-two pounds of polished granite, with a beveled underbelly and a handle that a human being can hold. Okay, so in and of itself it looks like it has no practical purpose. But it's a…a *repository*. Of possibility. And when it's handled just right, it exacts a kind of poetry."

"Poetry, Chris?"

"As close to poetry as I ever want to get. The way it moves. The way it can be moved. For ten years I've –

well, I've been around. I've drilled for oil on five conti-
nents. I've been in ninety-three countries and not once
have I ever done anything that equals the grace of a
well-thrown rock as it slides down a sheet. Seen the sort
of effort that a rink puts into guiding that stone. Not
once, in everything I've done, have I ever felt the same
wonder and humanity as when I'm playing the game of
curling."

Cutter stood and brushed off his cold ass. He picked
up the Coach's rock. With a grace that took Amy's
breath away, he glided effortlessly out of the hack, traveling with the rock for twenty feet before releasing it to
continue on its own. It slid on, curling toward the center, drifting slowly in an agonizing curve.

As if it knew where it belonged, it came to rest right
on the button.

13

As dawn crested the horizon, turning it peach-pink, Cutter dropped Amy off at her house. He leaned over and kissed her forehead. The Coach sat between them on the Impala's black vinyl seat.

"See you," he said. "You're the best."

As he drove away to find his teammates, Amy Foley thought she would faint from joy. He was going to play. The game was on.

Cutter knew where his boys would be. Trout Lake was more than just a place for cheaters to dump curling stones in a fit of remorse. It was also the place the boys had collected since the days their peckers were only used for peeing. There was a diving cliff, and despite the fact that the weather had turned past swimming days, Cutter knew they'd be there.

He stopped at the Tim Hortons and got four coffees – one double-double, one black no sugar, two just black – and drove to the Trout Lake Drop-Off, as they called it. Sure enough, fast asleep in the blueberry bushes, clutching their jackets around them, were the noble members of the Foley Rink.

"Get up, boys," he said. "Let's test our mettle."

It was a phrase they'd used as kids, to dare each other to jump into October water. Crazy stunt. Dangerous. But not as dangerous as risking the town's pride and self-worth on a drug dealer, a funeral director, an impotent bankrupt and a spineless cheater.

The tall cliffs and taller pines stood sentinel as they cascaded off the cliff, big naked hairless lemmings. They each shouted what they were, in defiance of the odds:

"I'm a dealer!" screamed Lennox. "Banzai!"

"I bury dead people!" Neil nearly landed on Lennox.

"I've got a single-digit sperm count!" Eddie's useless balls retreated into his body as they hit the freezing water.

Finally, Cutter leaped in among them. "I'm a naked cheater!" he screeched, arms and legs spiraling, dick waggling. Then he hit the freezing water in a cannonball. It was autumn-cold and not pleasant, but the shock was mind-clearing. Defying hypothermia, they forced themselves to gather together so they could leave the water together.

"That's it, then," said Cutter. "We're going as far as we can go."

"To the Broom, boys, to the Broom!"

Dripping and goose-pimpled, they emerged from the water, clinging to the rock face to commence their climb back up.

"It's freezing," said Eddie, teeth chattering. "We'll die of pneumonia before we even get back."

"Eddie, we're going to take the Broom," said Lennox. He glanced down at his privates. They had shriveled so far that all he could see was his pubic hair. "Shit, my gonads are gone," he said.

"Get your gonads back together," said Cutter. They struggled a few more inches up the cliff face, their lips blue and their fingers numb with cold. "We're gonna start training. You'll need gonads."

"How are we gonna train, Chris?" said Eddie. "Coach is dead."

"Yeah," said Neil, trembling very hard, since he was the thinnest of all of them. "And we're in terrible shape."

"Excuse me, gentlemen?"

A voice from the overhang above, a woman's unmistakable voice, called down to them. None of them could cover themselves, so they just pressed their cold bellies to the colder stone, except for Lennox, who'd already exposed himself to her and wasn't too worried about further exposure. For it was Lennox's rent-a-girlfriend, Joanne, who stood with their clothes folded over her arm, and her hands on her hips, Wonder-Woman style.

She wore a long baby-blue feathered scarf over shorts and a glittery halter, and silvery tights. There were feathers in her hair, too. She loved dressing up, and showing off her form. Her washboard stomach and trimly muscled arms would have been impressive even on a guy.

"Gentlemen," she called again. "I couldn't help but ease drop. But fitness does happen to be one of my areas of expertise, as I am an employee of the fitness industry.

In no time, I can whip you into shape. And I can do this in a plane, or a dentist's chair, or even in the back seat of a car."

Neil liked the back seat idea. But he kept that to himself. Why would such a delightful stunner as Joanne have anything to do with a lachrymose undertaker – and a married one, to boot?

He envied Lennox. Leaning over to him, he whispered, "She's a living doll, you lucky bastard."

"A *what?*" said Lennox. "What century do you get your vocabulary from?"

Neil glowered at him. "She's a really terrific girl, and you're lucky – that's what I'm saying– "

But Eddie interrupted. "We don't need a back seat," he offered. "How about a gym instead?"

"A *gym?*" said Cutter. "What gym?"

"Boys," Eddie replied, still clinging damply to the rock, "I'm going to ask you to *visualize…*"

Visualizing like crazy, the four men and a fitness bunny made their way through the minefield of failure that was Eddie Strombeck's yard. Eddie, though, saw it as a plain of possibility. He owned two acres. Those two acres were buried under the leavings of all Eddie's ventures: the double-decker bus that he'd planned to do tours with, but which he'd driven into a bridge and knocked the roof off of.

"Jesus, Eddie," said Lennox, looking at the crumpled upper deck of the bus.

"That bus is all the way from London. *England.*" Eddie

waved his hands in his characteristic summoning of an image. "Visualize! 'Eddie and Lily's Open-Air Tours'!"

The others groaned and turned away. "What the hell is that?" said Cutter, motioning toward a structure that was mostly collapsed frame and broken sheets of glass. Inside its wreckage, hip-deep plants and weeds were shriveling and dying in anticipation of an unprotected winter.

"I got a setback on that project. That freak hailstorm last spring made it all a bit messy. But I want you to visualize this. 'Eddie and Lily's Cucumber Galaxy.' You know how expensive produce can be. Here, you could pick your own– "

"Eddie," said Neil. "If I thought for a moment I could make a living with a greenhouse, I'd be out of that mortuary like a bat out of hell. You should have asked *me* about the potential of that project."

"Or me," said Joanne. "My parents owned a nursery."

Eddie looked puzzled. "What have babies got to do with it?"

"A plant nursery, Eddie," said Neil. "You got babies on the brain, boy-o."

Neil caught Joanne's eye and held it. He could see flowers blooming all around her. Big flowers with huge stamens and pistils, bobbing pink on their stems.

"Okay, okay," said Eddie. "You guys just have no vision. But look at this." He pulled a tarp from a bright yellow, hip-height, one-man submarine. "Direct from the Bolivian navy! It has a couple of leaks – Lily and I found that out pretty fast – but it'll be fine once I get it patched.

Visualize! 'Eddie and Lily's Submarine Tours'!"

"Eddie– " Cutter began.

But Eddie went on, telling them all about Eddie & Lily's Stationary Animal Safari (where guests would pay to pat animals fresh from the taxidermist's, and get a "guaranteed picture every time, or your money back") and Eddie & Lily's Helium Sucking Heaven. His faith was both discomforting and inspiring.

At last they reached the goal of their excursion. "Wait until you see this," said Eddie, stopping before the garage-style door of a semi-cylindrical aluminum hangar. He grabbed the door handle and rolled the door upward and open, in one mighty rumbling of counter-weights and chains.

"Visualize!" he cried, and Cutter smacked him across the back of the head. But it didn't deter Eddie. "Welcome to Eddie and Lily's Retro Gym!"

"Retro?" said Lennox. "More like wreckage."

The gym had a dirt floor but a decently high ceiling. It was filled with what at first glance looked like junk – piles of bent bars, big leather medicine balls, and a pre–Pearl Harbor version of gravity boots. As the dust cleared and Eddie opened the shutters on the windows, it became clear that not a piece of equipment postdated 1950. Parallel bars, medicine balls, rusty barbells – not a Stepmaster or a weight machine in sight.

Joanne cheerfully broke the dismal silence. "Wow," she declared. "This is perfect. When I'm finished with you, you will be a team. Come on, boys. Shirts off. We start with the smooth stick."

They glanced at one another, suddenly feeling silly to take off their shirts in front of her, when only an hour before they had been bouncing around buck naked. But now they were being assessed for their firmness of muscle, and they were supremely aware of their beer bellies, sagging asses, and stringy arms.

"I said, shirts off," said Joanne, picking up a six-foot smooth stick, and rapping it on the floor.

Slowly they peeled, tossing the shirts into a pile in the corner. They were indeed a flaccid and pitiful bunch. Only Cutter had any tone at all, and he wasn't exactly buff.

"Hey," said Joanne. "You guys all got beavers."

Eddie snorted in offense, while the others just looked confused. "There's no call for saying that," he protested.

"There, above your nipplies," Joanne explained.

Understanding dawned on them, and they each peered down at the tattoos over their hearts. Little beavers – fighting beavers. Each the same as the other.

Joanne slipped out of the sweater that she'd tossed on over the halter top. She stood as taut as a drum, hair perfect and befeathered, teeth gleaming: a rock-hard kitten, with a big stick.

"Grab a pole, boys," Joanne barked. "Over your heads with it. Arms. Legs. *March.*"

Feeling stupid – but not as stupid as they felt *weak* – the four of them fell in behind the apple-shaped buttocks of Joanne, former rent-a-girlfriend, now Marine drill sergeant. They were on their way.

14

I t was with mixed feelings, that Cutter rang the Foleys' doorbell. Winded and aching, nursing muscles pummeled from the workout, he had been charged with the duty of collecting the rest of the Copernicus stones. None of the others would do it, and as they pointed out, it was Chris who had started all this by dumping the stones and ditching the team in the first place. Chris knew what they were implying: coming home to the Foleys, to Eva and Amy and Julie, was part of his penance.

He hoped for the best: to have a cup of tea and a plate of Arrowroots with Eva, and maybe play a video game with Brandon while Amy sat on the back of the sofa, rubbing the knots out of his neck and shoulders. He could moan to her without fear of reprisal (although she might call him a wuss, it would be in the kindest possible way). Nor would he have minded seeing Julie, and making some peace there. The snubbing at the funeral home still stung him, and there had been few steps taken to correct that. She'd been civil enough at the reading of the will, but other than that, they were as polarized as ever.

But Amy was at work, Eva was on her way out to bowling, and Chris was on his own. "Stones are in the basement, ducky," Eva said, neglecting to mention what else was down there – Julie, that is.

Julie was not expecting Chris. In fact, she'd been in the very act of fingering the fabric on her wedding dress, which had stood on a dressmaker's dummy, gathering dust, for lo these ten years. Being caught dead to rights engaging in such a ridiculously sentimental act caused her to give the dummy a massive push, so that it tumbled backward into the closet. She slammed the door, and whirled to face the intruder.

"Hi," she said. "I was just going through his things. No one else seems up to it, and I thought– "

Cutter looked from where she was standing, to the pile of papers, photos, certificates, and keepsakes that she'd spread out in the middle of the rec-room's acrylic-pile carpet. It hadn't escaped him that she'd been beating up on her wedding gown. This left him in a delicate position. She seemed to be close to a clobbering mood, and he was close enough to clobber.

Or was that close to tears? It was hard to tell with Julie. He knew she had a soft side. As he watched, the brittleness on her face began to fall away, and her lower lip trembled. He knew what was coming next, and it came. Julie burst into tears.

Cutter was no idiot. He stepped forward at once, put his arms around her, and let her bawl against his shirt.

Julie didn't cry much, but when she did, it was a doozy. By the time she finally drew away, and looked wet-cheeked up into his face, he had a big damp spot on his T-shirt.

"I'm not crying because of…because…" she began.

"Of me," he filled in.

She waved her hand, warning him not to interrupt. "I'm crying because, you know, the past couple of years Dad and I barely spoke because I was – well, I was doing one thing or another – and now – now I just miss him, that's all. I would like to see him, have some tea and look at the stars, go for a drive on a Sunday….Cutter, I just *miss* him."

He nodded. "Me, too."

He held her again, but she was finished crying. She had slipped into the A-type mode, the directness, that had earned her so much in her life.

"You came for the rocks," she said.

"Yeah," Cutter replied. "I gotta do this. I owe him."

He could see the shift in her personality taking over. She was all business now. Information girl. "You owe him what?" she said.

"I owe him *me*. What I am."

She snorted. "You're a roughneck in an oil patch, Chris. That's not a debt to repay. That's a curse."

"Hey, not everyone can be an astronaut," he said, without rancor. He'd got a lot out of his travels – his "roughneck oil patch" life. He wasn't about to be ashamed of it.

Julie, on the other hand, seemed to have some issues

about being an astronaut. "You say 'astronaut' like it's a *fault*," she bristled.

"No," he said. "A *'fault'*? Come on. You know we're proud of you. He *was* proud of you. He loved you."

The tears were back, but the A-type woman was still there. A dangerous combination. "And you?" she demanded.

"Of course I loved him," said Cutter, believing himself to be reassuring.

"And me?"

"You loved him too."

"Did you?"

Something was wrong. She seemed to be getting madder. "Uh, love him?" he said, scrambling while alarms went off in his head.

"No."

That didn't help him any. 'No?' Okay, 'no', not her father. Whew. Okay. One down. Process of elimination. He could still get out of this.

"Who?" he asked.

Uh-oh. Her upper lip curled back over her perfect teeth. "*Me*, you moron. Did you love *me*?"

Lights went on all over the city as his mental blackout ended. Unfortunately, with the lights up like that, Cutter could see how much trouble he was in.

"Yes," he said, soothingly, truthfully. "Of course I did."

She absorbed this. The expression softened. He might be out of the woods.

Quietly, sweetly, she asked, "And now?"

But he couldn't answer. Nothing came. In an instant that seemed like a century, all sweetness vanished and she was nearly *throwing* curling rocks at him. One – she thrust at him – "Here, take it!" she cried – *whump* went the air from his diaphragm, and he stayed upright as *whoof* – two – another stone on top of it. His aching muscles struggled with the strain.

"Just go. Okay? Go!" she barked, attempting to load a third stone on the pile. Cutter, though, had had enough. Tight-lipped, confused, he backed away toward the stairs, losing the third stone en route. He would be back for the others later, when Julie was no longer lurking over them, asking questions he couldn't answer.

Julie sank to the carpet, regretting everything. The lost wedding, touching the dress, losing her cool with poor guileless Cutter, who couldn't tell a lie (surely!) if he were paid a million dollars. That was why he'd left her at the altar, after all. Because he'd found himself acting out a lie.

He might have loved her once, but he didn't love her now. Oh, she wished her dad were here. He'd make her a root beer float. They'd sit on the porch. He'd punch her in the upper arm and tell her about how wonderful she was. If only he were here.

But he wasn't. And he never would be again.

She picked up a shoebox – one of many – that she had not yet looked through. IN THE EVENT OF MY DEATH, read a faded pencil note, taped onto the cover. She frowned and opened the lid. Inside there was just one thing. A cassette tape. It too had a note taped to it.

FOR THE BOYS, it said.

She took the tape from the shoebox, knowing her dad's voice was on it, and burst once again into tears.

15

Julie sat in her kitchen, watching for the Foley Rink to run by. On the table before her was the cassette tape. She turned it over and over in her fingers against the tabletop, beside a few other scraps from her father's personal effects: photos of the Foley Rink, of Coach Foley as a twenty-year-old athlete, standing out on the river in silly pants and a thick sweater, with his curling broom held high.

FOR THE BOYS, the cassette's label reminded her.

Every day for two weeks, that parade of fools had run by the house, aimed a salute its way, and then jogged on. Behind them, dressed in a leopard-print leotard with black overthong fitness panty, ran Jim Lennox's rent-a-girlfriend. The first time Julie'd seen them she'd been embarrassed for them – the way they were barely able to jog, and Lennox running with a doobie dangling from his mouth. But for the last few days she'd noticed they were faster, sleeker and that the woman in the tights and the buttock-flossing panties was actually having to work. Even Eddie Strombeck looked fit. Cutter looked outstanding. But then again he always did muscle up easily.

The phone rang, breaking her concentration on the quite admirable backsides of the passing men. She reached for it, greeted the caller, and listened without speaking.

"Yes, sir," she said. "I understand. But I have to remind the Space Agency that I'm on compassionate leave."

The voice on the end of the phone went up an octave and several notches of volume, as the speaker pulled rank with all his might.

"Yes, sir," said Julie Foley. "I will take that under advisement."

She hung up. The men were long gone, having rounded the corner to head up to Eddie & Lily's Retro Gym. Julie sighed and sat down. What was she doing, sitting here for one moment longer? That call – that one she had just dismissed so blithely – was a demand from Mission Control, that she end her leave and report back...*now*. Why should she? They would just put her into another tank of water, or onto another g-force machine, or have her design another computer program to simulate re-entry with a simulated fuel leak.

She picked up the phone again and punched in the code numbers to block incoming calls from a particular source. That source was the number for the Houston command of the space program. She knew how serious it was – to shut herself away from Mission Control – but part of her felt as abandoned by her career as she had felt abandoned by Cutter. Men at the altar; men in the space program – they were all alike. If they wanted her, they were going to have to come get her. For once in her life, she wanted to stay still – and there was no place better for staying still than a place like Long Bay.

The Foley Rink's first scheduled match of its new incarnation was against Wally Walters' rink, which curled out of the somewhat posher curling club in nearby Glanford. The Glanford Curling Club was ordinary – like the Long Bay Memorial Arena, it had four sheets of ice, and a small observers' lounge – but the Walters Rink were real veterans. Some of them were veterans of World War II.

Their skip, Wally, led his team to the ice. The second had to carry his broom, since Wally used a walker. They approached the Foley Rink – or at least, the three members of that team that had shown up on time – and settled into the players' area.

Wally leered at Lennox with a face as wrinkled as a walnut. "Go easy on us, eh, boys?"

"My friend, we're gonna sweep your diapers clean off your withered asses."

"That's the spirit, young fella," chuckled Wally. In fact, the whole team chuckled. It was a somehow sinister comment.

"I don't like the sound of that," said Cutter, as their opponents shuffled and waddled off.

"Don't be ridiculous," said Lennox. "They're friggin' Methuselahs. Where the hell is Eddie?"

Neil sighed. "Lily showed up with her timer going

off. He had to go water the garden. He's sowing his bounty in the equipment room."

"Nice work," said Lennox, "if you can get it."

Joanne, who had come along to cheer her boys, exclaimed brightly that she couldn't imagine a garden needing watering this time of year.

"No, Joanne," Neil said gently. "He's having sex with his wife. They're trying to have babies."

"Ohhh," said Joanne. "Listen, I'm going to go sit with the other ladies in the spectators' lozenge. You boys have a good game. Knock 'em dead."

"They're dead already," said Lennox.

"Yeah, but Neil could use the business," said Cutter.

Neil laughed, but not wholeheartedly. Lately, "the business" had been unbearable. A line of work in which he'd always been able to find some sort of positive aspects – a certain escapism – had been overridden by a continuing fantasy of lowering Joanne (his buddy's girlfriend yet!) into a big field of flowers. Flowers he'd grown with her – flowers they'd grown together. He could see them bent over the beds, weeding and sowing together. The impossibility of it didn't make him a happy mortician. It affected his focus.

As Neil watched Joanne's admirable figure amble over to the stairs and up to where Julie and Amy Foley sat, Eddie Strombeck came running into the players' area, carrying his broom and panting. He'd been gone no more than five minutes.

"Sorry guys," he said.

"That's some hair trigger you got there," said Lennox.

"It's not the size of the army, it's the fury of the onslaught," Eddie replied, his complexion still ruddy from his efforts.

Cutter turned to wave at Amy and Julie through the glass. Julie had her nose in a sheaf of papers – her line of work wasn't one which could be long-neglected – and she didn't even see his greeting. But Amy waggled her fingers at him and smiled broadly. Joanne, coming up behind them, threw both arms in the air and yelled, "Go team!"

"Oh, hello," said Amy, a little taken aback by Joanne's sudden appearance.

"May I join you girls?" Joanne burbled.

"Sure. You're a big curling fan, then?" Amy asked, as Joanne pulled up a chair.

"I just know a little," said Joanne. "But I want to learn everything. Because I'm the team's Personal Trainer!"

"Well, get comfortable, because here we go." Amy nodded toward the ice beyond the glass, where the game had begun, the lead of the Walters Rink practically crawling into the hack.

"What inning are we in?" asked Joanne, trying to contribute, but forgetting pretty well everything Lennox had spelled out for her, the day he drew a curling sheet on her bare tummy.

"Well, we just started – and they're called 'ends,' not innings," said Amy. "This is the first end. They'll play ten of them – up one side and down the other. And don't be fooled by those old guys. Older players tend to have the touch."

"Touch?" said Joanne.

"That's right – *touch*. They'll lay that stone in just so. You see, every player has his own kind of style. Some guys have perfect weight. They throw the lead stones. Some guys set up guards well. At the end of it, comes the skip."

"What are all the brooms for?"

"Well, without even touching the rock, you can affect its speed and accuracy. You can, in fact, kind of *steer* a rock of granite – without touching it – down 146 feet of ice, landing it on an area the size of a dinner plate."

"Wow."

"I mean, it's not rocket science," said Amy, glancing at her sister, who had not yet participated at all in Joanne's education, said more than a hello, nor glanced at the action unfolding on the ice. "Not all of us can be rocket scientists."

Julie rolled her eyes. She had meant to ignore it all, but then Joanne turned to speak to her.

"May I just say what a thrill this is?" Joanne babbled. "I mean, I am a high school graduate – well, just about – but *you!* You've been to university I bet. I mean, I *don't think* they give astronaut degrees at college. Maybe I'm wrong. I'm wrong a lot. Can you learn to be an astronaut at college? Can you go to night school and get your diploma for it there? Not that I'd ever try. I'm devoted to the fitness industry myself."

Julie put her hand up to her face. But Amy saw no reason to spare her sister. She got a little weary, from time to time, of everything being the Julie Foley Talent Show.

"Actually, Joanne, Julie Foley has two doctoral degrees, which *no* does not mean she's a doctor who gives you breast implants, but who has a Ph.D. in a particular field of study. Julie in fact has a *double doctorate.* This means she's really smart. Her job is to operate the SPDM, which is the dual-armed robot that assists the larger Space Arm. You know the Space Arm. Canada's contribution to the space program, and Julie Foley from Long Bay, Canada, is part of that program. Why, with the SPDM, she can lift six hundred kilos."

Joanne had stopped understanding somewhere around "Ph.D." But she was still a big fan, and she understood power lifting.

"That's all amazing about the double doctor and stuff," said Joanne, "but what about your physical fitness! Six hundred kilos! I mean, girlfriend, who let the dogs out?"

Amy took a scoring pen and signed a napkin with Julie's name. "Want her autograph?"

"Thanks," said Joanne, not noticing the daggers Julie stared her sister's way. "Oh, look, that rock went onto the – uh – the target thing! Go, team, go!"

The Foley girls sunk down in their seats, while Joanne bounced right out of hers.

By the fourth end, the score was 4 to 1. The 1 belonged to the Foley Rink. The losing team was a little dismayed, but they figured they weren't really warmed up yet. Yeah, that was it. They were just a little stiff.

Eddie, the third, threw his rocks, leaving his rink

with a nice score: four rocks in the house, neatly placed. Wally and his ancient cronies hobbled up to examine the formation, while Eddie sat down and picked up his beer. He toasted the others, the bottles clinking.

"You never really lose the touch, do you?" said Neil.

"It's like riding a bike," agreed Eddie.

The third of the Walters Rink fired off a rock that curled the length of the ice with deadly precision. With four sharp bangs the Glanford rock removed the four scoring rocks of the Foley Rink. Cutter and the others watched in blank amazement as their Geritol-chugging opponent crept back to the players' area, weakly high-fiving Wally as he passed.

"Like riding a bike," Wally remarked to Jim Lennox. "What's that you're smoking, son?"

"Persian tobacco," said Lennox. "Want some?"

He proffered the joint to Wally. "I had a Persian cat, you know," said Wally, taking the joint and hobbling off with it, much to Lennox's chagrin. "Her name was Kitty. Legs from here to Los Angeles."

The game went on, rocks slamming into rocks. The score soared to 6 to 1. Cutter, as skip, focused on the strategy. He checked out the Glanford Rink's stones, and motioned to Lennox, whose turn it was to throw.

"Just tap it," Cutter said, pointing to a spot on one of the Glanford rocks. "Right there."

"Tap it," Lennox agreed.

Unfortunately, Lennox had bulked up some, and as the saying goes, didn't know his own strength. He let fly with a torpedo of a stone, which bulleted past the sweepers, focused in like a guided missile, and struck one of the Glanford Geriatrics' rocks with such force that the target stone shattered. The house was filled with chunks of granite.

"Whoa, Nellie," said Wally. "I think it's been fifty years since I seen that." He paused, mulling this over. "Nope, actually, I never seen that."

They consulted the rule book. In time, the Glanford Rink's PA system announced the finding: the largest piece of stone nearest the button wins the point.

"Hooray," said Joanne. "Does that mean they're going to do it?"

"No, Joanne," said Julie with great control, "it does not. It means that they're about to be beaten by a quartet of nonagenarians."

"A quart of *what?*" said Joanne.

"It means old people. Just hush and watch."

The Foley Rink reassembled, and indeed they had lost the point. Cutter scowled at Lennox.

"You call that a 'tap,' Lennox?"

"It was a tap with authority."

Cutter grabbed him by the sweater. Lennox took a swing at him. Cutter ducked it and pulled Lennox's jersey over his head. Eddie leaped in to stop it.

"Guys, guys, knock it off," he said. "Let's curl."

An hour later word had spread – Cutter's request that they keep this game a quiet, family-only affair had not survived Long Bay's porous veil of secrecy. A sizable crowd had gathered around the Long Bay/Glanford game. Wally was pulled away from his discussion with

Neil of the benefits of prepaid funerals so that he could throw his stone, the last stone of the game.

Wally set aside his walker and crept out onto the ice. But the Foley Rink were no longer fooled. Wally might not walk very well, but he could sure throw a curling rock. They winced as the old man slid out of the hack, released his rock, and rose achingly to his full five-foot-three of dowager-humped height. The stone described a perfect arc, avoided Cutter's guard, and snuggled itself right up to the button. The old men had won.

The men from the Glanford Club threw their canes in the air in celebration. "Huzzah," they croaked, and "Yippee." One of them took a long sip of oxygen from his portable tank. They shook arthritic hands with each other and turned to thank their opponents.

"Never mind, young fellas," said Wally. "Winners have to buy the beer."

"Yeah, well," said Eddie despondently. "I guess there's always an upside."

Cutter turned to the stands, to see what the girls were doing. Julie had left. Amy and Joanne sat together, Amy looking crestfallen, and Joanne applauding hard, in an effort to be encouraging. "Go, team, go," she offered.

"Go for beer, anyway," said Cutter. "Come on, guys."

Julie Foley was waiting for them in the parking lot as they loaded their gear into the back of Neil's hearse. She marched up to them with the stride of a woman who had trained to fly spacecraft. The men's testicles ducked for cover. Cutter tried to look brave.

Julie grabbed him by the sweater and pulled him to her, kissing him hard on the lips. The guys' balls dropped back into place, no longer afraid they were going to be kicked. But they were still confused.

"What's this about?" said Cutter, as Julie released him.

"I thought you might need it," she said. "And need...*this.*"

She handed him the cassette from her father's effects. Then she whirled on her heels and paraded off.

The men watched her go, their jaws on the asphalt. Lennox picked his up and asked the question they were all thinking.

"Spacewoman still got a thing for you, Cutter, my man?"

Cutter shook his head. "I didn't think so," he said. "All the vibes I get are hot and hostile, not hot and bothered." He looked at the tape in his hand. "It says it's for us, so let's listen."

It was appropriate that they'd be riding in a hearse to listen to the voice of a dead man. As the Foley Rink and Joanne rode the night roads back to the heart of town, Neil – who was at the wheel – took the cassette of "Funeral Top 40" out of the deck, and slipped in the Coach's tape.

Coach Foley's voice rode with them.

"Hello boys," he said, through the speakers.

"It's the voice of the dead," murmured Neil.

"Spooky," Eddie breathed.

"I imagine by now you've thrown a couple of rocks and are beginning to think this was a pretty dim idea.

Maybe it was. But it was important to me. So, I want to thank you for trying."

Lennox's eyes narrowed. "That's manipulation. He's trying to manipulate us."

"And I'm not trying to manipulate you," said Coach Foley. Lennox's mouth snapped shut, as Joanne's dropped open.

"*Very* spooky," reiterated Eddie.

The Coach continued. "But I know you're all trying to honor my spirit. Truth is, my spirit can only carry you so far. You need some temporal guidance. Chris, I think you know what that means."

The others all looked at Cutter. "What's it mean?"

"What do you think, you doorknobs?" Cutter looked out the passenger window, into the dark wall of trees flashing by. "Shut up now, he's not finished."

"I'm finished now," said Coach Foley. "I'll see you boys later."

"Like when we're dead?" said Lennox bitterly.

"Yes, Lennox, like when you're dead," the tape responded.

"That's sooo true," breathed Neil. "About the dead thing."

"Keep your brooms on the ice boys," said Coach Foley. "Keep your brooms on the ice."

The tape ended. No one spoke. They just listened to the hiss of the cassette deck and the hum of the tires on the asphalt. The glow of the hearse's high beams spread a carpet of light into the dark.

Just then, Neil cried, "Jesus!" and braked to a sliding

halt. Lennox and Eddie, who'd been in the back where the coffins normally rode, were thrown halfway into the front seat. There was a period of Three Stooges–style mutually offended slapping before they untangled themselves and saw what Neil had braked for.

Lennox peered out at the sight on the road, took his joint from his mouth, and tossed it out the window. "I think that stuff's gone bad," he said. "What do you see out there, boys?"

"Beavers," said Eddie. "The ones with teeth, that is."

"Beavers," breathed Neil. "There's gotta be a dozen of them."

"Two dozen," said Lennox. "Or more. This is really weird."

"It's nuts," said Eddie. "*Beavers* don't migrate. They don't travel in herds."

"It's an omen," said Neil darkly. "It's an unnatural omen."

Cutter leaned into the back and grabbed a broom. "C'mon, you guys, they're just beavers," he said. "I want to get home. Let's get the toothy little buggers off our highway."

They each grabbed a broom and headed out into the night. The beavers barely moved out of the way, regarding the approaching silhouettes with squinty-eyed beaverly disdain. Some of them slapped their tails against the pavement. Neil began to recite scripture, poking beavers in their asses and shoving them off into the drainage ditches beside the road.

"And the rivers shall bring forth beavers," Neil

intoned in the sepulchral tones that he reserved for eulogies, "which shall go up and come into thine house– "

"Knock it off, Neil." Cutter hit a recalcitrant beaver with his curling broom. It waddled off the road in a huff.

"It's from the *Book of Exodus*," said Neil defensively. "About the plagues in Egypt. This is an omen. Beavers will come into our bedchambers if we don't buckle down and win the Golden Broom. Coach's will, boys. It's the Coach's will."

"Wow," breathed Joanne, following close behind Neil. "'And the beavers shall come up both on thee and upon thy people and upon all thy servants…'"

Neil turned to her, puzzled. "How would you know scripture like that?"

She grinned back, and shrugged her shoulders. Her pink-and-yellow sheepskin shorty jacket hunched and dropped, fetchingly. "Believe it or not, I'm a preacher's daughter."

Working silently, they eventually cleared a pathway through the beavers, whapping their backsides to encourage a speedier departure. As the last few beavers slid down the embankment and into the streams running in the roadside ditches, swimming away into the dark, Lennox frowned.

"What if Neil's right?" he said. "Think about it. We just got our asses chewed off by guys who don't even have their own teeth, we're riding around in a hearse talking to a dead guy, and now our road is plugged with our national symbol."

"So what?"

"So all these events gotta add up to something! We have to fight our way through a herd of beavers? It *means* something. If we were Yanks, and letting our country down – you know, fixing the World Series or something – we'd get divebombed by bald eagles. But we're Canadians and we're curlers. So instead our hearse gets forced off the road by rogue beavers."

Cutter threw his broom into the hearse. He grabbed Lennox's from his hands and threw that in, too. Eddie and Neil hung back. The night air was filled with the sound of the beavers' tails slapping the water in the ditches, and the purr of the hearse's engine.

"What are you saying, Lennox? That because of an inexplicable event of nature, just a random anomaly in the grand scheme of all things earthly, I'm supposed to assume that I should get in touch with my crazed, mushroom-munching, no-balls old man, make peace with him somehow, and get him to coach four lunatics in an impossible quest to win the Golden Broom, so the town of Long Bay will have something to feel proud about, and another lunatic old man – who happens to be dead and gone, even though he speaks to us through the powers of modern technology, like *cassette players* for Chrissake – can have his final resting place in a big red circle on a sheet of ice? Is *that* what you're saying, Jim Lennox?"

Lennox smiled broadly, his delight genuine. "Jesus Murphy, Chris! I *knew* you could see things metaphorically. C'mon, boys. Chris is gonna get his old man onside."

Cutter stared off into the dark, beyond the hearse's headlights' sweep. He would rather wander about in the bear-infested Canadian forest than drive up his father's road again, to the place where he'd once lived, and see that old wreck playing with a barnful of cowshit and fungus. But he was a Canadian curler, and inside his friends' hearse they were all singing "O Canada," screwing up the words to the ending and slapping each other in punishment for the screw-up.

"Owww, Neil, that goddamn hurt," he heard Eddie say. "Put the broom down, man!"

Cutter smiled, in spite of himself, and climbed into the hearse. "Drop me off at my dad's, you dickheads," he said.

16

Lloyd Stuckmore sat in the mess hall of the Great Lakes freighter, the *Henry Allen*, his head wrapped in bandages and his stomach full of Tylenol 4's. Shortly after the ship passed the Bay of Chaleur, and was heading toward England, the lead hand had discovered that the supposedly empty ship's hold actually held one very annoyed, 345-pound former member of the Hells Hellions motorcycle gang. The crew had let him out (their first mistake) and then tried to be kind to him (their second). The ship's doctor had pronounced him severely concussed and directed him to go to bed and stay there until they got to Europe, but Stuckmore glowered at the doctor in that special way he had, causing the doctor to amend his prescription.

"This man should be up and around," said the terrified doctor. "Give him free access to all unsecured areas. He needs to move."

The doctor secretly hoped that this prescription would cause Stuckmore to drop dead in his elephantine tracks, but in fact Stuckmore really was made of very stern stuff. The brain that had been rattled around in the densely walled skull was small but tough, sort of like an Indian rubber ball. Stuckmore's brain told him that he had a headache, and to take all of the doctor's pills, and then it told him that his stomach said it was hungry. So Stuckmore followed the arrows on the ships' walls, found the mess hall, and settled down to eat a troughful of spaghetti.

In the mess hall, there was a pile of newspapers from their last port of call, Long Bay. The *Long Bay Herald* never did have much to go on in the way of news, and this edition – now nearly two weeks old – was no exception. It reported on a car pileup on the main highway, an attempted gas station robbery, a street sale on Wilbur's Road, the engagement of Deborah Louise McElroy (age seventeen) to "Dirty Bertie" Bertram (age thirty-eight), the escape of the entire stock of Jeff Fraser's beaver ranch via a culvert he'd thought he'd stopped up good and proper (his wife had *told* him beaver ranching was a stupid idea), and the news that Alexander "The Juggernaut" Yount would indeed be bringing his formidable rink to Long Bay for the Golden Broom.

But Lloyd Stuckmore didn't know how to read very well, and since this wasn't a Toronto paper with a pretty, half-naked, half-wit girl grinning at some old pervert of a photographer while wearing a few strategically placed dime-sized scraps of cloth, no doubt thinking *boy this will be good for my career,* he had no reason to try. He picked up the newspaper, tore off its first page, and wiped the spaghetti sauce off his face with it.

He ate an entire edition's worth of spaghetti, leaving a crumpled pile of red-blotted newspapers on the floor around his massive feet. The cook, like everyone on board, could hardly wait to see the end of Lloyd Stuckmore.

Gordon Cutter watched the Impala bounce up the driveway from his vantage point inside the first of his two, vast, connected barns. He wondered if he might be hallucinating. He was used to hallucinating. The medicinal effects of his special mushrooms had the side effect of colorful and spectacular visions. Some visions, though, weren't entirely pleasant, and Gordon had learned to walk calmly away when they appeared. He had walked away from a talking gargoyle who claimed he was from Revenue Canada, a gigantic-toothed snowplow clearing his driveway of hot pink snow, and the Dalai Lama at his breakfast table (he wouldn't have walked from the Dalai Lama, but this Dalai Lama was obviously a fraud because he asked for bacon and eggs).

Gordon was about to walk away from the Impala when he saw it stop and his son get out. So it was real – the boy had come.

Gordon grabbed his shotgun. It wasn't loaded, but only he knew that.

"What do you want?" he yelled, leaping out the barn door, wearing his collecting-and-spreading clothes, which were basically a set of shit-soaked overalls, a thirty-year-old shirt, and hip waders. He pointed the gun in the air, and pumped its action once, just for effect.

Cutter jumped back behind the car's open door. "Jesus *Christ*, Dad! It's me!"

"I know who you are," Gordon said. He put the gun down.

"Dad?" Cutter stepped cautiously forward. "Dad...can we talk?"

His father snorted. "Why start now?" He leaned the twelve-gauge up against the wall beside the barn door. "But since you're here, you can make yourself useful. Come into the shed. I need a hand with the spreading."

"Spreading what?" said Cutter innocently.

He found out soon enough. His father thrust a battered pail into his hand, and escorted him over to a stone stall, where a doe-eyed Jersey stood munching her cud.

Gordon Cutter instructed his son to hold the bucket beneath the cow's tail, while he rubbed the animal's rectum with a rubber-gloved hand.

"It's less messy if there's a second person involved," Gordon explained.

"Uh-huh." Cutter winced as the cow, reacting to the massage, moved its bovine bowels in a fresh, greenish spurt.

"There!" said Gordon. "The trick is getting her to move before she's fully digested. If it's not fully processed, it's better for the shrooms. I call them *shrooms*, Chris. You like that name? Shrooms?"

"I think it's not entirely novel," said Chris dryly. "Dad, you're not planning on selling these things, are you? Because that's trafficking."

"Nope." Gordon pushed open a low narrow door

that led to a wooden lean-to, and took both buckets of cowshit in his hands. "This is the critical growing period. There's nothing finer for it than what my girl delivers."

The mushroom room was low-ceilinged, dark, and fetid as a backhouse. Cutter breathed through his mouth as his father poured the cow's produce onto his crop. Then his father pulled a cord in the ceiling, and a row of yellow-tinted 40-watt bulbs popped into life. The room was filled with row upon row of long-stemmed mushrooms, sprouting from hanging bags and tiers of shelves, their feathery caps spreading like delicate, iridescent umbrellas.

"Beautiful, aren't they?" said Gordon. "Now I understand your scruples, but rest assured I have no commercial aspirations whatsoever. None at all. They're strictly medicinal."

"Can you just stop what you're doing for a minute? I'm not here about your mushrooms."

His father whirled on him, the buckets in his hands clanging together as he spun. "I know what you're here for," he snarled. "You got trounced, realized you needed a professional, figured you had to bury the hatchet with your evil old man, Mr. Bad Guy In This Story, in order to get what you need."

Cutter puzzled a moment. "How'd you know we got trounced?"

"Old men have telephones, bucko. Wally called me. Back when I won the Brier, you may recall, Wally was on my rink. You kids think the world started when you appeared on it. But there was a world before."

"Jesus, Dad." Cutter sighed heavily. "I'm thirty-fuck-ing-three."

"Watch your language!"

"All right, all right. I'll watch my language. But Dad, will you do it?"

"Do what?"

"Coach us?"

The old man sighed heavily and set down his buckets. "What makes you think I have anything to do with curling anymore? That I'm in the kind of shape to take on such a quest?"

Cutter shrugged. "I dunno," he said, shuffling his feet. "I just can't see you ever giving up curling. Even with what happened to Mom– "

"We shall not speak of her," said Gordon harshly. But then he softened – perhaps because of the wounded look on his son's face, that Cutter tried so hard to veil – and patted the boy on his arm.

"Come with me. And watch your step."

He led Cutter to a door in the far wall of the equipment shed, and held it open for him, motioning him to step through. Cutter did, and at once he found himself flat on his back, staring into the stars that sprinkled through his own concussed vision, thanks to the solid smack on the noggin he'd sustained. He hadn't counted on stepping onto ice.

But lying there on his back, as his vision cleared, he couldn't help but be amazed at what his father had built. Gordon had even hung high-power lamps, which he now switched on from the main panel, so that the whole place was as bright as a shopping mall. The entire hayloft had been removed, and the barn insulated, and a single perfectly maintained curling sheet stretched from one end of the barn to the other. A refrigerator unit hummed like a contented grandma in the corner. Rows of brooms were stacked neatly on their racks.

Cutter began to grin with inane pride. His old man had done this.

Gordon's face suddenly blocked his field of vision. "You alive?" he said.

"Uh-huh." Cutter sat up. "This is something else, Dad."

"Uh-huh."

The old man helped his son to his feet. They stood carefully on the ice, looking around the arena. The sum of their pride soared to the rafters.

"It'd be something to get a rink out using this place," Gordon said. "But I don't want any father-son bullshit. I only want bullshit on my shrooms."

"No bullshit," said Cutter. "I'm happy to leave all that in the drawer we put it in. I'm not asking you to love me, Dad. I'm not even asking you to like me. I'm just asking you to be our coach."

A bit of madman returned to Gordon's eyes. He raised one hand to the sky, and pointed a finger ominously at the ceiling.

"My word must be like unto God's!" he roared.

Cutter nodded.

"Well, okay, then."

They shook hands, and Cutter wiped the shit off his

hand from where his father's grip had smeared it. He might be as crazy as a bedbug, but he was their best chance for redemption. Cutter would do anything it took to make things right.

Except maybe forgive his father. He was still a long way from that.

17

"**G**entlemen!" Gordon Cutter boomed, as Eddie's feet went out from under him and he skidded, face planted against the ice, a full ten feet or more, before finally realizing he had to let go of his rock.

The members of the freshly renamed Cutter Rink all dropped to their asses, laughing. Lennox knocked over Cutter's beer in the throes of his delight.

Eddie got to his feet and brushed himself off. "Jerks," he told them.

"Hey, Eddie, next time let go of the *rock!*"

"Jerks!" Eddie repeated, advancing menacingly. He leaped on his comrades. Punching commenced. More beer was spilled.

Gordon Cutter covered the ice-covered ground between them in a few strides, and began whaling them with his curling broom. "Gentlemen!" he thundered once more, cracking his son on the knuckles with a solid cut of the broom handle. "Your attention!"

The laughter died away and Gordon stood among

the four still-twitching curler wannabes. But Gordon, semi-stoned as he always was, found nothing funny in Eddie's being so inept as to forget to let go of his stone. He found nothing funny in having to clean up the beer spills on the rink surface, or in the prospect of an injured player. When he took on this commitment, something in him had switched from directionless madman to Captain Ahab himself. He wanted that Golden Broom.

"We have less than two weeks," he said, in a voice that would split the Red Sea. "You might at least pretend you know how to play this game."

The overgrown kindergarteners who sat before him exchanged glances, trying to disperse the discomfort. But in truth, they each agreed. It was fear that was making them screw up. Fear they didn't have it in them after all. The whole town – the Muriels and the Ednas and the Berts, the guys filling up at the BP station and the women nattering away in the schoolyards – had their hearts set on this game. It was a bonspiel – it would bring in money, pride, purpose, activity. Long Bay was a curling town, and the boys had put themselves forward as *curlers*. It seemed right now that there was a solid possibility of the whole town being there to see them all getting dragged along the ice by their own curling stones.

"Get up," said Gordon, "and get yourselves in order. We'll not let ourselves be pushed around. We'll be aggressive, and we'll be hard-headed about this. We'll be up against skilled teams that play a touch game, and we'll answer that with power and heart. Are you with me?"

They all struggled to their feet, and Eddie prepared

himself in the hack for another shot. "Wait!" Gordon said, and came over to adjust his posture over the stone. "Like this," he said, molding Eddie's arm. "And bend your leg – support yourself – like *this*."

Eddie took his strides and swung. The rock slid from his hand. As it left it felt like angels taking off. A perfect stone, moving in a slow, purposeful arc, it glided at a consistent speed until somehow, as it entered the house, it seemed to know it was time to stop. As if it had the power over its own propulsion, it slowed to an imperceptibly spinning halt, precisely where Eddie had meant it to.

Ten years ago, Eddie had done that consistently. He had not done it that well in ten years. He stared at the stone in the silence of the handmade arena. For thirty seconds, nobody so much as breathed. And then, together, they all clapped – a slow applause of recognition. Recognition that this could be done. That they might be four assholes and a madman relic, but they could sure as hell throw rocks.

"I sure am learning a lot about curling," said Joanne good-naturedly, as she held Neil's feet for his sit-ups on the dirt floor of Eddie & Lily's Retro Gym. "Like, for instance, you can do so many different things with the rocks."

"Uh-huh," grunted Neil. The best thing about having Joanne hold his feet for sit-ups was the reward he got every time his upper body rose from the floor. Joanne's perky smile greeted him each time he pulled himself off the carpet.

"I could think of lots of things to do with the stones," she went on. "Would you like to hear some of them?"

"Uh, huh, huh," said Neil.

"A planter," she said. "I would hollow them out and make a planter."

"Can't…hollow…them," Neil grunted. His body stalled halfway in a sit-up, and only the promise of a nice big eyeful of Joanne kept him going. "They're…solid…granite."

"They hollowed out a little bit of that Coffernicus stone, to put in Coach Foley's ashes," she said.

"Copernicus," Neil corrected. "Gah…"

"Copernicus. So they could hollow one out completely," Joanne went on. She paused, waiting for the once-again-collapsed Neil to rise. "Come on, Neil, one more."

"ARRGGGH!" Neil's abs nearly popped as he completed what surely-to-God-in-His-heavens had to be the last damn sit-up he could do, would ever do, *Christ* did he hurt.

"Neil, why couldn't I make planters out of curling stones? You know what I picture? I picture a little house on one of the nicer streets in town, painted yellow, with a white fence. And in the backyard a little rock garden. But it wouldn't be regular rocks. I would make a curling stone garden. At the corner of each path is a curling stone planter. And there are curling stone edges. The stones are so nice and smooth, and if I took off their handles and turned them on their sides, I could do an edging with them, just their top halves showing, you know?

Then I could choose what plants to put in. Perennials and biennials and annuals and ground cover and stuff."

Neil couldn't help but notice that she had no trouble getting the word *perennial* right. He lay on his back, panting, as Joanne came up and sat beside him. She put her hand on his arm, stroking the soft skin of his bicep, almost absent-mindedly.

"I can see the garden," said Neil, closing his eyes. "There could be a fountain, too. A rock garden with a fountain. If the place was big enough there could be a place to pour a sheet of ice in the winter." He sighed. "A real garden of live things. That would be so wonderful."

Joanne nodded. She did not move her hand. Neil lay there, listening as Lennox and Cutter threw a medicine ball at each other, an exercise which was quickly deteriorating in an attempt to knock the other son-of-a-bitch over. Eddie, attempting to do a vertical lift on the parallel even bars, slipped his grip and brained himself on one of the poles.

"Shit," said Neil.

"No, it's okay," said Joanne. "You guys are gonna do it for us. Go team go."

She leaned over closer, and Neil felt her breath brush against his ear.

"By the way," she whispered, "my name's not really Joanne. That's just my professional name. I wanted you to know…because I like you."

But before he could ask anything further, she had leaped to her feet and thrown herself in among the other men, calling out directions and blowing her whistle, correcting their posture and insisting on higher, faster, firmer. Neil closed his eyes again, imagining the touch of her fingers, the curve of her cheek and chin, and what her real name might be.

The warehouses by the Long Bay docks were largely empty. The brickworks that had relied on the gravel pits, which had relied on a building boom in a distant city, had closed down when the boom faltered and the builders found cheaper materials closer by. The copper mine had been bought out by incompetent management, who'd failed to find copper quickly in a very competitive market. There was still an active dock for the smelter plant's production, but it had been cut back considerably in the last eighteen months. And as for fish…well, that never was much of a going concern. That ships stopped at Long Bay at all was becoming a matter of habit, manners, and even pity.

Julie Foley jogged along the cracked pavement in front of the warehouses, thinking of curling and spaceships. There was incredible dexterity, planning, and training involved in manipulating something inanimate into doing something precise. Wielding the space arm, and wielding a curling rock – there were parallels. The biggest difference is that she was actually involved with curling now, even though it wasn't a source of great interest to her. At least she felt part of it. The space missions were (you should excuse the expression) absolute pie-in-the-sky.

She heard the grumble of tires approach. Even a

backwater like Long Bay had its threatening element, and she stiffened. But then she saw that the person in the back seat of the approaching cab, leaning out the window and waving *yoohoo*, was her mother.

"Honey, you're not planning on running all the way back to Houston, are you?" Eva Foley called.

"Mom," Julie sighed, slowing to a walk, "I may not go back to Houston."

"Good God in all His outfits!" Eva slapped the cabbie across the back of his head. "Stop this car, Derwin. My daughter's lost her marbles."

Julie stopped too as the taxi braked sharply, and Eva leaned farther out of the window. "What're you on about now, missy?"

"I'm going to take full leave from the program. Try to find something here– "

"Nonsense!" Eva nearly fell out of the cab.

"No, Mom. Nonsense is thousands of hours underwater, simulating weightlessness. Spinning around in a g-force machine, around and around the same circle. I'm sick of simulations and endless, pointless circles. I want something *real*."

Eva shook her head forcefully. "Honey, there is nothing real left in Long Bay. Nothing except curling."

"I *hate* curling," said Julie.

"Well then, you don't belong in Long Bay, my sweet darling," Eva replied, not without sadness.

Julie inhaled sharply. To her shock, her lower lip began to quiver. Her own mother, saying such a thing!

She took off for home, no longer jogging, but

running – running as fast as her legs could carry her, as fast as the days when she was six years old and had thought, *if I run fast enough, maybe I'll start to fly.*

18

But as Julie Foley flew home, the ordinary earth-bound citizens of Long Bay went through their paces, overshadowed by the excitement of the approaching Golden Broom. In the Long Bay Curling Club, the bartender ordered extra beer, as did McTeague in his tavern. In the fresh meat aisle of the Safeway, Primrose Turner and Yolanda Sterling revealed to each other the different versions they'd acquired of what had become known to Long Bay as That Kiss In The Parking Lot. Although tempers flared during their analysis, in time they came to the consensus that Cutter might have talent, but he had no business forcing his kisses upon Long Bay's Astronaut when he was supposed to be training for the Golden Broom. In Milt Lakehead's Muffler and Brake Shop, the well-greased Hi Wilkins came close to blows with Milt's son, Hughie, when Hughie advanced the proposition that Neil Bucyk might be able to stuff a cadaver, but the Juggernaut would eat him alive. And in Belle's diner, a covert operation unfolded between Frances Darte and her "eyes on the street," the omniscient Belle Doppleman.

Belle made sure no one was listening before she whispered the latest status report to Frances, under pretense of pouring her coffee. Frances, alone at the counter, listened carefully to the crucial information.

"Bets are laying that the Cutter Rink doesn't make it to the fourth end."

Frances Darte lifted one eyebrow as Belle's aproned bosom came intimately close.

"I'm your eyes on the street, Frances," said Belle. "That's all I am. Unless you wanted more, of course." She put her hand on Frances's shoulder, to steady herself as she pretended to pour.

"Cream would be nice," said Officer Darte, laying a twenty-dollar bill on the counter. "That's on Cutter."

There was one place in town, however, where attention was not being paid to curling. It was in the Club Council Room of the Long Bay Country Club, where the draperies were velvet and the carpet was thick as moss. Behind a polished teak desk as broad as God's own heaven sat the Membership Committee of the Club, assessing the worthiness of two new applicants, Mr. and Mrs. Neil and Linda Bucyk.

"Can you tell us, Mr. Bucyk," said Randal Tournot, chair of the committee, "in fifty words or less, why you think you should become a member of our club?"

Neil felt Linda's nails pressing sharply into his hand, where it was held prisoner in her hand. Linda had said they had to hold hands, to show togetherness, and the unity of their marriage. He looked at his wife, who was

PHOTO: MICHAEL GIBSON

Peter Outerbridge as Jim Lennox and Polly Shannon as Joanne.

PHOTO: ALEX DUKAY

*Kari Matchett as Linda Bucyk and James Allodi as Neil
Bucyk with their kids, Philip played by Barrett Cribbey
and Andrew played by Kenney McCoy.*

PHOTO: MICHAEL GIBSON

*George Buza as Stuckmore, Peter Outerbridge as
Jim Lennox and Polly Shannon as Joanne.*

All photos from scenes or the set of *Men With Brooms*.
Directed by Paul Gross. A Robert Lantos Production.

Michelle Nolden as Julie Foley and Paul Gross as Chris Cutter.

Michelle Nolden as Julie Foley.

Jane Spidell as Lily Strombeck and Jed Rees as Eddie Strombeck

Jed Rees as Eddie Strombeck, Paul Gross as Chris Cutter, Molly Parker as Amy Foley, Leslie Nielsen as Gordon Cutter and Peter Outerbridge as Jim Lennox.

Paul Gross as Chris Cutter, Peter Outerbridge as Jim Lennox, Jed Rees as Eddie Strombeck, and James Allodi as Neil Bucyk.

Molly Parker as Amy Foley and Paul Gross as Chris Cutter.

Leslie Nielsen as Gordon Cutter.

Paul Gross as Chris Cutter, Jed Rees as Eddie Strombeck, Leslie Nielsen as Gordon Cutter, James Allodi as Neil Bucyk and Polly Shannon as Joanne.

Leslie Nielsen as Gordon Cutter and Polly Shannon as Joanne.

Peter Outerbridge as Jim Lennox, Leslie Nielsen as Gordon Cutter and Paul Gross as Chris Cutter.

Jed Rees as Eddie Strombeck, Paul Gross as Chris Cutter and Peter Outerbridge as Jim Lennox.

Paul Gross as Chris Cutter and Leslie Nielsen as Gordon Cutter.

Paul Gross as Chris Cutter and Leslie Nielsen as Gordon Cutter.

*Jed Rees as Eddie Strombeck,
James Allodi as Neil Bucyk,
Paul Gross as Chris Cutter and
Peter Outerbridge as Jim Lennox.*

*Greg Bryk as
Alexander Yount.*

Jed Rees as Eddie Strombeck,
Paul Gross as Chris Cutter,
Peter Outerbridge as Jim Lennox
and James Allodi as Neil Bucyk.

PHOTO: MICHAEL GIBSON

PHOTO: MICHAEL GIBSON

Paul Gross as Chris Cutter.

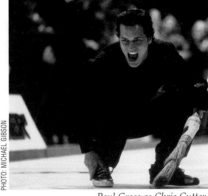

PHOTO: MICHAEL GIBSON

Paul Gross as Chris Cutter.

Paul Gross as Chris Cutter and Michelle Nolden as Julie Foley.

James Allodi as Neil Bucyk, Peter Outerbridge as Jim Lennox, Jed Rees as Eddie Strombeck, Leslie Nielsen as Gordon Cutter and Paul Gross as Chris Cutter.

Molly Parker as Amy Foley and Paul Gross as Chris Cutter.

regarding him with a bovine but perfectly practiced smile, the one she trotted out when she wanted something very badly. Linda wanted this very badly, badly enough to make puncture wounds in her husband's palms.

Neil turned back to Randal Tournot and his band of renown lined up like a buffet at the three-thousand-dollar desk.

"Mr. Bucyk?" said Tournot. "Fifty words or less, Mr. Bucyk. Why do you think you should be a member of this club?"

"Because she wants us to," Neil blurted.

Linda Bucyk's middle fingernail sank into Neil's palm to its root, a most effective little dagger. But Neil didn't cry out. He was a dead man now, and he knew it.

The Long Bay Rehabilitation Center was a busy place, owing to the number of people who were on workers' compensation, and who needed therapy for their injuries. A rumor of a plant closing, mine shutdown or mass layoff was always followed by a surprising number of boxes dropped on toes, backs going into spasm, and forklifts pinning workers against walls.

Gordon Cutter's presence at the therapy center was owing to his having found himself, the evening before at the practice rink, in a difficult position.

"How does my form look?" he had asked his son, after demonstrating a flawless slide.

"Very fine," said Cutter, suitably awed at the old man's prowess.

"That's good," Gordon Cutter had said, "because I think it could be permanent."

Of course, it was not permanent, but it was damned uncomfortable, and Cutter unbent his father and pushed him moaning into the back seat of the '66 Impala. Now Cutter lay on a therapy pallet in the waters of the physio pool, suspended from a hoist. Amy, his therapist, was torturing him. Or at least, that was the effect. The pool water seethed around Gordon as he tried to pretzel himself in Amy's hands. Moans and bellows of agony rose in the steamy air of the pool room.

"Jesus Murphy, woman, where did you graduate from? The Idi Amin Therapy Academy?"

"Quit whining, you suckhole," she said cheerfully. "Your leg can go higher than that."

"Oh, yeah, sure, if I remove the bone from it."

"Suckhole."

"Madame de Sade."

"Hey, Dad," Cutter called. "That is a medical professional."

"So she's Nurse de Sade," Gordon Cutter snarled.

"Well, could I have a word with her on an unrelated matter?"

Amy handed Gordon the support rope and told him to keep his legs raised while twisting them from side to side. Then she swam over to where Cutter was now crouched at the edge of the pool.

"He is a suckhole, you know," she said.

"Yeah. Listen, I need some advice."

Amy brightened at the prospect of such intimacy.

"Sure thing. About what?"

"Your sister."

Boom went Amy's brightness. "Jesus wept," she said, pushing herself away from the poolside.

"What? Come on, Amy. You're a woman."

"Oh-ho!" she snorted. "You noticed."

"Excuse me," said Gordon, "I'm drowning over here."

Amy and Cutter looked over to see that he had indeed slipped beneath the water. He surfaced long enough for Amy to tell him to pull himself together and get back to work.

"See?" said Gordon, dragging himself up with the rope, his drenched hair hanging in silver strands around his haggard face. "She only *looks* like a woman. Oh, she has all the requisite curls and swirls. But you get caught for two seconds in her clutches and you will come to know – she is in fact the Spawn of Satan!"

Cutter ignored him and addressed Amy. "All I'm asking is whether Julie's said anything about me. That's all."

"I'm not doing this, Cutter." Amy started back toward Gordon.

"What? What?"

"*This.* It was almost bearable when I was your drinking buddy. But I'm not your drinking buddy and I'm not your errand girl. I'm not playing go-between. You got something to ask my sister, you go ask her yourself."

Cutter rose from his squat by the pool, a dim light dawning on his face. "Ask her myself," he mused.

"Thanks, Amy. Good advice. You're the best."

Amy gawped at him as he strolled out of the center, his shoulders erect, the picture of resolve. She looked back at her patient, who was clinging to the rope and moaning.

"Your son's a creep," she told him.

Gordon nodded. "No argument there." As she approached, he gestured for her to come closer, as if to tell her something secret.

"That creep's got it for you," he whispered. "He just doesn't know it yet."

Amy felt herself flood red from her fingertips to her scalp. "Get away with you," she told her patient, as she took his hands and stretched his arms back over his head. But she didn't even hear his screams. All that rang through her head were the words *that creep's got it for you*, repeating like a chorus, giving her a tiny spot of hope.

Meanwhile, the cook of the *Henry Allen* had just nervously placed another bowl of chowder before the unfillable hole that was Lloyd Stuckmore.

Stuckmore upended the bowl and slurped it down, dribbling white fluid into his beard. But most of it made it down his gullet. He thrust the bowl at the cowering cook.

"Another one," he said.

The cook scampered away to find a bigger bowl. Stuckmore hunched down in his seat, picking scraps of chowder out of his beard and eating them. His eyes fell on the mess hall television set, which was tuned to the Sportsco Network. The sound was off, but the event in play was a curling match.

Stuckmore's eyes widened. He rose to his massive feet and clomped over to the TV, turning up the volume and cocking his head like the RCA Victor dog.

"…in curling, the Golden Broom is set to get underway in Long Bay, where a local rink is drawing considerable attention. Skipped by Chris Cutter, son of bonspiel champ Gordon Cutter, his second is Jim Lennox– "

A rumble sounded in Stuckmore's chest, sort of a growl but with a bit more organization. A careful listener standing nearby would have been able to discern that it was indeed a word.

"Curler," Stuckmore was growling. *"Currrrrrrler."*

Stuckmore forgot his soup. He had something else to focus on: getting off this ship, and getting the hell back to Long Bay.

19

The doorbell at the Foleys' sounded, and Julie was the one home to answer. She opened the front door, and there stood Cutter.

"I was thinking of getting a bite to eat and don't like to eat alone," he said.

She gawped at him for a moment, as he stood there expectantly. Then understanding dawned.

"Oh," she said. "You're asking me *out.*"

Cutter looked at his feet, grinding the toe of his boot into the wooden slats of the porch. It occurred to him that she would probably say no.

But she didn't. She went and got her coat.

In McTeague's, Joanne sat struggling to open her tin of Mug root beer as she watched a curling match on the television. Six weeks ago she wouldn't have known which end of the curling sheet was which. She might even have found the game – unbelievable as that may seem – a kinda boring thing to watch. But now she saw every nuance, every whisper, every delicacy. She saw as well the power in the curlers' arms and legs, and the team-work as the sweepers pushed their brooms, melting the ice with the heat of it. She no longer saw anything odd about it at all.

"Go team go," she murmured.

"Go where?" said Neil Bucyk, sitting down beside her. He had come out of the Men's room and had seen her sitting there, gazing into the TV like a real Long Bay curling addict, her folded arms tucked comfortably under those lovely little boobs. Then Nug had brought her root beer, and Neil had seen a chance – she couldn't cope with the snap-top, owing to her long nails.

He was about to offer help when suddenly, one of the nails snapped off at the tip, ruining her manicure.

"Aw, shit," she said. "I could just blow a gasket."

"I'm a gasket," said Neil lamely. *Oh please God what a STUPID thing to say,* he at once thought, but Joanne didn't seem to mind.

"Okay," she said. "So you're Gasket."

"And you're *not* Joanne." He smiled, a little slyly, since he knew her secret. "What's your real name, Not-Joanne?"

She looked a little embarrassed. "Andrea," she said.

"Andrea," he breathed. "It sounds kind of floral."

She blossomed into smiles.

"Bastard," said Julie Foley.

Cutter winced. "I'm sorry."

"Never mind sorry. You abandoned me, you prick. You scumbag son-of-a-bitch."

"More coffee?" said Belle, appearing suddenly at their booth.

They were getting a little sick of her obvious attempts to eavesdrop. "No thanks," said Cutter.

"Well, I wonder…Miss Foley, can I have your autograph?" Belle handed Julie a napkin.

"Sure," said Julie. She signed the napkin, handed it back to Belle, and turned back to Cutter.

"*Rat* bastard," she said.

"Julie, how do I put it?" he said, his head in his hands. "I had a meltdown. A full-blown, old style crack-up."

"You just didn't love me enough, that's all."

"Okay."

"How *dare* you agree with me!"

"I'm not agreeing," said Cutter. "But I'm sitting across from an astronaut. It's not like I'm going to win an argument with a woman with enough letters after her name to start her own alphabet. And don't think that there's not a connection– "

"No," she interrupted, seething. "If you're suggesting there's some causal relationship between your ditching me at the altar in front of two hundred guests, and me winding up in the space program, forget it. It was not my fault. You get no absolution for dumping me, just because I had some ambition."

"Miss Foley?" another voice interrupted. This time it was the cook, seventeen-year-old Darrel Merrill, carrying a camera. "Miss Foley, could I get a picture?"

"Here," said Cutter, taking the camera from Darrel,

and gesturing for him to sit down. "I'll get you guys together."

"Oh, no," said Darrel, half-pushing and half-guiding Cutter into the booth seat beside Julie. "I'll get *you* guys together."

You and whose army, Julie thought, but her thigh felt warm against Cutter's, and she smelled his aftershave and light perspiration as he slipped his arm around her – just for the photo's sake, she thought. For the sake of Darrel Merrill's scrapbook, she could suffer being under the taut, muscular, great-smelling arm of that rotten lying abandoning son-of-a-bitch bastard, Christopher Cutter.

Just for that, and for nothing else, she snuggled up to him and smiled.

Neil Bucyk returned home to the simultaneous slamming of the back door. He sighed in recognition of the sound. As he had before, he parted the windows over the kitchen sink to see Ronnie in the dark yard, fleeing over the sea of mud, past the fleet of silenced earthmovers. Ronnie was barefoot, shirtless, with trousers pulled up but fly still down. He was struggling into his shoes and socks.

Linda came into the room, every hair in place except for one strand, which she'd missed in her effort to put herself in order on such short notice. She wore a slick grey skirt and expensive hose, a cream-colored cashmere sweater set, and a silk scarf, perfectly knotted. It occurred to Neil that he'd never seen anything quite so monstrous.

"Where have you been?" she asked.

"Out."

"Curling, no doubt," she spat, "while the honest business my father handed to you goes unattended. If it weren't for Ronald, that is."

"Ah. Yes. Good ol' Ronald." He poured himself four fingers of Scotch and looked his wife up and down. "Linda, you're looking at me as if you asked a question. But you actually made a statement."

"Here's another one, you rock-throwing waste of human skin," she said. "Shape up, or ship out."

Both of them ignored the sound of Ronnie's car starting up in the street outside.

A few streets away, a black '66 Impala sat with engine running in the Foley driveway. In the front seat, Julie Foley was talking, and Cutter was quietly listening as she talked.

"Next thing I knew, they went and put my name on the town's sign, as if I actually do something in the space program. The truth is, I am a carbon-based interface for the Space Platform Deployment Module. A robot with periods."

She shifted around to pull Cutter's jacket open, then began to unbutton his shirt, as she lifted herself onto his lap, so that she sat astride him, facing him.

"I'm good at what I do," she said, her voice low. "I can work that baby to within a hundredth of a millimeter. But on the simulator. It's all virtual. It's not real." She bent to put her mouth to his naked chest, where it lay exposed in his opened shirtfront. "I've never been to space."

"What are we doing?" said Cutter, as she reached for his belt.

"Well, it's slightly complicated," she replied, tugging at him. "Because I actually think I hate you. But this hate is good. It's at least something I can feel. I can feel it. I can feel it. Chris, Chris…I can feel it…"

Inside the Foley house, Amy was putting Brandon to sleep. As she turned out his light, she saw a black '66 Impala in their driveway. Its windows were fogged, but the dome light inside was on. She could see the blue-white silhouettes inside. Julie, and Cutter.

The palm of a man's hand pressed against the steamed-over window, pushing his imprint against the glass.

It was Saturday night. Amy was due for her weekly meeting at AA. Funny, but she never made it.

20

The management had not yet repaired the damage to the Seahorse Motel, but had agreed not to call the police if the guys in Units 3 and 4 agreed to pay for new drywall. The proprietor of The See Whores (as the locals called it) was in no rush to call in the cops, in any event, and Lennox and Cutter knew it. So they agreed they'd fix it themselves, just as soon as the Broom was over.

The mention of the Golden Broom had got the Seahorse's Owner and General Manager (as she called herself) all wriggly with excitement. In a grotesque version of flirting she sidled up to Lennox and Cutter, asking them double-edged questions about their wrist technique and how slippery they liked their sheets.

When she asked how much their rocks weighed, they both bolted.

So when there was a knock at Lennox's door at 2 a.m., he fully expected the Owner and General Manager – all 232 pounds of her – to be standing there in a nightie, carrying a bottle of bourbon and a packet of Trojans.

Hence he was cautious and kept the chain on as he opened the door.

The woman was indeed carrying a bottle, but not of bourbon. Amy Foley was a Scotch drinker. She held up the nearly drained bottle and waggled it at him suggestively, tugging at the Juicy Fruit in her mouth, stringing it out between her lips and purring.

He had hardly managed to open the door before Amy lurched forward and fell drunkenly into his arms.

"Good to see you, too," he said.

Somewhere near dawn, Cutter woke to the sound of his name being stage-whispered from the hole in the drywall. He dragged himself awake to answer the call.

Jim Lennox was leaning through the gap, his face mildly concerned, but not terribly. "Hey Cutter," he said. "It's 5 a.m. Have you seen my girlfriend?"

Cutter groaned and rolled over. "No, " he said.

"Man," muttered Lennox, shaking his head. "I gotta get one of those tracking collars like they put on caribou or something."

Cutter, barely listening, heard the sounds of a woman stirring, even thrashing, in Lennox's bed. He even thought he heard her speak his name, but maybe she just belched.

"Isn't that her?" he said.

"In my room?" Lennox looked back over his shoulder. "Nah, that's Amy."

"Amy!" Cutter jumped out of bed, threw on his jeans, and pushed Lennox aside as he stepped through the portal into Lennox's unit. Amy, shirtless and lying there in jeans and bra, had stopped her mumbling and slipped into a drunken stupor.

Cutter advanced on Lennox. "You got her *drunk*, you asshole. She's AA! What else did you do?"

"Whoa!" said Lennox, putting his hands up before him, as if to ward off a swing. "I resent that implication. I do have some principles, you know. They have to be conscious, for one thing. And for another, I'm in training. I have to preserve myself. Thirdly, I didn't get her drunk. *You* did."

"Me! I wasn't even here!"

"Exactly. You were in your car. With her sister."

Cutter's stomach dropped a few storeys, and he leaned back against the wall. Shit, of all the times not to keep the equipment in its locker. Of *course* Amy would have seen the car; she would have known. They were parked right in her driveway. He could have at least had the decency to park down the block a little.

He went over and smoothed Amy's hair away from her perspiring brow as he tugged the sheet up over her. She opened one eye groggily, and then the other. A big, rowdy, hammered smile spread over her face.

"Chris Cutter," she said. "You are such a sweet man."

The smile faded into a look of dismayed surprise two seconds before she leaned over the bed's edge and whoopsed onto Cutter's bare feet.

"Sorry," she moaned.

"No, Amy," he said. "It's me who's sorry. Come on, let's get you home."

Brandon Foley, awakened by voices in the hallway, crept out of his room to see the silhouette of Chris Cutter heading into his mother's room, carrying a limp form in his arms. Brandon's Grandmother and Aunt Julie were in the kitchen, talking. He could hear them, too.

Grandma said, "Julie, honey, your room's not the only one that faces the driveway."

Sneaking behind, he watched as Cutter settled his mother onto her bed, took off her shoes, and covered her up. Amy Foley snored lustily throughout the exercise.

Cutter sighed as he turned around. The presence of the little voyeur startled him.

"Hell – oh, Brandon! Uh, don't worry about your mom. She's just tired."

Brandon nodded sagely. "It's nice that you're lying to me, Cutter," he said. "But we both know she's shit-faced."

Amy let loose with a huge snort of inebriated exhalation. "He's a nice man," she muttered.

Cutter winced. "I gotta go to practice," he said. "Look after your mom, okay?"

"I will. She's the only mom I got. And Cutter?"

"Yeah?"

"You're gonna win that broom thing, right? Beat the Juggernuts?"

Cutter laughed in spite of himself. "The Juggernuts is *toast*," he said. "Promise."

He went out the back door, so as not to have to see Julie, sitting at the kitchen table with Coach Foley's widow. He had to focus hard. When he lost that vision, terrible things happened. It was all about the curling, now. It was all about the game.

PART TWO

1

For years, curlers have journeyed to take part in their art. They have journeyed to Scandinavia, to the Alps, to the Hebrides, and deep into the heart of the Canadian Shield. From professionals – like Alexander "The Juggernaut" Yount – to amateurs like Cutter and Lennox and Neil and Eddie, they are drawn to test themselves, one squadron against the other. There may be bigger tournaments. There may be bigger prizes. But to the people of Long Bay, the legendary tournament is the Golden Broom. To them, the Golden Broom is to curling what St. Andrew's is to golf. So they come, one and all, to watch their hometown boys. To hail them – the conquering heroes.

On Thursday – the day before the opening morning of the Golden Broom – Joanne ran the boys until they should have dropped. But they didn't drop. She ran them their entire route, through the town, past the Foleys' two-storey brick house with Brandon's bike on its porch and the Foley women waving through the window, and she ran them through the perfectly conical, gravel-textured slag heaps that lay in monotonous rows outside the smelter like manufactured Grand Tetons. She ran them down to the docks, along the piers, then back along the concession road where they had seen the ominous influx of beavers. A month ago these men would have dropped like sacks of wet meal. But now, each of them – even the chain-smoking Jim Lennox, who had cut back to half-a-pack a day, and smoked in the evenings only – was a hardbodied, taut-bellied, broad-shouldered, curling hunk of man.

"'*Curling hunk of man*'?" said Lennox, when Joanne pronounced him such.

"Yes, you are," trilled Joanne, handing out towels. "You are all just the most amazing specimens. I could eat you all up."

Me first, thought Neil, and then, *me only – please, Andrea, me only?*

After their last run before the bonspiel, they assembled on Gordon Cutter's indoor ice, carrying their brooms and wearing their sliders. Gordon Cutter pushed them again, as hard as Joanne had when she ran them. Late into the evening, until the moon rose and shone through the cracks in the barnboard, they threw rocks; they walked the balance beam; they swept until their biceps throbbed.

Gordon Cutter watched them, expressionless and (for once) unimpaired by homegrown pharmaceuticals. He barked out his Godlike orders and smiled – inwardly only – as they were obeyed. The boys were ready.

At 11 p.m. he called them to him, and they assembled in a row before him, their brooms held swordlike to their chests. Gordon Cutter spread his arms to encompass the members of the rink: his still-estranged son, dark-haired and blue-eyed, solemn and determined when playing, but recalcitrant as hell in private; Jim Lennox, who (training having ended for the day) was already gratefully sucking on a smoke, his faded decade-old jeans bagging off his newly toned ass; Neil Bucyk, as skinny as a ferret despite weeks of high-protein food, his long face and beaky nose practically shouting *"I am an undertaker!,"* yet probably the fittest of them all. And Eddie Strombeck – compact, bearded, elfin, naive – who did his training in suspenders, a checkered flannel shirt, a toque, and (when not on the ice) steel-toed boots. They looked nothing like champion material, but to Gordon Cutter – even a non-stoned Gordon Cutter – they looked outstanding.

Which didn't mean they would win.

He raised his chin and made his final pronouncement. "Tomorrow," he intoned, "we face the best. May God be with us."

The men with brooms saluted.

"What the hell is this shit?" said Jim Lennox, his cigarette dangling from his lips, as he stood with his rinkmates awaiting their introductory announcement from the arena loudspeaker. "Yount has *fireworks?*"

"It's like the NBA," an awestruck Eddie breathed.

"Eddie, for Chrissake."

It wasn't the NBA at all, but something much more

important to Long Bay. It was the opening day of the Golden Broom. The plain, cinder-blocked walls of the Long Bay Memorial Arena had disappeared under navy-and-red flag banners, trimmed with gold fringe, and the official seal of the Canadian Curling Federation hung above the high-quality metal bleachers that the Sportsco Network had brought in. That Sportsco was on hand was an indication of Alexander "The Juggernaut" Yount's drawing power. Annoyingly handsome, built like a Bolshoi ballet dancer, the quintessential showman: that was Yount. He was a walking, rock-throwing, Hilfiger ad, and he knew how to make an entrance.

In through the main doors, where the beams from specially installed spotlights spun around the darkened arena, flashing across the crowd and the red carpets threaded over the ice, came the Yount Entourage, in advance of its leader. First, prancing like circus ponies but wearing what would have been considered skimpy on a beach in Rio, came the Jugger-Ettes, four pompom girls in Juggernaut colors. They did pelvic spins and one-arm walkovers, whipping the loyal Long Bay fans into a frenzy of applause. Meanwhile, on either side of the entrance hall, a half-dozen installations of fireworks sprayed colored sparks into the air. Anyone seated near the edge got nipped by the fallout.

"Good evening, ladies and gentlemen, we'd like to extend a warm welcome to all our viewers," the Sportsco announcer boomed over the PA system, which had to be cranked up to the *deafen* setting to be heard over Yount's fanfare soundtrack. "This is Greg Guinness and joining me is Paul Savage, our color commentator, and this is the opening day of the Golden Broom of Long Bay. The teams are entering the arena, and making his typically understated entrance is two-time Brier winner and the current curling world champion. Ladies and gentlemen, put your hands together and welcome – *Alexander 'The Juggernaut' Yount!"*

The crowd, hypnotized by the swell of music and of pompom-girl bosom, and blinded by hype and the magnesium splurt of the fireworks, egged on by Greg the Sportsco Guy shouting instructions over the PA, rose to its feet in one hollering lump of applauding mayhem. When Yount, seconds later, made his entrance, wearing a black mink coat over a sparkly uniform that was more spacesuit than jumpsuit (and followed by his identically dressed teammates and a trio of videocam guys from Sportsco), the audience practically fell over itself in ecstasy. The spectacle was the biggest display of excess Long Bay had seen since a minor pro-wrestling league had come to town two years ago, and driven a ten-car motorcade down main street, pulling one of their fighters in a gold-painted cage, while a trio of bottled blonds in a hot pink '67 Caddy convertible dispensed complimentary passes and Tootsie-pops.

Cutter's lip curled a little, but somewhere inside him, fear twitched. Alexander Yount might be a self-aggrandizing, overblown, spangle-outfitted spire of pomposity, but he threw a wicked curling rock, and he *was* a world champion. Cutter's rink didn't have matching uniforms, or travel around with six professional breasts and a pyrotechnic expert. They were an undertaker and a pothead and an impotent bankrupt and a cheating quitter, and they dressed the part. Eddie wore his toque and his flood-pants and his suspenders over a dyed long-john shirt, his steel-toed boots replaced by soft-soled curling shoes. Lennox wore his flattened, tan-colored, wide-brimmed hat, squashed onto his thinning eighties hairstyle like a drunkard's afterthought, his volleyball-player kneepads pulled over tartan pants. Neil was primly dressed in a mono-grammed sweater and stretch slacks, but he looked nervously about him for the sight of his wife, who would kill him if she found him here, wasting valuable time on a game only riff-raff would choose over golf. And Cutter just wore his favorite trousers and loose-fit-ting cotton shirt, with a sweatshirt tossed over it to keep off the chill. Not only did they not look like a match for the shimmering, smile-flashing Alexander Yount, they didn't feel like it.

"Hey, Beautiful Dreamer! Wake up," Cutter heard Lennox saying. It was time for their own big entrance.

Neil, behind him, gave Cutter a push as the Sportsco announcer introduced the local heroes. Out into the whirling spotlights the Cutter Rink marched, trying to keep in a line but not practiced in the art, so Eddie lost his stride and wandered off the carpet and fell on his butt on the ice. Jim Lennox lost his focus on the complex task of walking a straight line, and headed instead directly to the nearest pompom girl.

"Hi, what's your name?" he oozed.

The girl, obviously not familiar with Jim Lennox, replied, "Available."

Cutter grabbed Lennox by the elbow and dragged him back with the others, just as Coach Gordon Cutter came out onto the carpet and joined his boys. The lights and cheers struck at Gordon Cutter in a way he hadn't expected: it was both familiar and agonizing, for the last time he had heard such a sound he had won the Brier himself. But then he had gone home to find his wife had died. Gordon Cutter winced and waved.

Greg the Sportsco Guy – who had got right into the spirit of the event by lining up a bar's worth of plastic cups of beer on the broadcast desk before him – recited in his trained baritone the names of the Cutter Rink. Each name drew shrieks of approval from the crowd, who were well-warmed up by their excitement over the Yount Circus and Light Show.

"The local boys!" cried Greg Guiness. "Chris Cutter, Eddie Strombeck, Neil Bucyk and James Lennox – they're coached by former Brier Champion and true local hero, Mr. Gordon Cutter himself." He slugged back a beer, and turned to his sober and somewhat surprised booth partner. "They're here to win, Paul, despite their hometown wardrobe."

"They certainly are, Greg," said Paul.

"What's that about our wardrobe?" said Eddie, who had removed his toque for the singing of "O Canada."

"Nothing, Eddie," said Cutter soothingly, painfully aware that they were the only rink that didn't even vaguely coordinate their attire, let alone tailor it precisely to match. They could have at least gone to the Discount Heaven and bought the same red tracksuits or something.

But their clothing was the least of his problems. His father's eyes were suspiciously glazed. Cutter leaned over to Gordon.

"Dad, are you eating *mushrooms?*" he whispered.

Gordon Cutter chewed furiously on something grey and gummy, growing pop-eyed as the effect spread through him like a hallucinogenic warm toddy. "Son, I'm not throwing. I'm the one who's gotta see the big picture."

"Jesus," said Cutter.

Greg the Sportsco Guy's hyperbolic exclamations led the other six Golden Broom teams onto the ice, while Paul the Color Guy basically spoke when spoken to, a little overwhelmed by his broadcast partner's bug-eyed enthusiasm, and trying not to get any beer splashed on him. But it wasn't just Greg the Sportsco Guy who was bug-eyed. Although each team had imported its own supporters, none was greeted with the insane screaming that first Yount and then the Cutter Rink had enjoyed.

As each team took their places Cutter couldn't help but notice how well-turned-out they were – how they looked smooth, coordinated, professional. This was a "cashspiel," and it attracted good curlers. Twenty grand was a fair bit of money in itself, but there were promotions to be made and products to endorse as well – perqs for the winners that could add up to a lot of dough. A successful curler could make some respectable loot from this, so curlers came. Very good curlers.

Saskatoon, Saskatchewan. Medicine Hat, Alberta. Kingston, Ontario. Moose Jaw, Saskatchewan. Sarnia, Ontario. Rocky Mountain, British Columbia. Long Bay, Ontario. And Butte, Montana. Eight rinks, four sheets of ice, thirty-two curlers, sixty-four rocks. The Golden Broom used house rocks – the rocks belonging to the Long Bay Memorial Arena and its curling association. For now, the Cutter Rink's stones – Coach Foley's Copernicus stones, which Foley had died retrieving from the lake bottom – remained at the Cutter barn. Their time, if it were to come, would not come this first day.

The draw had been made for opponents for the opening rounds, and Greg the Sportsco Guy sounded like Lorne Greene's Voice of Doom as he announced the bad news over the system.

"The opponents are drawn, ladies and gentlemen, and the Yount Rink has drawn – oh, that's a nightmare for them – the local rink, skipped by Chris Cutter. Sorry, boys."

"I feel a general sense of dread," moaned the lugubrious Neil Bucyk.

Gordon Cutter wheeled on him, his vision stoned but narrow. "You want an easy ride, then go play a bonspiel for the gutless. You want the Golden Broom? Then find your spine. Do not diminish this! You are up against the Empire of Evil." He drew a flared-nostril breath, and turned to the others. "Good luck," he said.

"Thanks." They all shook his quivering hand, and watched him weave his way back to the stands to sit with Amy, dodging barriers that only he could see.

"Coin toss," said the official.

"Just to put things into perspective, Paul," Greg the Sportsco Guy informed all present, "no local rink has won the Golden Broom since its inception in 1937." He took a gulp of beer to reward himself for his acumen.

"That's right, Greg. Now, they're making the toss for who throws first – and who'll get last-rock advantage."

Cutter stepped forward on the red runner, shaking hands with Yount, who moved like a panther even in that single stride. Yount was as tall as Cutter, with that solitary coiffed curl pressing against his smooth, white brow. The quasi-sneer that brushed across Yount's lips, passing for a smile of friendly competition, made Cutter shudder. The guy was a weird combination of obsessed nerd and vampire – downright otherworldly.

He also looked like someone capable of pulling out Cutter's entrails and playing jump rope with them.

"Call it in the air," said the official.

"Tails," said Yount.

The official snapped the coin out of the air and flipped it onto the back of his hand. "Tails it is. Mr. Yount?"

Alexander Yount's gaze never left Cutter's. "Good game, Cutter."

"Good game," Cutter replied. *Creepy,* he thought.

And the Golden Broom began.

2

The Cutter Rink played their first game of the Golden Broom tournament against the Yount Rink, skipped by the man known as the Juggernaut, on an autumn morning in northern Ontario, on Sheet B of four sheets of ice, in a small-town arena that had been dressed up like a prom date for the occasion. On the other sheets there was mere serious curling taking place, but on Sheet B, there was the first stage of the ultimate struggle. Cutter's Rink had a solid chance against every other team present. They had virtually none against Yount.

But virtually none is not none at all. And if they played in top form and made no mistakes, they could not only pay Lennox's debt honorably, and make amends for Cutter's cheating a decade before, and lead the town to the happiest moments they'd had for years or would have for years to come – not only could they achieve all that, and give each of themselves a sense of pride in their largely empty lives in the doing – but they could do what Coach Foley had decreed. Having won back the lost Golden Broom, they could slide his burned remains out onto the ice and put the whole matter, at last, well to rest.

To do this, they had to play very well indeed. Playing well hadn't seemed such a tricky thing to do when they first walked out on the sheets that morning. Neil, who was to throw the lead rock, looked from his place in the hack to where Cutter stood in the house, his arms folded across his broom. They had discussed the strategy: Neil would simply start by setting up a guard. He should be able to do it with his eyes closed.

But as Neil Bucyk threw his rock, the others grimaced and the Yount Rink's lips tightened into pleased smiles. It was an appallingly bad shot, the sort of thing someone who'd never thrown a rock before would make. Neil watched in horror as the wayward stone sailed on through the target area and out of play.

Neil, cringing, returned to his teammates. Lennox looked at him, aghast.

"What do you call *that*?" Lennox demanded.

"I call it a miss, Lennox." Neil snapped. He sank to the players' bench and watched as Barnhart, of the Yount Rink, lined up his shot.

Barnhart's shot floated perfectly into the house, spinning like the Belle of the Ball in a hoop skirt, and settled right in on the button.

It didn't get any better after that. Eddie's first throw was far too light and curled too sharply too soon, heading straight for Neil's second rock, which had been well placed as a guard. Eddie panicked and began to shout insane, contradictory sweeping instructions – *hard off off hard leave it off shit oh shit off hard line hard hard hurry hard ooooohhhh noooo* – leaving Neil and Lennox to spend more time peering questioningly at each other than to sweep. They settled for haphazardly and uselessly brushing their brooms over the ice. Eddie's rock glanced off his own team's guard, knocking it aside before wobbling off out of play.

Eddie crawled back to the hack. In the house, Yount stood beside Cutter, watching the pathetic display with icy disdain.

"He's got a nice touch," said Yount.

Cutter bit his tongue and turned away.

More than an hour later, Greg the Sportsco Guy's assessment of the situation blared throughout the arena. He was about halfway through his allotment of free beer, and although his speech was still slur-free, his neck above his collar had began to glow an inebriate's shade of red.

"Whoo, baby!" he crowed. "Things are looking grisly on Sheet B, where at the end of six ends the Yount rink is leading Long Bay by a score of four to zip."

"Zip yourself," said Jim Lennox. "Four to nothing ain't so bad."

"You're right; we can come back." Cutter looked up into the stands, seeking reassurance from the crowd. It was the wrong place to look. Anyone local was either grimly quiet or leaning into a neighbor, post-morteming the game and the last rocks thrown. The studious analyses that Cutter saw unfolding only served to make him more nervous. He sought out his father, and found him sitting with Joanne, who had her arm wrapped through his to hold herself down and keep the bouncing to a minimum.

She waved with great good cheer at Cutter, and gave him a mighty thumbs-up. Gordon saw her do this and decided to explain how things were really going.

"See there?" he began, trying to point at the scoreboard, but quickly alarmed by the fact that his hand was bright blue and feathered. He put it quickly back in his lap, and continued. "Uh, that's a – if you're in a situation – uh, they…"

Joanne leaned closer, trying to understand, nodding encouragement.

"I'm *very* stoned," said Gordon Cutter.

"Oh," said Joanne. "Okay!"

She turned back to the game. Cutter and Lennox were standing in the target circle, Lennox having thrown his rocks. Now it was Lennox's turn to set the target for Cutter, who moved around the house assessing the lay of the rocks. He looked like he was strolling calmly, but inside he was a nervous wreck.

Cutter could see some potential. If he could glance off the Yount rock that lay at the rear of the twelve-foot target circle, he could both take that rock out and push his own rock into the button. That would earn them a point.

"I'm gonna take off some weight," Cutter told Lennox. "Back twelve. Roll inside. Okay?"

"Okay," said Lennox. He remained in the house

while Cutter jogged back to the hack, and set himself up to throw. He took a long, calming breath, and sized up the shot, focusing on Lennox's target broom. And on staying calm.

"Come on," he told himself. "Come on, come on."

He pushed himself out of the hack, releasing the rock with a long soft swing of his arm, spinning it as he released it so that it would curl inside, avoiding the guard but taking out that stone on the back twelve. Taking it out, though, wasn't the end of the question. He had to rebound back inside, so that he finished closer to the button than any Yount rock.

Finally – at last – a Long Bay rock was looking good. Cutter barked sweeping orders at Eddie and Neil, but the rock moved like it had eyes, and he called the brooms off. It slipped through the guard and around the button, striking Yount's rear stone and bouncing neatly inside, coming to rest right in the center of the house. There were half-a-dozen Yount Rink stones in the house, but Cutter's was the only one on the button. The score was 4 to 1. Things were looking ever so slightly up.

The Cutter Rink men met in a hopeful high-five. It wasn't particularly intimidating to Yount, but it was a point and Yount didn't care for it much. He was experienced enough to know that some of the most oddball teams could have a certain bite to them. Yount might have looked merely cocky, but he was – like all curlers – one hell of a strategist. Good strategists never underestimate their opponents.

But that didn't mean Yount had to be social. When

Cutter's gaze passed over him, Yount turned abruptly back to his team. It was easier to crush people when you didn't care about them. Yount could see how much this tourney – and that ridiculous-looking foursome of ragtag hosers – meant to the town. Yount didn't actually need another $20,000. In fact, twenty g's would just about make him break even, after paying the entourage. It was only twenty thou *Canadian*, too. They might as well have paid him in Monopoly money. No, this was about pride in being the best, and staying the best. If Yount cared about things like small-town feelings, and about the struggle to survive in some backwoods burb that even God had forgotten about, he might not be completely on his game. Yount was never off his game. He always knew exactly what he was doing.

He watched as Cutter ran over to shake hands with the old man – Cutter's father. Yount knew Gordon Cutter. He would never let anyone know, but years ago he had been an admirer of Gordon Cutter. He had, once upon a time, been a kid in a small town himself – a cattle settlement in Montana that had experienced its own downward spiral. But that Montana town was a curling town, and curlers know all other curlers. Borders disappear. Alex Yount was a kid who loved to curl, and he knew all the champs and pros, both Canadian and American and the Swedes and the Scots, too. When he watched the Brier, he couldn't help but idolize the lithe and silver-haired bombast, Gordon Cutter. The Brier Champ's flamboyance and flair were inspiration to a skinny kid on a semi-destitute cattle ranch in the middle of West Armpit, Montana.

Yount couldn't care about those old feelings now, though. This wasn't personal. This was business. There were bottom lines – lines as clearly drawn as any on the ice. Nothing mattered but winning.

The Cutter Rink was going *down*.

3

Hungover and violently nauseous, Amy sat alone at her mother's kitchen table, too sick to head to the rink. She was surrounded by the bits and pieces – the knickknacks and memories – of the sixty years of Foley Family Life. Sometimes her own life seemed like a long stretch of hard work, of struggle, and a big dollop of loneliness too. *Why do you do this to yourself, Amy Foley?*

When Chris Cutter had promised to marry her sister, that was bad enough, but Amy had been able (tough little good-natured thing that she was) to see the up side of having the man she loved married to someone else. If the best she could do was have him as a brother-in-law, that would have to be what she got. At least he would be close, and she would have him as a devoted friend. She could settle. She could cope.

But then, he'd left. He'd left them all. It was of scant, small comfort to her that she was the only one in town who knew why he'd gone, and why those curling rocks had ended up in their watery grave, because soon after he'd disappeared from town, she'd started receiving postcards. Cutter kept in touch with his Amy. She got postcards from everywhere – Saudi Arabia, Malaysia, Texas, Chile. Every one of them he signed "Love, Chris." Every one of them, she kept.

Without Chris, curling had pretty well died in Long Bay. People still played recreationally, but most of the town had lost its taste for it. Amy had missed not only Chris, but curling. Sometimes it seemed that the only thing that brought a spark to life had been the game of curling – the preparation, the skill, and the beers with the gang afterwards. A tournament made it even more magic, turning the spark to a bonfire. The Golden Broom made everything electric, and there hadn't been one for such a long time.

But the Golden Broom was finally here again, and where was she? Still unsteady from having drunk herself into a state of near toxicity. In the post-binge clarity, she could see why she'd done it. Cutter and Julie were together again, and she – Amy Foley, good ol' buddy Amy, who got friendly little notes from faraway places, but never any more intimacy than a chummy hug – was so far off their radar screen that they'd had the gall to consummate their reunion right outside her kid's bedroom. The Impala's windows hadn't been the only thing that was steamed.

But, of course, she had no right to be angry. Amy Foley was a fun girl, and a good sport, and she had a get-along personality, and she knew her place (to wit: ten paces behind her sister's solid-gold ass). Oops, there was that anger again. That hurt. A drink always made her feel better – made her feel more like she could be fun-loving all the time, and everybody's buddy, and not mind being eclipsed. But, of course, there was a practical problem to coping with pain by drinking. One cannot be drunk *all the time*.

Amy did not want to be drunk all the time. She just wanted the hurting to stop, and the sight of Cutter's palm pressing against the misted-over window of the Impala had hurt more than she could bear.

Perhaps the town had been right: Cutter could not be trusted after all. When the Golden Broom was over, maybe he would dump them all again, pull up stakes, and leave them all waving delicate white handkerchiefs in his wake. Or maybe he would marry Julie, who had recently announced that she was taking extended leave from the space program, past the ordinary compassionate period. Amy would have to smile and nod throughout the whole wedding thing again. Or maybe Julie and Cutter would go back to Houston, where Cutter could work on the oil fields, and Julie could fly to the skies…

If that happens, Chris, will you still send me postcards signed "love"?

The various scenarios spun through her imagination, but Amy couldn't help but notice that none of them included *her*. She was Amy, and she would stay here. That would be okay. Long Bay was home. She just wouldn't drink, that's all. It would be easier not to drink if Cutter wasn't here.

Her stomach lurched, and the small motion of that

lurch shook her body. The shaking caused her headache to scream in protest. Amy could almost hear her mother: *Dear God in His Sunday Suit, sweetheart, why do you do this to yourself?*

There had been no call for Amy to answer that question for a while. In fact, she hadn't done this to herself for months. Those corny twelve steps had cast their special spell. Amy was not Julie; she didn't have any urge to see the world from two hundred miles up. She didn't have enormous abandonment issues or a brain the size of a front-end loader, that made it impossible to be content with ordinary things. Amy actually liked her mother's kitchen, and the curling-rock kettle, and the collection of colored badges and buttons stuck to a cork panel in the wall, and all those refrigerator magnets, and Brandon's finger paintings Scotch-taped to any free space. She liked the mismatched crockery, the dangling oven mitts, the hysterically flowered curtains. They all smacked of home and hometown. It didn't matter to her if she never saw a big city, not really it didn't. She wanted a home like her mother's, and an eccentric and fun-loving man like her dad had been, as a life partner. It wouldn't hurt if the guy was a curler, too.

Gee, funny, but wasn't it just the golly-gosh-darndest irony that Chris Cutter was just such a man, but, of course, he belonged to *Julie*, whom he still panted after while she – Amy, the official Chopped Liver Girl – sat around mooning and trying to be a *pal*…

The thought of chopped liver made her stomach do a roller-coaster move. She had just thought that maybe a cup of tea might settle things, and filled the curling-rock kettle and put it on the burner, when the doorbell rang. Something about the tone of the bell – the precision of the length of time the caller kept his finger on the button – made Amy think, *that sounds official*. Like the taxman was calling, or Officer Frances with a summons for an unpaid ticket. Like whoever was at the door, was wearing the uniform of a Very Important Institution, and had come a long way on a High Profile Mission.

"Good day," said Scott Blendick of the American Space Agency, as Amy opened the door and stepped out into the blindingly bright day. "I'm Captain Scott Blendick."

Amy squinted at him blankly, trying very hard not to whoops on his shoes.

"Of the Space Agency?" Blendick coaxed.

Amy nodded. Julie might have mentioned his name. It explained the trim blue uniform with the silvery braid. Space agency, come to get big sister Julie…

The roller coaster in her stomach finished its long climb up her esophagus, and reached the nice big opening at the back of her throat. Its ascent was ill-timed, emphasis on the *ill*. Amy opened her mouth to say hello, just as the carnival ride that was her hangover forced her nausea into full-blown puke.

Scott Blendick of the Space Agency leaped nimbly back as the volley of barf hit the porch floor. Nevertheless, his uniform did not escape unspotted. He glanced at his companion, evidently a Space Agency minion, who was still on the front walk, and very glad indeed to be down there and not up on the porch of this house where a rather unpleasant local greeting custom had just been demonstrated.

"Sorry," said Amy, her fingers to her quivering lips. "I'm Amy Foley."

Blendick just gawped.

"I'm with AA," she explained.

"Okay," said Blendick. "Okay. Well."

From the front lawn, his companion, Cpl. Friesen, spoke.

"Captain Blendick," he said. "Are you sure this is *Doctor* Foley's house?"

If the floorboards could have peeled away, and given Amy a place to crawl and hide, Amy would have thanked the stars for the chance. But instead, she gathered herself together, and offered to clean and press the Captain's uniform. She could do it while they waited for Dr. Foley to come back from the curling club.

"She's getting her hair done?" said Cpl. Friesen.

Amy sighed and ushered her sister's guests into the house, trying to remember whether Americans drank tea.

Baie Comeau, Quebec, is a big, busy port, like Long Bay except successful. Freighters roll in and out all day and long into the night, and in the night their prow lights blink as their elephantine bodies slide into the docking slips. Their horns blow like dirges.

It takes great expertise to dock a Great Lakes freighter. As delicate as a sailboat but weighing as much as a skyscraper, a freighter requires the touch of a true pro, who is in charge of his nerves and faculties, and is undistracted by such things as wheezing, apoplectic, grizzly-bear-sized drug enforcers banging on the wheelhouse door. It's hard to drive an iron boat as long as a city block with a homicidal maniac stomping around the decks.

When Stuckmore demanded the boat turn around, the captain made a judgment call. He figured the best thing to do was comply: get the bastard off the boat and get him off fast. It could be done without too much expense, and it would be a lot more risky to raise hell and radio help. By the time help arrived, someone could be wearing their guts for garters. Someone like *him*.

So the captain posted a guard outside the wheelroom, and turned the boat toward the nearest port. Baie Comeau, that was.

But despite the presence of ship security outside the cabin, the captain of the *Henry Allen* was still shaky as he commandeered the hulking vessel into port. Even the ship's horn sounded shaky. When he glanced out his window, he saw standing by the rail, looking into the black water that slid by beneath the ship's flanks, the enormous lurking shadow of Stuckmore.

It was almost over: a few more minutes and the nasty big man would be gone. The captain could have notified the Quebec police, and had them waiting to gather Stuckmore to their bosom the moment the ship landed. But he wanted to be sure of this. Stuckmore was the sort of person who had connections. Stuckmore knew the captain's name. The captain had a family. He had an expensive car with new whitewalls. He had a split-level home in a nice suburb in Sarnia. He had lots of reasons not to piss off a man like Stuckmore.

Stuckmore paced like a caged bear while the crewmen strung the gangplank. They didn't even have it fully secured before Stuckmore pushed one of them out of his way and stomped, lurching for balance as the gangplank swayed beneath him, down toward solid ground.

The captain heaved a huge sigh of relief. He couldn't help but notice how quickly the crew pulled up the gangplank again, as if Stuckmore might change his mind. But from his eagle's nest, the captain could see that some other poor bastard was now in charge of the balding, bearded behemoth.

An eighteen-wheeler with a big cab-over sat quietly under the floodlights of a nearby parking lot, looking for all the world like a dozing buffalo. Stuckmore headed straight for it, splashing through murky puddles and tromping over the low brambly grass that separated the largely vacant lots. He grabbed the door rail on the passenger side, and hauled himself up, reaching through the partly open window, which the driver would now regret having left that way, so that he would have a little fresh air on his nap.

The driver woke to the feeling of a fleshy, powerful palm closing on his throat. When he opened his eyes, there was a big ugly monster looking right at him. The monster had spaghetti in his beard and bits of clam chowder in his eyebrows.

"This truck is going to Long Bay," the monster said.

"*Quoi?*" said the driver. "Qui est– "

"Long Bay. You drive. *Now.*"

"Okay, okay," said the driver, regretting deeply ever having paid attention in his English classes.

The driver had two thoughts as he pulled onto the Trans-Canada: that he wouldn't be getting back to Montreal on time for dinner after all, and he was going to miss the Sportsco broadcast of the opening morning of Day 2 of the Long Bay Golden Broom. He didn't mind missing dinner, but he sure hated to miss the Golden Broom. Dinners came and went, but missing that bonspiel – *merde! That* was a drag indeed.

The rig rolled up the highway, heading back the long way to Long Bay.

4

Cutter wasn't shaking inside anymore. They had a solid chance to come back with a win now. The score was 6 to 4 for the bad guys. Cutter could see an out. A very tough shot, but not an impossible one. He knew he could do it.

Several Yount rocks lay just inside the hog line, between the hack and three Cutter stones on the near side of the twelve-foot circle. Inside that, surrounding the button in a triangulation, were three more Yount rocks. There was a space – a port – between two Cutter rocks and a Yount one, which would have to be squeezed through by Cutter's throw. Then, the Cutter rock would have to nestle right onto the button. It would have to stop itself by hitting the far Yount rock, but not so hard as to take it out, because that would mean it would itself likely bounce out of play.

This would be like maneuvering the space arm. It would be as delicate as brain surgery, except it would involve a forty-two-pound hunk of granite instead of a computerized simulator or a hair-thin surgical tool.

Cutter and Lennox stood with heads together in the house, surrounded by the spread of rocks. Lennox chewed on his lower lip as Cutter described the plan. The configuration they had in mind would leave Yount in a position that in order to get Cutter off the button, Yount would have to make the same shot, but hard enough to strike two rocks out of the way – his own as well as Cutter's. That would be particularly tricky, since that much force would carry himself off the button as well, unless he went to the outside, in which case he would take out his own point-scoring stones with the rebound. But Cutter knew he couldn't anticipate what Yount might do, or be capable of. He had to stick with his own capabilities.

Cutter returned to the hack and set himself up. The minute he released the rock, he knew he'd hit the broom: he'd sent a perfect stone out. Its aim was precisely what he'd wanted. "Off it, clean!" he called to Neil and Eddie. "Don't even breathe on it! Leave it!"

Neil and Eddie backed off, but stayed ready, brooms aloft. Cutter crouched, watching the line and waiting for the moment the stone began to curl. At that moment, he would have to get them sweeping – and hard – to control the curl so that the stone moved through the port, at the proper speed.

There! It was curling.

"HARD!" screamed Cutter. "Hard now, *HARD!*"

Eddie and Lennox swept like madmen. The crowd rose to its feet as the rock picked up speed and its aim stayed true. It was going fine, it was going well…

...and Cutter saw Eddie's foot touch the rock...

...and the rock shifted just so slightly, so very slightly, improving its path from near-perfect to dead-on...

...and Cutter's heart turned to stone, and he had to put his hands on the ice to keep himself from collapsing.

Shit, Eddie burned the rock.

But the rock didn't know it was a burned rock. It delicately curled into the target, nudging Yount's rock out of the way as a lady might gently move aside a rival belle. It sat on the button like it belonged there. Which it didn't.

The crowd hadn't seen the touch. Only those watching the stone and the sweepers' feet, would have seen it – and those with expert, eagle eyes. Like Gordon Cutter.

Gordon was by his son's side in a moment, taking him by the elbow, fairly, gently, but still insisting. "Time out!" Gordon called to the official. "Son, that was a burned rock."

Cutter couldn't look at his father. He found interesting things to look at in the banners and the signs advertising Swiss Chalet and Tim Hortons and the Canada Curling Stone Company.

The official made his way over to Eddie, covering his headset's mike with his hand. "Is there a problem?" he asked him.

Eddie stood with his broom, looking to his skip and his coach for guidance. Eddie had no way of knowing whether he'd touched. The call was entirely Cutter's.

Cutter didn't look at Eddie, or his father. His skin felt tight and itchy. It was another ten seconds before he could find the resolve to speak. He raised his face and looked right at Eddie. His expression spoke a bald-faced lie.

Eddie knew what he was to say, and he said it. "It was clean. No touch."

The official called the game back on and motioned to Yount to set up for his last rock. Yount almost imperceptibly nodded back. But inside, he was seething. He'd seen the touch. He'd seen the foul. That was a burned rock, and it was sitting on *his* button.

His vice-skip whispered to him. "What do you want to do?"

They had the right to challenge the rock. The Yount Rink could declare the foul and demand the rock's removal. There were rules about these things.

Or, they could just keep playing, and blow the cheating hicks right out of the arena.

Yount chose the latter path. "Crush them," he said.

Greg the Sportsco Guy had plenty to crow over when it came to announcing Yount's final shot.

"As is so often the case, it all comes down to one stone. And you have to pity the Cutter Rink, because the man throwing that stone is Alexander Yount – the Juggernaut himself."

Considering that the last shot Yount made was pretty well one-in-a-thousand, he didn't take long to set it up. What's more, it was over in seconds, for the rock he threw traveled the length of the ice without aid of sweeping. It hit one of Yount's own rocks, which hit one of Cutter's rocks, which took itself and one of its fellows out of play. The Yount rock which had been hit proceeded with the same bulletlike speed as the stone that had struck it, sailing up to strike one of the three rocks that surrounded Cutter's on the button. It struck that rock on the outside edge, which moved it sharply into the Cutter rock. That last rock spun neatly off the button, making way for the Yount stone.

Not a single Cutter rock remained in the house. The Yount rink scored three points. The final score: Butte: 9, Long Bay: 4.

"Okay, it's not the end of the world," said Cutter, after it was all over for the day and the Sportsco equipage had all trotted off after Yount to his tour bus. The Cutter Rink men stood around staring at those useless, misguided excuses for curling rocks, which hadn't had the good sense to go where they were supposed to at the speed they were supposed to, or to stay out of the way of Eddie's feet, and were now just sitting there looking embarrassed. Gordon Cutter, escorted out onto the ice by Joanne, stood there too, aware that the mushrooms' effects had now completely worn off, and not liking the feeling of reality at all.

"He's right," said Lennox. "It might be the end of our goddamn chances, but not the world." He fixed Cutter with an accusing stare. "And you...how could you do this to us, man? How could you do it *twice?*"

"Guys," said Eddie. "C'mon. Think positive. Visualize."

"Eddie, if you say that word one more time I'll– "

An ear-splitting shriek, like the cry of a banshee heralding the death of some poor Irishman, sailed across the arena. At first, it was not clearly recognizable as a human sound, but when it repeated, it took a certain form and became identifiable. It was a name – a man's name, screeched by a woman whose voice was so fraught with thwarted rage that it had achieved a register just below the point where the sound becomes audible only to dogs.

The name was Neil. Or rather, it was *NEEEEEEEEEEEEEEEIIIIIIIIIIIIL!*

"Fire in the hole," said Jim Lennox, bolting for the stands.

Eddie backed off, but Cutter stood his ground. Neil was visibly trembling, as Linda – holding the two boys by their hands – marched up to them in her Italian leather loafers. She looked, as always, absolutely perfect, with her sharp nails polished and her figure trim and her slacks ironed into a razor's-edge crease. The most perfect thing about her was her fury.

She came to a precise halt before Neil, and despite having to look up to him, seemed to tower over him. Or rather, he seemed to shrink below her.

"Neil Bucyk," she said, as if his name were a malediction. "There are straws, and there are camels, and there are backs."

This confused Neil. But so beaten was he that he didn't care if she knew it. "Linda, that's so cryptic," he said. "Just say what you want to say."

But it was his oldest boy who replied. Philip had

regained his balance after having to slide across the ice to keep up with his mother. He was obviously exhausted, too – the picture of his father in bearing and in personality, although he looked nothing like him physically.

"Dad," said Philip. "She could be talking divorce."

Out of the mouths of babes come harsh truths. Neil, who up until then had been half-an-inch from telling Linda that if she ever came hollering at him like that again, she'd be sliding across the ice on her silk-pantied backside, suddenly withered at that word. Divorce. He had been about to get in touch with a tiny feeling – little more than embryonic – that he'd been having lately. It was the feeling that he should be able to do the occasional thing *he* wanted to do, instead of scrambling around in pursuit of the Linda Bucyk Life Plan.

And then, that word struck him. *Divorce.*

God almighty, not a divorce. The kids always suffer in a divorce. He didn't want the kids to suffer. He couldn't bear the thought of moving out, and of losing those beautiful, red-haired boys. He wouldn't wake up in the morning and come down for coffee to find them eating their Sugar Wows and spilling their orange juice and asking if they could play baseball that Saturday with him, could they, huh, hey Dad, are you gonna be home on time tonight? Hey, Dad, are you coming home?

Neil turned to his rinkmates. He could hear Linda's breathing behind him as he spoke. She was practically panting, so tightly was she holding in her fury.

"I'm out, guys," he said. "I'm done."

Cutter nodded. This was hard enough for Neil,

without the rest of them letting on about what would become of the team without him. He tried to keep his voice even.

"We understand. You've got a family."

Neil laughed, not too bitterly. "That's what I'm trying for," he said. "Listen, do me a favor. Don't die in Long Bay. I don't want to bury you."

"Like we aren't buried already," said Eddie.

Neil backed away from them, then turned and rejoined his wife, who said nothing to the others as she victoriously whirled and started back across the ice toward the exit. Neil managed to slip in one more remark, very quietly, as he too left. He spoke to Joanne.

"It was nice to have met you…Andrea," he said.

Linda had made it as far as the exit doors. At that point she noticed Neil hadn't kept up, and was about to call him to heel, but he broke into a run and she never got the chance. The doors opened, and the doors closed.

Now, they were only three. Gordon Cutter smacked his cane against the ice. Lennox emerged from where he'd been hiding under the bleachers, and sized up the situation. It was hopeless.

"Come on, Jackie," he called to Joanne. "Let's hit the road."

Joanne whirled around to face him. "Hel-*lo!*" she said. "I told you, my name is Joanne. Can't you even remember my name?"

"How?" said Lennox, genuinely baffled. "It keeps changing."

Joanne let fly with a little wail of frustration. That

Neil guy knew her name. Heck, he knew her *really-truly* name. She bet he'd remember it forever. Just like she'd remember how goofy he looked when he made that lame dirty joke about him being a gasket…he was like some Grade 8 kid trying to impress the prettiest girl. Joanne would know. She spent three years in Grade 8.

She took Gordon's arm to help him off the ice. Lennox hadn't waited for her. Well, what did she expect? The only person who'd she'd really, truly bonded with here was gone. But at least they were all nice, and she still had the curling – at least they still had the Golden Broom.

She nearly burst into tears when she remembered that what had just happened meant a lot more than her not seeing that big sweet undertaker guy again. It meant that the Cutter Rink was finished. Neil was their lead. He was crucial. Sure, they still had a way to make it to the finals – mathematically, it could be done – but not without Neil. After all their work, the Cutter Rink was dead in the water.

Not long after they'd left, the arena custodian switched off the lights for the night. He hadn't even noticed Cutter sitting alone on a players' bench, watching the stones expectantly, as if they might somehow speak, and tell him what to do now.

5

Eddie and Lily Strombeck didn't have much money, so they bought the Shoppers Drug Mart low-cost line of pregnancy test sticks. Even so, those were nearly ten bucks a box, or five bucks a stick. Five bucks, for the monthly bad news that Eddie's little spermies still hadn't made it to the button. Five bucks, literally pissed away.

Eddie was feeling bad enough when he got home. Lily helped him out of the car and up the stairs to the house, practically holding him up, much as she had held him up at Coach Foley's funeral. It felt a lot like the funeral: as if the Coach had died all over again. Somehow, the Golden Broom had brought him back – the whole ridiculous business of carrying the Coach's mortal remains around in a curling rock, and the excitement, and the crowd, and the constant buzz of rumor. The bets flying in Belle's diner. As if they were really gonna do it this time.

"I'm gonna test," said Lily, pushing one of their cats off a kitchen chair and sitting Eddie down on the flower-print vinyl seat. "Then I'll make you some nice Kraft Dinner and wieners. Don't worry, baby, this'll work out somehow."

"I'll come watch you test," Eddie said.

"Okay."

They headed into the bathroom together. Eddie always watched her test. He found the whole process fascinating. It reminded him of watching the litmus paper change colors back in Grade 9 science class. He'd never understood why, but he liked the magic of such things. The sign that something was present that otherwise wouldn't be seen, like a hidden talent. Or a business opportunity. Or a little baby…

With these test sticks, all Lily had to do was pee on the stick, and then wait one minute. The stick was about as long as a Popsicle stick, and twice as thick, and made of plastic, with a little half-inch-wide opening in it that exposed the testing paper. That was the part Lily had to hit with her pee. After one minute, the window would produce the results: one colored line, or two. One line meant failure. Two meant success.

There'd always only been one line.

But at least Lily was getting very accurate at hitting the window, sitting on the toidy holding the stick with her thumb and forefinger, reaching down between her plumply rounded thighs.

She'd been testing once a month for years. It was a huge deal to her, and she always made like there was a real chance the stick would come up with the magic sign that meant there was a baby inside her. But Eddie didn't understand why she had to use the sticks, when the other signs that she might be pregnant were never there. Like barfing, or a missed monthly.

Eddie knew that the instructions on the box said that the maybe-pregnant lady was only supposed to pee on these sticks when her time of the month was late. Eddie didn't know anything about ladies' monthlies, but he knew it said right on the box *"use on the first day of your late period!"* Well, Eddie himself didn't have a period, but he kind of figured that there was no point in Lily testing unless she'd missed her monthly. That was the biggest sign, the one ladies always waited for: the late monthly. If *that* was late, then came the peeing-on-sticks.

But Lily was never late. If she waited for her monthly, she'd have never tested. She'd never have a *reason* to. Because you could set a stopwatch by Lily's monthly. But Lily had trouble accepting that all her work, all her prayers, all her trips to the doctor and making poor Eddie whack off into a bottle and then get told he had deformed sperms – she wanted the same thrill other women get, of seeing that test come up positive. There would be no chance at all of it ever coming up positive if she followed the rules and waited for a late period. So, two days before her monthly, Lily tested. Eddie was not going to question her logic.

But sometimes her optimism, and her faith, nearly broke his heart. Lily always approached these tests with the same blinkered anticipation of a really poor kid coming downstairs for Christmas year after year, thinking that this is the year that Santa's gonna bring that bike. Lily was like that kid. She never gave up.

Besides, hadn't the doctor said to pray? Praying did make miracles. Little baby Jesus was a miracle. He didn't have any sperm-giving daddy at all, and still He was real. Now, Eddie wasn't saying that Lily was going to have a holy child, but that if God could make a baby out of nothing, then He could certainly make one out of the lame-tailed, raggedy-assed, low-motility sperms that Eddie's balls were chock full of. They had even been told to consider *artificial insemination*, but Lily had decided against it. Not only was there a lack of suitable donors in town, she *knew* she was going to get pregnant. And it would be by her husband. Eddie was the only guy on the team for her.

So, if it made Lily feel better to pee $5 away every month, and to have that one minute's soaring hope as she watched for that paper in the window to show those two magic colored lines, he wasn't going to go against her.

The dog and several cats gathered around them on the bathroom floor as Eddie and Lily settled in for the test. Lily sat down on the toidy, skirt hoisted, and got a stick from the Shoppers Drug Mart box. Eddie sat down on the bathtub's edge, which was directly across from her. The bathroom was tiny, so their knees touched. Eddie's knees nestled within the spread of her legs.

"Here goes," she said, a big, brave smile on her face.

"Yep," said Eddie. He was surprised how quietly he said it.

There was the soft tinkle of pee, and Lily pulled the

stick back out from beneath her, and held it in her lap, counting to sixty while Eddie massaged the outside of her legs. She liked that. Today would be the day that it would come up roses, that it would be the real thing, and Eddie would leap around the bathroom with joy, and then they'd go learn childbirthing stuff like Lamaze classes and massaging her back against back labor and bringing her ice chips, and getting the nursery ready. Trips to Toys 'R' Us and to Storkland. They'd have to teach the cats not to jump into the baby's crib. The dog should be okay, though. The dog was too fat to jump anywhere.

"Fifty-eight, fifty-nine, sixty. Okay, Eddie-ready?"

"Okay, Lily-dilly." He could hardly say the foolish pet name, the traditional salute of hope. Something was really choking him.

She held the stick before her closed eyes, a quiet smile of confidence on her lips. Then, her eyes flew open and she absorbed the news, the wonderful news. She was – surely she was! – pregnant.

Eddie watched as her face fell, her smile collapsing. The pain raced across her pretty face like a storm cloud. But as fast as it came, it was gone. She tossed the stick in the overloaded trash, and cocked her head brightly at Eddie.

"Not this time," she said.

To her shock, Eddie slipped off the edge of the bathtub, falling to his knees before her. He wrapped his arms around her chubby calves and clung there, his shoulders shaking.

"It's all so futile!" he bawled.

"Honey, honey, come on," she cried, patting his hair and trying to pull him back to his feet. "Don't cry, please don't cry. Hey! Success is just failure turned inside out. And that's what we're good at, you and me!"

"What?" said Eddie. He wiped his nose on his sleeve, and looked up at her. She was crying too, but trying very hard to smile for him. "Failure?"

"No, turning failure inside out, silly. You just gotta have faith that things will happen. I'll prove it. I'm gonna test every day of the Golden Broom. Tomorrow and Sunday, I'll test. And we'll be pregnant, okay? That's faith."

That's ridiculous, Eddie thought, but he was still enough in control of himself that he wasn't going to pop her bubble. There were two more tournament days, and her period would start on the last day, the Sunday, somewhere around noon he would look at his watch and she'd be off in the Ladies', taking some Midol and tending to herself. She'd be bringing out the sanitary pads, not the Shoppers Drug Mart pregnancy home-test strips.

Eddie sighed. She really had got carried away. She wasn't going to test every day of the Golden Broom – for them, the Golden Broom was over.

"Didja forget, Lily honey?" he said. "We lost Neil today. We're gonna have to step out."

"Aw, I don't believe that," said Lily, making a dismissive little gesture with her soft, plump hand. "That's another failure that's gonna get turned inside out. Eddie Strombeck, your ship is gonna come in. Our ship. You just wait and see."

The car parked outside the Foley house was an obvious rental: an over-long blue-black quasi-limousine, the kind that very important men phone ahead to ensure will be waiting for them at the airport. Of course, at the Toronto airport, the very important men from Houston had not realized that they still had a ten-hour drive ahead of them to get to Long Bay. They went from teeming urban metropolis to an endless stretch of blacktop heading deeper and deeper into a land that comprised nothing but rocks, trees, lakes, rocks, trees, lakes, rocks, oops there's a moose, trees, lakes, rocks and more rocks.

It was a comfort to them to have leather seats to soothe their confusion.

Eva and Julie were confused too, but Julie only briefly. Like Amy at the ringing of the doorbell, she had a semi-psychic whiff of officialdom strike her when she saw that car. She knew at once that the Space Agency was here. But why? Couldn't they just phone?

Not if she'd blocked their phone number. And they couldn't wire or courier, either. Not if it was crucial. Top secret. Urgent. They could travel as fast by plane as a Purolator package, and Lord knows neither Canada Post nor the U.S. Postal Service were exactly trustworthy with time-sensitive material. There were men from Houston in her house. They wouldn't be here to can her. They'd be here to tell her one thing. One improbable thing...

"Mom," she said, taking Brandon's hand, and slipping her other hand through Eva's arm, "There are astronauts in your kitchen."

"Humph," said Eva. "I've had an astronaut in my kitchen for the last month. *You*, dear."

"Oh. Right."

But when they opened the kitchen door, they were greeted by the sight of Amy standing over the ironing board, cheerfully pressing the trousers of a dark blue suit. The jacket of the suit, still slightly damp from the sponging off, and its crisp linen long-sleeved shirt, hung over the back of a kitchen chair. On another kitchen chair sat a man of late middle age, wearing an undershirt and striped undershorts, and dark socks held up by knee garters. His shoes, cleaned of the spots of Amy barf, sat by his feet, ready for a final polish.

Corporal Friesen, who stood behind Captain Blendick at near attention, saluted as Julie came in. Julie saluted back, accustomed to Friesen's near hysterical compliance with procedure. "Hello, Corporal," she said. "Captain Blendick. What a surprise."

"Don't talk about surprises," said Blendick. "I've had enough of those. I was surprised to find the only way I could reach you with mission information was to attend upon you personally. I was surprised that this attendance would require a trip beyond the Arctic Circle. I was surprised to be vomited upon by your sister." He softened a little. "But I am *pleasantly* surprised by how this afternoon has turned out."

Julie looked aghast at Amy, who could barely meet her sister's eyes, but who gathered herself together almost at once and proudly swallowed her embarrassment. She was damned if she was going to be scolded like a toddler.

Julie launched in anyway. "Amy, what's going on? You– "

Eva put her hand on Julie's arm, and Brandon ran to his room and slammed the door. Captain Blendick put his hands up to calm Julie.

"Dr. Foley, you might rest assured that my distress over your sister's digestive incontinence is considerably less than my distress over discovering that you have deliberately rendered yourself incommunicado, which was not a term of your compassionate leave, and which is grounds for internal action." There was a certain protective smugness in his tone as he folded his arms, glanced at Amy, and continued.

"The Space Agency has seen vomit before," he said. "But it doesn't like to be stood up like a teenager waiting for her prom date. Is that clear, Dr. Foley?"

The shoe being suddenly on the other foot, Julie grew formal. She was in deep shit. These men could only be here for one reason: somehow, she was needed in Houston, and not for some sort of computer simulation exercises. She didn't know how, but she was probably being bumped up the list – to standby, even. They'd have to have their standby onsite, not off in the middle of nowhere.

"Captain. I apologize for my unprofessional behavior. I have been under considerable personal stress, owing to the passing of my father and his being placed in a – uh, owing to the nature of his final wishes.

Will there be disciplinary action?"

Captain Blendick shook his head. "Not under the circumstances. Indeed, there should be. But we have news, Dr. Foley. Please sit down."

Eva, fussing, offered everyone tea, but Captain Blendick had already had eight cups, owing to sitting with Amy and Friesen watching a very strange game called *curling* being played on the TV. Captain Blendick understood that somehow, everyone in this place was completely committed to the tournament, which had even attracted Sportsco Network, and which involved people sliding around on ice, tossing big rocks at a target, like a gigantic slippery game of crokinole.

In fact, Captain Blendick had very happy memories of crokinole. His Nana Parker had a crokinole board in her living room. He remembered the knocking *crack* sound the crokinole chips made when they struck each other, and the thrill of getting his little chip in the circle, and how when they all were spread out around the crokinole bulls-eye, they often looked just like that map of the solar system in his science textbook at school. He loved his science textbook, and his *Fantastic Journeys* and *Amazing Voyage* comic books, and he loved his Nana, who'd been dead for years and years. Strangely, Eva Foley's kitchen had the same creeping-vine wallpaper that his Nana had. She would stand in the kitchen and iron, too, while he had tomato sandwiches and chocolate milk...

"Captain Blendick?"

"Hmm?"

"Milk and sugar in your tea?"

"Yes, that's fine, thank you, Mrs. Foley– "

"Captain Blendick," said Julie, drumming her fingers on the tabletop, "you were saying– "

"Here's your pants, Captain," said Amy sweetly, handing him his folded, pressed trousers.

"Thank you," he said. "Oh, and thank you," he said to Eva as she put down the teacup.

"I hope I didn't make the crease too sharp," said Amy.

"I hope the tea's got enough sweet in it," said Eva.

"HEY!" Julie slammed her hand down on the table. "Captain Blendick, Mother, Amy, if you please. What is this news?"

Blendick finished buckling his trousers before he sat down again, and took a good long slurp of the foreign beverage before settling in to his announcement.

"It has transpired that Dr. Olsen has developed a hypertrophic prostate," he said.

"In layman's terms," Corporal Friesen offered, "a plumbing problem."

"We're all quite familiar up here with prostates," said Julie evenly. "Canadian men have them, too. Captain Blendick, I take it that means I am now first alternate."

"Uh, nooo," said Blendick, stirring his tea, and Julie's heart sank. Now she was really confused. She'd been wrong. The Agency hadn't sent the big brass all the way to Long Bay to tell her that she was required back in Houston, right now. It was something else. She didn't know what, but maybe it was a transfer – maybe out of the space program itself, into instructional.

"I'm not first alternate. Then what am I?"

"Dr. Foley, protocol moved us to Dr. Marx. You know Dr. Marx."

"Yes, of course."

"Close to him? Know him personally?"

"Not particularly. I know him in passing, profession-ally."

"Good. Good. Because he's dead, Dr. Foley. He received the news of his appointment to the flight deck with such enthusiasm that…well, suffice it to say that there's an inquest pending."

Eva and Amy looked aghast, but Julie caught on to what this really meant. She was not next in line. She was no longer lining up at all.

"Just like that?" she said. "Just like that, I'm going– I'm going– "

But the penny had dropped for Eva, too. And Eva had less trouble speaking. "Good God and all His grand plans!" she hollered, clasping her hands together and raising them to the kitchen's spackled ceiling. "My baby's going up in space!"

Julie felt her sister's congratulating hand on her shoulder. "You'll miss the rest of the Golden Broom."

Julie didn't think it was the best time to tell Amy that there wasn't going to be any Golden Broom, that Neil had been yanked by his wife, putting an end to the town's dreams. Besides, she didn't really care that much what happened to it now – now that everything she'd put a decade's work into was suddenly reaching fruition.

"I take it we're going to leave tonight," said Dr. Julie Foley. "I'll just pull a few things together."

"Actually, Dr. Foley," said Captain Blendick. "After spending such a delightful afternoon with your sister, watching the television here, and considering it's such a grueling drive back to – what's that city called again, Friesen?"

"Toronto, sir."

"Topronto, yes, back to Topronto, that it would be pleasant to stay here another day and see how this curling tournament unfolds."

"Sir," said Friesen, wringing his hands. "We can't stay beyond that. The mission is in lockdown– "

"Well, actually," said Julie, "there won't be anything to watch, if you're a Long Bay fan. It seems that Long Bay is out of the Golden Broom. We lost a key player today."

"What!" cried Amy. "Was someone hurt?"

"His missus gave a good yank on Neil Bucyk's leash, is what happened," said Eva Foley.

"I see," said Julie, ignoring her mother's metaphorical relating of the event. "So we can leave directly, then."

Blendick looked genuinely disappointed. "Oh," he said. "I was just getting into it. Well, then, yes, we'll leave at 0900 Sunday. That will give you a day to collect yourself and your effects, resolve whatever you have to resolve. Correct, Dr. Foley?"

"Yes, sir."

"And I'll have one more day of watching curling." He glared at his Corporal, who was now tugging anxiously at his sleeves, running the time parameters in his mind. How many hours' drive back to Toronto...how long a flight...how many asses would be in how many slings if they weren't back in a timely fashion...

"Captain," he began.

But the Captain ignored him, as Eva topped up his cup with more tea. "You'll stay here, and have a nice dinner, Captain," she said. "And we'll tell you all about the game of curling."

"Oh," said Captain Blendick, picking up his cup like a man who'd drunk the stuff all his life. "I'd like that a lot. Tell me, how much do those rocks weigh? What sort of training do the players need to effect that curl with such accuracy? I tell you, Mrs. Foley, it's poetry in motion."

Julie Foley and Corporal Friesen stared slack-jawed at Captain Blendick. The man had been on a lunar mission. He was involved in the planned excursions to Mars. He'd spacewalked. But what was fascinating him right now? How a group of hicks in wooly sweaters managed to get big round rocks to travel in an arc across a sheet of ice. It was like he'd been kidnapped and brainwashed. Corporal Friesen rubbed his face with both hands, hard, trying to wake himself up.

And when Julie stood up and left the room, nobody noticed. That was not something she was accustomed to. But strangely, she didn't mind too much. The space program had never, for her, been about attention and adulation. It had been about going up in space.

Which was now, at last, really going to happen.

6

Just before sunset, not far north of Kearney, Ontario, in a roadside second-hand store that sold all manner of junk, the elderly proprietor was just locking up for the night when he heard a shattering crash. It was the unmistakable sound of his front window breaking.

He'd heard that noise before. A couple of times the wind had blown the darn thing right out, just from malice it seemed to him. Another time, some teenage punks on a ripsnort heaved a brick through it, then took off in somebody's father's station wagon without grabbing so much as a used electric mixer. So he wasn't too shook up by the sound. He kind of figured his insurance premiums would be going up, but that was no big deal.

On the other hand, when he headed slowly to the exit to check out the damage, he did not expect to see a bear rooting through his window display. At least he thought it was a bear. In fact, bears were a lot tidier. This guy pawed goods aside, oblivious to the big chunk of glass sticking out of his forehead, trying to reach an item on the back shelf.

The shopkeeper decided to exercise caution and hang back to watch. He certainly wasn't going to go up and offer to help him find what he needed.

The bear grunted with accomplishment as he seized the back-row item. It was a small, battery-operated, obsolete B&W television, the kind that plugged into an ordinary outlet, or into the lighter on a car's dashboard. The proprietor knew that the TV was in pretty crappy shape, offering a 6" diagonal screen and a very grainy image. It was worth about $10 tops. But the bear seemed to want it pretty badly. Ergo, he would let the bear take it.

The bear climbed into a waiting tractor-trailer, still unconcerned with the broken shard wedged into his scalp. Inside the truck, the driver – who looked like a trembling aspen – sat with his hand on the gearshift and his eyes bugging out of his head. The shopkeeper knew a man who was operating under a threat when he saw him. It made him even gladder he had not approached the bear and asked for the $10.

As the rig pulled away, he slipped up to the door and shot the bolt. It was a rather pointless act, considering his front window was gone, but it made him feel a little better. He would call the insurance people Monday morning. There was a local agent down the road, who could have come and taken the claim info, but there was no point in calling him until Monday. Everybody would be glued to their TVs tomorrow.

They'd be watching the Long Bay Golden Broom. Everything else could wait.

Julie came down the cellar stairs to find Amy sitting in the middle of the papers and leftovers that she herself had already gone through - where she'd found the cassette tape that her father had left for the boys. She cleared her throat, to let Amy know she was there.

Amy glanced up and smiled weakly. She set down the photos she'd been going over – family snaps, mostly, and some of neighbors and curling teams long-gone-by.

"Hi," said Amy.

"Hi."

"Thanks for taking Brandon to the arena. I was feeling pretty bad."

Julie nodded and sat down across from her. The papers formed a pile between them. "He's a good kid." She thumbed absent-mindedly through the slips in the pile. "Amy," she said at length. "Why do you do this to yourself?"

Amy stiffened defensively. "I'm an alcoholic," she said.

There was an uncomfortable silence, and then Julie broached the unspeakable topic. "Listen, the other night, in the car– "

She got no farther. Amy interrupted her. "We don't have to talk about that," she said.

"Yeah, we do. You know we do."

Amy shook her downcast head. "I have no claim on that man."

"This isn't about you and him, or me and him. This is about me and *you*."

Julie was getting a little close for comfort. Amy

scrambled for a joke, a smart-ass line, anything to defuse the proximity. "Oh, like, a lesbian incest kind of thing?"

"Why do you always have to be so flip?" said Julie quietly.

"I'm an alcoholic!" Amy cried again.

Julie's quietness broke. She slapped her hands down on the pile of photos. "Would you *drop* that woe is me thing? I'm sorry for having a brain and for working that brain to the bone...no, you know what? I *don't* apologize. I'm proud of what I am. I am an astronaut. And I worked like hell to become an astronaut. And you! You sneer at me."

"Sneer!" Amy gawped at her. "Sneer? I envy you. You...you have everything. You even have Chris."

Now it was Julie's turn to gawp. She was speechless for several seconds. Then she said, "That's very funny."

Amy frowned – an expression that meant, *what do you mean?* And Julie reached into her back pocket for the answer. A bundle of aging postcards, from the past ten years, wrapped in a crumbling rubber band. Amy's postcards, from Cutter. They were stuck together at the corners, some of them, but that was to be expected. They had been living all this time in a drawer in the kitchen, where things sometimes got a little damp.

"Dear Amy," Julie read. "Signed Chris Cutter. Ah, here's another. Dear Amy. Chris. Amy, from Chris." She put the cards down gently, and took her sister's hand and put it on top of the bundle. "I was supposed to marry the guy, but really...he clicked with you. Friends first. It's you, Amy. You have this – this *thing*. Something special. And with you and Dad, too. You just clicked."

Amy shook her head, frowning, unsure. Julie continued, hurriedly, onto the next – and toughest – topic.

"The other night, in the car." Her voice dropped, becoming almost inaudible. "I was trying to…to go back in time, maybe…"

Amy took Julie's hands in her own. "But you can't, can you?"

"No." Julie chuckled, in spite of herself. "Not even in the space shuttle. No matter how far or fast I go."

They leaned over the pile of paper that summed up the last ten years, and hugged each other goodbye.

7

Cutter sat at Nug's bar, trying to drown a sorrow that was one of those big fat things with an unbelievable buoyancy. An oversized beachball of miserable disappointment. He kept shoving it down in his vat of beer, and it kept popping back up again.

After an hour of this, Cutter grew weary. "Nug," he said, "how much for the beer?"

"Buck fifty," said Nug.

"And how much for this mug?" Cutter held up the cheap glass stein.

Nug frowned. "One fifty, I guess."

Cutter nodded. He looked at the television set, on which the Sportsco guys were soundlessly moving their lips over scenes from that day's Golden Broom. Yount's triple raised takeout had been re-broadcast eight times.

"Nug?"

"Hmm?"

"How much for the TV set?"

Nug *really* frowned this time. "One hundred fifty," he said firmly.

Cutter pulled out his wallet and emptied a pile of tens and twenties onto the bar. Then he picked up his mug and hurled it, with all that Joanne-trained force, at the television. The glass burst as the vacuum tube imploded. Broken bits of TV screen cascaded to the bar carpet.

"Good one," said Nug.

Cutter nodded thanks and sat down again. But he wasn't there two seconds before he felt a hand on his arm. He looked up. Amy. *Amy*. Thank God.

"Hi," he said.

"Don't talk," Amy replied. "Just come on." She glanced at the Copernicus stone that sat on the bartop in front of Cutter, and frowned. "Don't forget to bring Dad."

He barely had time to wave a quick so-long to Nug, before he was in Amy's red pickup, on his way to he didn't know where, listening to the Tragically Hip wailing on her cassette deck. He felt so much better, just being there.

The red pickup pulled to a stop outside the gates of the Long Bay cemetery. Evening was just around the corner, lengthening the shadows and throwing all the hedges and shrubs into dark. The headstones shone, though – grey-white in the fading day, they stood row upon row, like soldiers at the last post.

"What are we doing here?" asked Cutter.

Amy leaned across him and opened his door. "Your dad's visiting your mom, Chris," she said. "You go, too."

Cutter stepped out. The gravel beneath his feet

crunched – a loud and intrusive sound in the evening silence – and somewhere in the graveyard Cutter saw a quick responding movement. His eyes tracked it. It was his dad, all right, standing in one of the far back rows, alone in the shadows. Looking down at a stone.

Cutter tried not to make too much noise crossing the lawn of the boneyard. Its grass was cropped as short as a military haircut, and each stone he passed had a name he recognized. This town was tight and small, and everyone knew everyone else.

"Hi," he said, taking his place beside his father. Before them, the headstone had their name carved into its granite: CUTTER. Another use for granite, other than curling stones. For holding down the dead, so they don't come back, complaining.

She wouldn't have complained, Cutter thought. I would have. But Mom was not *me*.

"I don't want one of those shitty father-son conversations," Gordon Cutter said, his voice tense with controlled and sober anger. "But what you did today– "

Cutter didn't want to hear this. His father would never understand what it was like to live under the umbrella of his influence, and his neglect. "It's not just today, Dad," he said.

"What?"

"I've lived my whole life terrified that I was exactly like you."

Gordon turned on him. "Well, you're not. I never cheated. Son, you had a chance to clean house. And instead, you brought more dishonor to the game."

Cutter couldn't argue with that. And it wasn't like it was the only time he'd done it. He focused on the name on the stone, trying not to think of what lay beneath it.

"You know," he said, his voice cracking a little, "when she was dying…this place she was in…the smell, Dad. You can smell it in the walls, and her room stinks with it, and she's got all these tubes and…all she wants is a TV. And I'm just a kid. I can't afford one." He took a long breath, making one more statement without a quaver in his tone. "And you were off at the Brier."

"You don't think I live every hour, of every day, with that!"

"I'm not trying to blame you!" cried Cutter. "I'm just trying to tell you that she wanted a TV. So she could see *you* play."

Gordon's face crumpled in confusion. "She…saw it? Peggy saw the Brier…?"

"No, Dad. She died."

In the silence their shoes brushed against that soft, short grass. Cutter could see his father's head hanging lower than he'd ever seen it before.

"But she wanted to see it, Dad," he said gently. "For the longest time, I didn't understand that. But now I think…you know, it's not about forgiveness, because she didn't *forgive* you- "

"And you don't either- "

"I don't know one way or the other! But what I'm trying to say is that she loved you! She loved *you!*"

Now they were both suffering, but it was a good pain, a sweet relief. A dead woman's love, so overpowering that it had driven one of them away and another into hiding. But they had to look at it, and then at each other, before they could go on.

Cutter reached, like a shy kid, for his father's hand. Their fingers, just at the tips, interlocked briefly, in a brief, soft, touch.

"You know," Gordon said, "when you were a little boy, you were my best friend. I carried you everywhere. Hugged you all the time. All the time."

Cutter remembered. He nodded.

Gordon straightened up; wiped his eyes. "Get back in that truck," he said, regaining his self-control. "And when you do, you take a good long look at the woman that brought you."

Cutter frowned. The nature of this directive was unclear. He looked at Amy all the time, didn't he? But Gordon had turned back to Peggy Cutter's stone, and was lost in some conversation, some ancient moment, that Cutter had no part of. So he slipped away, across the now-black graveyard, heading for the single pole lamp under which Amy's truck was parked.

She was watching him expectantly as he climbed inside, as if waiting for a report. He was about to tell her, but then he remembered his father's instructions. He looked at her: a good long look.

Familiar, wonderful, freckled, soft hair, warm eyes, big smile (a little confused), elegant somehow…Amy. And she was looking back, as if she was seeing something in him. He didn't know what. After all, what on earth could she see in him? What had Julie called him…a roughneck from an oil patch…*cursed?*

But that was Julie who called him those things. Not Amy. Amy had never judged him. Amy had always…always…always *loved* him.

Before Cutter's mind could seize on this, and grasp it solidly, the silence was broken by Gordon Cutter's *arooga* horn blasting as he drove by in his own truck. He yelled out the window to Cutter as he passed.

"Sweat lodge!" he said.

"What?" said Cutter.

"Sweat lodge! Seven a.m., sharp!"

He drove away in a spray of gravel. "What's that mean?" Amy asked.

"I think it means he has an idea," said Cutter. "And if I know that old bugger, it means we're not out of the game just yet."

They drove off together, unsaid things hanging in the air between them.

8

I n the grove of maples and horse chestnuts out beyond Gordon Cutter's back forty, through a cow pasture strewn with cows and their patties, sat an igloo-shaped bark hut. Many cultures globally have experience with bark huts. In Australia, they are celebrated in the songs of Banjo Patterson. In other parts of the world, such huts house entire extended families. In still other environs, young boys who are coming of age spend days in such structures, preparing themselves mentally for the rites that will mark their passage into manhood. Indeed, they are a structure with an honorable history.

In a patch of hardwood trees, outside a dying mining town, such a bark hut stood. It was Gordon Cutter's sweat lodge. Therein, he would ingest a brew of mushrooms and beer, boil a cauldron of water and herbs on hot stones, and commune with the higher spirits that guided his existence.

The boys – by now – were pretty accustomed to the sweat lodge, and to getting up at ungodly hours to attend at it. But they had thought it was part of their training. Training was over. The game was over.

"Over!?" roared Gordon Cutter. "It's not over!"

"Why not?" said Eddie. All of them were naked, with towels over their laps, and they sat on half-log benches around the glowing coal pit dug into the earth in the lodge's center. Their skin gleamed with wet.

"Why not!" Gordon Cutter rose to his feet. "I'll tell you. Men, curling doesn't quit just because men quit curling."

"Neil quit," said Lennox, wishing he had a cigarette.

"That's right. Who's going to replace Neil?" said Cutter, quietly. "You, Dad?"

"Yes, as a matter of fact," cried his father, pointing a finger to the heavens, and practically breaking it against the roof of the lodge. "Oww."

"Dad, you have a bad back – you went through all that physiotherapy– "

"Now you listen to me, son. In the town of Stirling, in the country of Scotland, a man took a block of granite, cut it, rounded it, and carved a date into it, 1511! Yes, 1511, men. The first known curling rock. And since that day, curling has been a game of the people. It has foregone the trappings of commerce, embraced all comers, and in its heart has cherished the truth that all who play, in any rink, on any given day, *can be victorious!*"

Gordon Cutter turned in his seat and uncovered a tarpaulin from a pile of eight curling rocks – the Copernicus stones. Nodding to the others, he made it clear that they were to be placed on the furnace burning at the lodge's heart. Each man took two stones, and placed those stones in the fire.

They all sat back, watching as the stones absorbed the heat. Those directly on the coals began to glow at their bases, as tiny flames licked up their polished sides.

"Wow," Eddie breathed.

"On this day, in our rink, with our brooms and Donald Foley's dust in our stones," Gordon Cutter intoned, "we can do this. We shall be victorious. It's us, men. Agreed?"

They put their hands together in the boiling air above the stones. In an hour, they would be curling. And they would be curling to win.

"Good morning, ladies and gentlemen," Greg the Sportsco Guy announced, as he lined up his broadcast's worth of beer on the panel before him. "Welcome to Day 2 of the Golden Broom. Today we'll see the world champion team from Montana up against the Sarnia Rink, who defeated Moose Jaw yesterday. Fighting for its life is the Cutter Rink, in a hole after going down yesterday to the Juggernaut. And speaking of the Cutter Rink, we have a change of lineup – Jim Lennox moves to second, Eddie Strombeck moves to lead, and oh, hey! This should bring a thrill to the hometown fans – rounding out the foursome will be a former Brier winner and living curling legend, Gordon Cutter!"

Amy, sitting in the stands with Brandon and Eva, whistled sharply through her teeth and applauded madly. She wasn't too thrilled about all her physio work with the old coot getting shot to hell, but if he had to spend a month in the sling after this, whinging like a toddler, so be it. Besides, Gordon never looked better as he strode confidently onto the ice, waving at the stands and smiling a big, natural, crowd-pleasing grin, his grey hair properly coiffed and combed. He wore the same outfit he'd always worn curling: tartan pants and a red sweater, and a flat Scots cap that looked a bit like a tam o'shanter, although you better not tell *him* that if you care to live on. It was as if twenty years had melted off him.

Lily was in the seat beside her. She'd drunk a fair bit of coffee that morning, as she often did on testing days, so that she could pee a good steady stream just before noon. But today either the cream had been going bad, or she was getting that flu that was going around, because not only did she feel she had to pee pretty badly already, but she also was a little off in the tummy. She'd kept it from Eddie when she woke up feeling crummy because he was going to that sweat lodge meeting and at that point he'd thought the whole jig was up, so there was no point moaning about a sour stomach. And when he'd come back, he was over the moon – *gimme my broom, Lily, we're back on the ice!* – so she wasn't going to bring him down by saying she still felt pretty yecchy and what's more, she was afraid that she'd give him her germs. That would be just dandy – he overcomes all these obstacles to get back into play at the Golden Broom, and then gets laid to waste by his wife's flu bug. So she kept her mouth shut about it.

"Hey, what's all that about?" Eva said, pointing at a

commotion commencing on the ice – one involving the Cutter Rink. "Good God in a motorcycle sidecar, are those your father's curling rocks?"

"And the old corn brooms, too," said Amy. "What are they up to?"

What were they up to indeed, thought the game official, coming over to intervene as the Cutter Rink unloaded the ancient stones and brooms onto the rack. "Gordon," the official said, "this tournament plays with house rocks."

Gordon rolled his eye at the approaching minion and at once pulled godly rank. "Indeed it does," he said, handing the man a folded sheet of yellowing paper. "These rocks, known to my rink as the Copernicus stones, after the great seer who saw possibility and truth in the stars above, are registered as house rocks for the Long Bay Curling Club!"

The official frowned. "When was this done?"

"Nineteen fifty-two," said Gordon primly. "A very good year it was."

The official handed the paper back to Gordon, praying no one else would object. He didn't feel like dragging out the rule book and getting into an angels-on-the-head-of-a-pin argument. It was all right with him if it was all right with everyone else. The point of the day was the game.

Gordon Cutter rotated slowly on his heels, scanning the opposing rinks for objections. The Yount Rink looked suspicious and hostile, but that was nothing new.

"I'll allow it," said the official.

"Ladies and gentlemen," Greg the Sportsco Guy pronounced, "we are curling!"

The four men of the Cutter Rink slapped their brooms on the ice, a single blow in unison, in a thunderous clap of straw and power.

With Gordon Cutter off with his boys on the ice, the duty of explaining to Joanne what was going on fell to Amy.

"We've got one chance left," Amy said. "We have to beat Moose Jaw. We should be able to do that, if Coach Cutter's form holds out. That'll take us to the afternoon, where we'll have to beat whoever wins between Kingston and Rocky Mountain. My money's on Rocky Mountain. Yount will no doubt wipe the ice with poor Sarnia. But the question is going to be whether Medicine Hat beats Saskatoon. Medicine Hat has to go down – they're the only ones who have any chance against the Juggernaut in the semis. That would put Saskatoon up against Yount in the semi-finals. Then on Sunday, it'll be the one game for all the roses. That's gotta be us against the Juggernaut, it's just gotta. But, of course, it's all pie in the sky if we don't beat Moose Jaw right now. Okay?"

Joanne's lower lip quivered. "I guess," she said. She wasn't completely recovered from yesterday and the shock that her friendship with that loveable Neil was over, so she was close to tears despite everyone else's happy attitude.

"Hey, don't worry," said Lily, catching Joanne's mood, and putting her hand over Joanne's big pink fuzzy-bunny mittens. "All you have to think is – go team go!"

"That I can do." Joanne applauded, her mittens going puffpuffpuff. "Go team go!"

Lily settled down to watch the opening rocks of the day. The Cutter/Moose Jaw game was on Sheet A, and the boys were revved. Gordon hadn't ingested so much as a single mushroom since his morning ceremony, and in the afterglow he was a clear-eyed, clear-headed, curling machine. By the fourth end, they were up over Moose Jaw 6 to 4.

"I have to pee," said Lily. It was nearly noon, and she always used morning pee, which the box said was the best.

"We'll keep an eye on things for you," said Eva, as Lily sidled her way out to the Ladies'. Ten minutes later she was back, looking crestfallen. In those ten minutes the boys had set up a beautiful spread of rocks, and the Moose Jaw players were struggling to figure out a strategy.

"It's all over but the shouting," said Lily.

"Go team go," offered Joanne.

A cheer went up from the far end of the stands, as the Saskatoon contingent celebrated its waltz over the Medicine Hat rink, which had been touted as being the toughest contender after Butte. Amy slapped her knee.

"The Hat went down," she said. "We can do this."

"Now, you three don't be counting your chickens," said Eva. "We have another team to beat before we can face off with the Juggernaut. And then, of course, we have to beat the Juggernaut. Which won't be a cake-walk, now will it?"

"No, Mom." Amy put her arm around Brandon and hugged him as he smeared a candy floss all over his face. At that point, it didn't seem possible they couldn't win. These men could do anything.

The Cutter Rink beat Moose Jaw 8 to 6. Not a cakewalk, not a rout, but a clean game and a good one. They were on the move now.

So, it would be the Cutter Rink against Rocky Mountain House in the afternoon. Yount had steam-rolled Sarnia, leaving the men of that team reeling in shock: a humiliating loss of 12 to 3. Sarnia had planned to stay for the whole tourney, win or lose, but they were so dispirited they all headed to their team van right after the match ended and pulled out of town. They didn't even hang around for the free team-luncheon buffet, featuring burgers and egg salad as catered by Belle's diner, the Spotty Apron Take-Out Luncheonette and Grill.

But the Cutter Rink boys were always happy to have free chow. In the arena's common room they piled their paper plates (printed with a red-and-white maple leaf print), loading them high with dogs and coleslaw. They helped themselves to tins of Pepsi (into which they funneled a little splash of rye), and plunked themselves down on stacking chairs to toast one another.

Alexander Yount, whose personal assistant was preparing a low-fat/hi-carb meal for him in the comfort of his tour bus, paused by the meeting room entrance to watch the riff-raff gorge themselves. He did indeed scorn these bottomdwellers. But he was not a stupid man. He saw how linked – how tight – the Cutter Rink were. It was impossible to see any of the fractures that had existed between them, only weeks ago. Yount knew that that sort of teamwork, and loyalty, can make up for a lack of ability. Not that the Cutter Rink lacked ability, either.

He leaned in to whisper to Barnhart, his vice-skip. "Keep your eyes on them," he said.

Barnhart nodded. He agreed. Curling was the sort of game that attracted some pretty talented losers. Canadians often looked bizarre, but they could surprise you, quick as a snake. And that old man was a former Brier champ. Nobody on the Yount Rink was underestimating anyone from Long Bay.

Meanwhile, not too far away, a long-faced, beak-nosed undertaker stood in the preparation room of the basement morgue of his wife's father's family business, leaning over a corpse. The corpse was motionless. Decay was already setting in. Its heart wasn't beating. It had nothing left.

The undertaker's red-haired son, who was used to playing in the funeral home the way a carpenter's kid might play in the woodshop, came bounding in, the control for his electric car in his hands. He buzzed the remote-control car up to his dad's foot, where it crashed to a stop.

"Hey, Dad," said the man's son. "Whatcha doing?"

The man pulled a sheet over the corpse's head.

"Looking in a mirror, son," he said.

He ruffled the boy's hair before climbing the stairs to his office. He and the dead guy in the basement were the only men in town who weren't out watching the curling.

Indeed, even men from *out* of town were watching the curling. About three hundred miles south of Long Bay, a giant named Stuckmore had not taken his eyes from the static-sparkled TV screen of his purloined portable TV since he acquired it. Now, hunger had taken over, and the rig needed fuel. He instructed his cowed chauffeur to pull into the next stop.

They drove into the lot of a Tim Hortons for a cup of joe and a breadbowl full of soup, leaving the rig to be fueled. The driver was not feeling very good. He didn't really want to eat anything. Even though the hideous bully who had precipitously acquired the use of his truck had not yet physically hurt him, the implication of hurt was very present. Stuckmore was an animal. He even sounded like one. Every time the Juggernaut Rink players were shown on the screen, a low grumbling sound, a sort of throaty snarl, came out of the nasty facial gash that was Stuckmore's mouth. Other than that, he spoke only to give instructions, and indicate the consequences of non-compliance. Which were not pretty.

But the rig's driver, now out of his rig and in the normal-looking, brightly lit doughnut store, started to do some simple math. He was two hundred miles north of Toronto. He was hundreds of miles away from his wife's casserole. He was also about four hundred miles from

Long Bay. He was the kidnap victim of a madman. Here, now, was his chance. They were in a public place, and he could yell for help, or get to a phone and dial 911. Did they have 911 this far north? Okay, he'd dial the operator. Hopefully he wouldn't get one of those recordings…

He'd been too scared to exercise his narrow chances back when the crazy son-of-a-bitch had smashed that junkstore window and shoplifted the portable TV. Now he was a little more confident. Except the coffee shop was full of elderly people having a pick-me-up on their way to visit the grandkids. If something went wrong, there really – practically speaking – was no one to help him.

Stuckmore plowed through the small lineup at the counter, sending geriatrics scattering.

"Can I help you sir?" trembled the counter-help kid.

"Jumbo decaf latte, no sugar," Stuckmore ordered. "And one of them sprinkly crullers."

He turned to the driver, who was checking the exits and looking for fire alarm boxes to pull. "Tell the kid what you want," he said.

You mean, other than a SWAT team? the driver thought. But he said, "Uh, a black anything, as long as it's ninety-nine percent caffeine."

Stuckmore turned back to the cowering counter-help, who was a pimpled fifteen-year-old. The counter-help's Tim Horton training had not encompassed the protocol involved in dealing with draft horse–sized, leather-clad, bug-eyed maniacs with pieces of glass sticking out of their foreheads.

"You heard the man," the maniac said to the pimply boy. "Get him a coffee."

The pimply boy did all he could think of doing. He filled the order.

"Here," said Stuckmore, thrusting the coffee at the driver. "You're off duty."

"What?"

"My turn to drive."

"*Quoi!?*"

Stuckmore put his hand on the driver's neck, and began to unmistakably guide him back to his truck, applying just enough pressure to frighten without causing a disturbance.

"But it's my truck!" the driver protested.

Stuckmore shrugged. "Not until it gets to Long Bay, it ain't."

About ten miles further down the road, as Stuckmore slowed the rig in a grinding clash of gears, the driver – now the passenger – had had enough. Stuckmore drove largely up the middle of the highway. He oversteered. And he kept watching the friggin' curling game on the TV as much – if not more – as he was watching oncoming traffic.

As the rig crawled slowly up an on-ramp, Stuckmore's chauffeur abandoned ship. Stuckmore barely gave it a second's notice as the driver opened the door and leaped out of the cab, landing in a rolling heap in the long grass and Scotch thistles by the on-ramp.

For Stuckmore, the desertion was no problem. It would mean taking a few back routes to Long Bay, to avoid the OPP who'd be onto him, now that the driver would be out blabbing. Big deal. It didn't matter. Stuckmore could handle the OPP.

What he couldn't have handled was not making Long Bay by morning. That would have *really* pissed him off.

9

Beating the team from Rocky Mountain House looked like the cakewalk that Eva had spoken of. The game started on time, after all the wiener dogs were chowed down, and the boys were slightly tipsy from their rye-and-Pepsi. But that tiny bit of drunkenness served only to sharpen their aim. Shot after shot hit its mark, and the Rocky Mountain Men stood with knit brows and folded arms, hardly believing what they were seeing. Rocky Mountain was a first-rate curling team. It made no difference. Cutter's Rink was eating them alive.

But toward the last few rocks of the final end, Rocky Mountain had rallied, largely because the Cutter Rink had sobered up some. The score was briefly tied – or at least, the Cutter Rink felt the tie would be brief. While Rocky Mountain felt hopeful and inspired, the Cutter boys felt no pressure. Gordon Cutter and his son walked confidently around the house, deciding what to do.

"Freeze him?" suggested Gordon, gesturing to a rock with his broom.

Cutter shook his head. "No, take him out."

Cutter remained behind to set a target broom for his father. This was a slam-dunk, textbook takeout shot, and Gordon almost nonchalantly sailed out of the hack, taking a breath and releasing the stone. At the same time, exactly, he felt something twist in his spine – a sharp pain, but also a wrenching one. He instantly knew he was in desperate trouble. But there was no dealing with that now. It was a badly thrown stone, owing to his back giving way just as he released the handle. Now he had to fix it. He had to get the stone to where it belonged.

"Line, line!" he yelled to Eddie and Lennox, who swept as instructed, thwacking the ice with their scary-witch brooms. Amy stood up, and her mother tugged her down again.

"This isn't even the exciting part yet," she said. "Keep your fanny out of the faces of the folks in back of us."

"Go team go," yelled Joanne.

"Hurry hurry HARD!" Gordon bellowed, although the force of the yelling – which involved taking a lungful of air – caused the combination of pinched nerve and deteriorating disk in his spine to scream in outrage. Nevertheless Gordon himself didn't scream. He stayed frozen like a pointer dog, watching the line, as the shot missed its mark, leaving their opponents no longer exposed, but in reach of dominance.

Cutter scowled at the resulting layout, then turned to his dad to question why he'd thrown such a balls-up of a stone. But his distress dissolved as he realized that

Gordon Cutter was frozen on all fours, stiff as a coffee table.

"*Medic*," he groaned.

"Shit," said Lennox, motioning to the others for help. "Come on, guys, pick him up– "

"NO!" Amy cried from the bleachers. "Don't move him. Just push him back to the hack."

Lennox and Eddie applied their hands to his shoulders and slid him backward off the ice, as Amy scrambled from her seat and out onto the ice.

"Uh-oh, looks like a spot of trouble for the Long Bay Rink," Greg the Sportsco Guy said.

"Understatement of the century," grumbled Chris, as they gathered around their rigid coach. "Is he going to be all right?"

Amy, who had dropped to her knees beside him, shook her head.

"Oh, this is a nightmare!" cried Greg the Sportsco Guy, about as understated as a Yount entrance. "The Cutter team has sustained a terrible blow! This could be fatal! This could be their *death!*"

"Never mind that idiot," said Gordon. "Son, listen. I figure you roll in behind the guard, you force the extra end."

Cutter got down in a squat beside Amy, and peered into his father's pained face. "Or I could throw the in-off, go for the deuce, and win it right here and now."

Lennox and Eddie looked at him as if he'd gone insane. "Say *what?*" said Lennox. "Chris, are you– "

"Well," said Gordon Cutter, as the paramedics

arrived with a stretcher, and Amy began to help them manipulate Gordon onto his back, "SWEET JESUS WOMAN YOU'RE KILLING ME – I guess if you're on thin ice, son, you might just as well dance."

Cutter grinned like a lunatic. He jumped to his feet and leveled his teammates with a commanding regard. "Let's do it."

"They're both unhinged," Lennox muttered.

"Like father, like son," Eddie agreed. But they both slid obediently into sweeping position. Cutter would line up the shot without a target broom.

"Look at this," said Greg the Sportsco Guy, "I could be wrong but it appears Cutter is lining up for a double takeout, but he's doing it blind, choosing to keep both his men on the brooms. Which is…well, what would you call it, Paul?"

Paul the Color Guy mulled this over. "I'd call it risky, Greg. But if it works, they've wrapped it up. They're in the finals."

Cutter took a breath and placed his foot in the hack, glancing up at his sweepers. Lennox and Eddie leaned over expectantly. Starting with a gentle movement, like a glider soaring into the clear blue, Cutter pushed out of the hack. He released the stone in one smooth swoop.

It curled toward the target, a well-thrown stone with a mind of its own. The sweepers slapped the ice, fast and furious, until Cutter called them off. The stone continued on its own, having been sent well on its way. It bumped two rocks en route, which graciously slipped aside, unprotesting, hardly affecting its trajectory. It looked like a throw that was child's play, but in fact it was the result of knowledge, training, skill, and a little luck.

The stone nestled happily onto the button.

Up went the crowd. Gordon Cutter, on his back on the stretcher with his legs and arms in the air like a dead June bug, attempted to cheer. The medics put him down so they could jump up and down and scream. The crowd jumped up and down and screamed. Eva and Brandon embraced. Lily nearly wet herself (geez, she had to pee again!).

And Joanne yelled *go team go*.

"A lunatic long shot puts Cutter over the edge!" Greg the Sportsco Guy shouted, squeakily hoarse from all his shouting. He went largely unheard anyway, except by his broadcast partner, who covered his headphones with both hands to quell the racket.

"It wasn't a *lunatic* long shot," said Paul the hapless Color Guy. "It was skillful, Greg, and– "

"And it was the longest of long shots, long *and* lunatic, these guys are crazy as coyotes and now we're going to see the little guys, the boys from Long Bay, up against the formidable rink of the mighty Alexander Yount, tomorrow morning starting at 10 a.m. Eastern Standard Time, in the finals of the Long Bay Golden Broom! What have you got to say to that, Paul?"

Paul the Color Guy sighed. "It's not all peaches and cream, Greg," he said cautiously. "Remember it looks as if they've lost a player."

"Well, this is all too much excitement for me!" crowed Greg the Sportsco Guy. He poured the rest of his beer down his gullet. "First they're in, then they're out, up and down and up and down! This is curling at its finest! This is curling for the *people*, Paul! Curling at its rock-solid best! I tell, you, Paul, I'm *spent*."

Paul Savage nodded, watching as the medics carried Gordon Cutter from the ice. The stands had emptied themselves onto the sheet, and everyone was trying to dance, with the natural result of a lot of people falling down. Probably the only people not out there dancing and falling down were the members of the Butte Rink – the teammates of Alexander "The Juggernaut" Yount. They were already back at their bus, preparing for the battle that would unfold the next day, with meditation, fasting, and discussion of potential plays. This was not their time to dance on the ice.

Their time would come tomorrow.

10

reg the Sportsco Guy wasn't the only one who was spent. Nug's bar – normally a zooful of inebriates every Saturday night – was virtually deserted. Everyone had crawled home to recoup for the big day tomorrow, when the Yount rink would get its ass whupped by the local boys. Really.

But the local boys had a very practical problem. They were once again short one man, and this time there was no replacement.

Amy, Gordon Cutter and the three remaining members of the Cutter Rink bellied up to one of the tables, Gordon wearing a neck brace and walking as if someone had kicked him in the family jewels. When he lowered himself carefully into the seat, Amy held out a steadying hand.

"I'm fine, woman!" he barked. "Get your gore-splattered Spawn of Satan hands off me."

She sighed and sat down hard, glaring at Gordon – a virtually immobilized geriatric curler who fully intended to try to throw rocks in the morning. "Gordon, look. I don't even know how you're sitting upright. But play tomorrow? Out of the question." She pulled a pamphlet out of her knapsack-sized handbag and thrust it at Cutter. "Event rules," she said. "Page 65."

"Page 65?"

"Clause C." Amy swept all of them with her gaze. "Read it. And listen, boys."

Cutter read out loud. "'In the event of an injury, a team can elect to continue as a threesome.'"

"There," said Amy. "You see? You can still play. You're not out of it."

Eddie slammed his fist on the table, causing Gordon to wince. "She's right!" Eddie cried. "We just gotta believe."

Lennox and Cutter looked long and hard at each other.

"Believe," said Cutter. "*Believe.*"

"Well," said Lennox. "I got a little something I believe in, at moments like this." He levied a devil-take-the-hindmost wink at Amy. "Let's drink up, everyone, and maybe some of you might join me in a little recreational self-abuse down by the slag hills."

"Not me," moaned Gordon. "I'm going home to abuse myself in the safety of my own bed. You young people simply do not know how to engage in recreational abuses. There are creature comforts to be observed in the process."

"Teach us, mighty guru," said Lennox. Cutter kicked him under the table.

"Fie on the wretched lot of you," replied Gordon. He slurped a mouthful of beer from the mug Amy held to his lips. "Thanks, Mrs. Mengele."

And so it came to pass that a few beers, a couple of hours, and a great deal of pot later, the stalwart and solid men of the Cutter Rink, who stood to earn the Golden Broom on the morrow (should they hold their course and pursue their noble goal to its culmination), gathered on the peak of one of the mountains of slag that peppered the wasteland behind the smelter. Thus they had gathered for years, since they were mere lads in short pants, and now they were men with brooms, except that their brooms were in the hearse and they were *way* stoned out of their heads.

Lennox, being Lennox, took the opportunity to expound on the deeper questions of life: the prime movers that drive a man to quest onward and upward, against all odds and opposition, for values and things that sometimes are misunderstood by those outside the sphere of his spiritual acumen.

Lennox's eloquence was unparalleled. He formed a striking figure, silhouetted against the slag dumps pouring their molten mess down the hills, much as the statue of our Lord and Savior rises above Rio, as he recited the Gospel According To Lennox.

"We can believe, sure, but what? I mean, believe, I don't even think we can begin to even, to begin to fathom what it is – but there *is* this pool of *everything*, you know – like, all people, like Einstein are, is, someone. No! this is even, uh, I'd like to say something."

"What?" said Cutter, staring into the grey sky, which seemed particularly grey this evening, but in a good grey sort of way. Boy, was it grey. Look at that. Cool.

"I'd like to say that Jesus Christ is...has...is someone who has incredible– "

"Insight!" cried Eddie, who was flat on his back on the slag, his eyes closed.

"It's raining a little," Amy observed. She was the only unimpaired individual present, and as a result, the only one aware of the current meteorological shift. "I'm getting wet. Uh, boys?"

"Incredible insight!" squealed Lennox, bounding down to Eddie.

"Like he was, like he was like Uri Geller, walking among us," offered an awestruck Eddie, very pleased with this insight shit.

"Very wet," said Amy resignedly.

Other than insight, Lennox had been touched by the gifts of loquacity and enlightenment. It was his duty to expound his learning so that his friends might share in the glow of his epiphany.

"But Jesus wasn't any *better* than Einstein," he said. "If Einstein had been born in *his* time, then I think Einstein would have become the savior."

"If he got in touch with the right kind of people," said Eddie. "He'd have to visualize."

Cutter slid down the mountain on his ass, coming to a bumping halt beside the recumbent and thoroughly blitzed Eddie. "And then the question of it," he said, surprised at how hard it was to form simple words when one's lips were made of big flaps of foam rubber. "You know the genius question? Like Beethoven, and Shakespeare, someone who could just sit down with a pen, and boom, but then there's that other guy over there, like…he can't do it, like, it's like those two guys?"

"Salieri and Mozart," said Eddie, surprising everyone, including himself.

Amy, who was the only one the least aware of the transformation of drizzle to downpour, sighed and cuddled up into her coat.

"Wow," said Cutter. It seemed to him Eddie had read his fuzzed-upped mind, in one of those totally real experiences one only gets when one has moved beyond the egotistical, isolated, logical state and into the glorious morass of the unified unconscious. "Salieri and Mozart. Riiight."

"Yeah," said Lennox, not knowing who this chick Sally Airy Ann Mozark was, and not caring to admit it. "Why is one person *better* than another?"

Eddie grew cross at the injustice of it. "Because *this* person was able to grab some knowledge out of the pool!" he cried.

"But it's common knowledge," protested Cutter.

"Right!" cried Lennox, suddenly realizing they were agreeing after all, and touched deeply by this accord. "Einstein isn't any different from, you know, uh, Tiger Woods, or William Shatner, or Boutros Boutros Galli!"

Rivers of hot slag poured orange tongues down the night-drenched mountains. The boys, thrilled by the brilliance of their metaphysics, and by Lennox's use of the name Boutros Boutros Galli, lay back in the dirt and observed that beautiful grey sky. They were stoned silly, and playing a four-man game with only three men, but nothing could stop them now. Because they believed.

n the crepuscular moments before the doors to the Long Bay Arena were flung wide to the public (some of whom had been in line for hours, to ensure good seating on the bleachers), a grizzled alchemist known as Shorty walked backward down the length of the sheet where the finals of the Golden Broom were to be played. On his back he wore a large canister of water, from which a thin rubber hose emerged and snaked across his shoulders and down his chest. He held the nozzle of this hose in his two experienced hands, and as he moved backward he sprayed in his wake (in a sweeping, graceful, figure-eight ballet of the hands) a mist of water. The mist was set to emerge from the spigot in just the right density, at precisely the right speed, to fall properly upon the ice and to freeze thereon, smooth as silk and hard as iron. This thin layer of fresh ice was instrumental to the game, and Shorty was a key man. When those rocks spun toward their target, the men with brooms would sweep at that ice, the friction from the brooms' action creating an ever-so-shallow pool of water in the stones' path. The stones would use the water to aquaplane to their destination. The ice could not just be any ice. It had to be magic: the child of expertise and alchemy.

And while the quiet but essential wizardry of the Old One known as Shorty rained gently down upon the curling sheets, the television crew from Sportsco worked to set up their cameras and check their angles and sound, and the Sportsco broadcast team, Greg and Paul, climbed up to their broadcast booth. The security guard opened the doors and in rushed the entire town, one soul at a time squeezing their sometimes hefty hips through the turnstile, carrying noisemakers and flags and wearing red-and-white toques. Onto the bleachers they poured, politely but anxiously arranging themselves. They were not particularly loud, although there was a lot of excited conversation, and much mutual arranging of bottoms on benches. Their heavy boots stomped on the wooden stairs.

In the locker room, Cutter sat on a bench too, with Eddie on one side of him and Lennox on the other. They were speechless, the three of them, mentally preparing for the game, their hands clasped as if in Sunday prayer before them. They were not just praying, though: they were wringing their wet palms dry. They could hear Hoser Dave warming up the bagpipes in the hallway. Soon they would be piped into the arena, like brides or sacrificial virgins. In a few hours, the three of them would either accomplish everything, or they would be nothing at all. There was no middle ground.

There was a tap at the door. The trio inhaled deeply, thinking it was the signal to assemble, but then the door opened a crack and in stepped Julie Foley.

"A word, Chris?" she said.

"Sure." He brushed his hands across the backs of his teammates before joining her in private behind a bank of lockers.

"You know, the only thing wrong with getting a second chance would be not taking it."

"Hey," he said, shaking himself to loosen the stress. "Look at me. Lurking in a locker room, worrying about a *game*, and I'm getting advice from an astronaut. Who's going on a flight deck." He laughed at himself. "I am proud of you. When are you leaving?"

"I'm leaving right away," she said. "We aren't staying for the finals. We've overstayed as it is. T-minus time, you know."

He nodded. Amy had told him at lunch the day before that Julie would be leaving Sunday morning, but somehow, it hadn't mattered that much to him – personally – what Julie was doing. He was happy, very happy, for her: that she had achieved so much, and pleased to have known her. He knew it meant a lot to her. But that was all. There was no connection at the level of the soul. It seemed as if he had read a news story – a human-interest piece – about a woman everyone knew and liked, who had finally made it to her big dream.

"If you're leaving, uh, that quickly," he said. "We should probably talk."

"Not exactly our strong suit." She smiled at him. "Listen. I wanted you to know. It's okay. Between you and me. All of it. I'm okay. We're okay."

He frowned. "It's okay?" He got the feeling she was trying to tell him something, send him off with a blessing, but she wasn't being entirely clear. Or he was missing the point.

"Yes," she said. "It's okay. You. Me." She paused. "You. Amy."

"Oh." Now he understood completely. He had hoped that was what she meant.

"You win that...thing," she said. "For my dad. Okay?"

And so it was clear: she really cared nothing about curling, and had only come along in an attempt to recapture something she thought she'd once had, and because (most of all) for the love of her dad. It hadn't been a natural thing for her, but it had been gracious. She was not a Long Bay girl. Her home was among the stars.

He hugged her tight. "I'll be looking up for you," he said.

"First week of June, right beneath Venus?" she said. "That little dot? It'll be me."

He thought the better of wisecracking about blown O-rings – one never knew with Julie – and they kissed a friendly kiss. A goodbye kiss. Julie backed away from him, taking one last look, absorbing his features.

"What are you staring at?" he wisecracked.

"Just memorizing the face of the skip of the Long Bay Golden Broom Championship Rink," she said.

"Get out there and do it, Chris."

"You too."

Then she was gone, slipping away from him like a leaf in a river, and he didn't feel anything more than a wisp of nostalgia for a time ten years past. He smiled to himself as he returned to the boys, who had quickly retaken their places on the bench, struggling to affect nonchalance.

"As if you weren't listening to every freakin' word," said Cutter. "Doofuses."

"That's 'doofi,'" said Lennox. "Shit, they're ready for us."

A high-strung Sportsco event organizer – the only kind of Sportsco organizer – flung open the locker room door, revealing a blare of camera lights and flashbulbs. The boys stood up, squinting and smiling and waving as they were swept into the squadron of media-men crowding the hallway. Hoser Dave sounded the opening squeal of the bagpipe version of "O Canada," and the three surviving members of the Cutter Rink fell in behind their kilted escort. This time, there was no goofing around with the pompom girls; no falling on one's ass while trying to keep a straight line. They kept time, and they stayed straight, and when they came out onto the ice, shoulder-to-shoulder, the spotlights hit them and the audience burst from their seats, onto their feet, waving banners and spinning noisemakers, while singing "O Canada" at the top of their fractured voices. Cutter and Eddie and Lennox – just three to Yount's four – stood at attention, genuinely proud, as Hoser Dave's wretched instrument squawked their country's anthem into the air.

Across from them, standing quietly and with only the minimally requisite display of respect, were the four perfect men of the Juggernaut Rink.

"I wish Neil was here," Eddie whimpered, as the ovation that marked the final notes of the anthem rang through the arena.

"Us too, Eddie," said Cutter. "But we can do this. Okay?"

As the assembled settled once more into their seats, and the cameras and the piper left the ice, there was an odd moment of preparatory near-silence, a sort of calming breath that everyone required in order to deal with the next two hours. Cutter and his teammates took that moment to find in the crowd the faces that meant most to them. Cutter found his father, and Amy too, with Brandon snuggled up to her (the kid already had a candy floss – Amy must have suspended all rules for this day). Eddie saw his Lily sitting at the edge of the bleachers, beside the stairs: she'd be popping up for a pee, he knew, at 11 a.m. – the game better be over by then, or she'd be in one hell of a quandary. Lennox, the lone wolf, took comfort in the sight of all of them, Amy and Eva and Coach Cutter and Eddie's Lily, and even what's-her-name, who had long since stopped charging him for her time. What was her name? Ah – Joanne. Her name was *Joanne*. He smiled to himself. Well, danged if she hadn't become a friend.

The silence was broken by Greg the Sportsco Guy,

totally encaffeinated and preparing to become inebriated, blaring into the loudspeaker a sentence that brought everyone once again to their feet, so that the bleachers groaned under the strain:

LADIES AND GENTLEMEN, WE ARE CURLING!

12

A t the Mr. and Mrs. Neil Bucyk's, preparations were in order to attend the Sunday brunch at the country club, where the new membership list would be read. Since the Mr. and Mrs. Neil Bucyk had been invited to said brunch, it was clear that the reading of the list was merely a lovely formality. A touching welcome for those applicants who were of a caliber to be accepted to the country club's roll. Linda should have been over the moon at this surefire ticket. But instead, she was taut with anxiety. Her own hair, stockings, fingernails, attitude – her *person* – she could control. What was beyond her was how Neil might behave. Neil might mention that blasted idiotic game. He might mention his…his association with those…those fools!

"If you so much as open your mouth, Neil Bucyk," she told him, as she slipped her white-gloved hand through the crook of his arm, and he escorted her to their car, "I will serve your kidneys to you for dinner. Is that clear?"

It was quite clear. Neil opened the driver's side door

for her, and she climbed behind the wheel. He sighed and got into the passenger's seat. It didn't matter. He didn't really want to drive himself to his own funeral.

All the way there, although he never opened his mouth, he screamed and screamed and screamed.

The string of remarkably creative expletives that poured from the lips of the man-mountain known as Stuckmore would have earned prizes, were there a competition for such things. Stuckmore called the truck a mother **** butt **** pile of **** blue-black**** tincan **** that didn't **** deserve **** bloody **** a horse and what the **** was he going to do now?

Black oily smoke streamed from the seams and grille of the cab-over's engine. Stuckmore, who could do just about anything with the engine of a Harley, was quickly flummoxed by the seized guts of the Freightliner. He stood there, the foul plumes of smoldering engine-smoke settling grittily upon his face. He blinked to clear his vision, dimly aware that the action caused a certain stinging pain in his forehead. It had not yet sunk in that he still had a chunk of glass sticking out of his forehead – a single horn, a little left of center, the presence of which his underdeveloped limbic system had failed to as yet inform him.

Well, he was eighteen kilometers from Long Bay. It was 9:05. Inside the truck, he could hear his precious little TV broadcasting the Sportsco station's opening theme for the event. He could hear Greg the Sportsco Guy announcing the lineup. Every massive muscle in his massive body tensed. A vein in his neck throbbed grotesquely. He reached into the hot guts of the Freightliner and, his bare hands sizzling at the contact with overheated engine-parts, pulled the battery clear of its connections.

Stuckmore was a get-things-done kind of guy. He actually would have made a fine corporate executive, except that he looked like something out of a very scary fairy tale. And then there was that part about the Grade 5 education. But nevertheless, Stuckmore's problem-solving abilities, and his determination, served him well that Sunday morning. He retrieved his little TV, and ripped the wires clean of their insulation, hooking them up in a shower of sparks to the battery. Then, he collected the battery under his arm and, carrying the TV in one hand and its power source in the other, he focused on what he had to do now.

Alone on the highway's shoulder, ignoring the occasional car that swept by him, Stuckmore began the last leg of his trek into Long Bay.

Lily Strombeck held her breath as Eddie stretched out along the ice, watching his stone curl toward the house. "A fine stone! This game is underway!" Greg the Sportsco Guy bellowed.

"Way to go, Sweetie," she said to herself. She then hiccupped a big bile-producing hiccup, one that drew Amy Foley's attention.

"You okay?"

"I still feel a little pukey," she said. "And I have to pee."

"Pee!" said Eva. "Good God and His garment bag, Lily! Why didn't you go before the game?"

Lily didn't want to explain about her ceremonial testing, which she knew in her heart was just a waste of a pee-stick, but which meant the world to her, since it included her in the ranks of Women Trying To Get Pregnant. She didn't want to be a Woman Who Couldn't Get Pregnant. Women Who Couldn't Get Pregnant didn't buy pee-sticks. Anyway, she knew that her period would be starting that afternoon, and she wanted desperately to pee on one of those magic sticks before it did. Faith, for her, was evident in ritual. Which ritual meant a fair bit of pee, and good morning pee, which was supposed to be the best pee for being rich with pregnant-lady hormones. Not that Eva Foley needed to know any of that.

"I forgot to," Lily said.

"Well, you better hold on until the game's over," said Eva.

"If you want to maintain urinary continence, as well as vaginal control that will please your bed partner, do some elevator exercises," Joanne offered, in a recitative from one of her fitness picture books.

Lily looked at her quizzically. Eva and Amy just gawped (and Amy covered Brandon's ears).

"Raise and lower your vagina muscles like they're an elevator," said Joanne, as if this were something people said every day. "Like this." Her face went blank (even blanker than usual) and she sat perfectly still for a count of ten. "There," she announced, rejoining the social group. "I just went up and down five floors."

"Uh, okay," said Lily. "Maybe some other time."

This momentary distraction, however, had meant that the girls missed a blindingly clever shot by the Yount's vice-skip. It left an unbeatable pattern of rocks in the house, with an ominous blockade lying across Long Bay's access route.

"The Juggernaut appears to be very much in the driver's seat," said Greg the Sportsco Guy, gesturing dramatically toward the action with his beer. "What the hell does Cutter do now? It's like he's staring at the Great Wall of China."

"Yes, indeed," said Paul the Color Guy, sighing as he wiped the drops of beer from the sleeve of his blazer.

"Great Wall of Granite, more likely," said Eva. "Good God and His All-Girl Orchestra. Come on, team."

The ladies hunkered down to watch and pray.

In a limousine with leather seats, cruising comfortably down the highway on its way back to Toronto, Corporal Friesen turned down the radio broadcast of the Golden Broom, so that his superior officer and Dr. Julie Foley could hear him.

"Parenthetically," he said, "the Great Wall of China is the only man-made object that can be seen from space."

"Shut up, Corporal," said Captain Blendick. "I'm trying to listen to the curling."

So intent were the men on the game, that they didn't even notice when they passed the northbound grizzly who marched at an even pace along the highway, a truck battery under one arm, and a portable TV held before him like a guiding lamp. Julie saw him, though. And the thought that came to mind in response to such a sight was, *well, at least I'm heading in the right direction.*

When the limo hit the town limits, Julie Foley never looked back.

13

"**T**his is ugly," said Eddie. Cutter stood, rubbing his chin, for a full minute, unrolling a blueprint in his head – a spread of calculus and trig, of grids and arcs and angles. Finally, he went with both his knowledge *and* his instinct.

"Around the guard, and raise this one to the button," he said, pointing at the stones he meant to move.

Eddie examined all the stones in the house carefully one more time, trying to imagine how they were going to accomplish their skip's strategy. Lennox joined them in the powwow.

"Did you say 'around the guard,' Chris?" said Lennox.

Cutter frosted him. "I'm the skip," he said. "That's the call."

Lennox shrugged mightily and slid back to the hack, followed by Eddie. Yount, who had been quietly standing aside while his opponents mapped out their war plan, now appeared at Cutter's shoulder. Without looking at him, as if he were merely speaking to the air, he observed that it was a pretty tough shot.

"Yep," said Cutter.

"No one's curled that side of the ice," said Yount.

Cutter concentrated on setting his target broom, not looking at Yount, either. "Hey, we're amateurs," he said.

Yount snorted and moved out of the play, drifting like a ghoul back to where his teammates stood. "Guy is truly *creepy*," Cutter muttered to himself.

Lennox sized up his shot, and then glided out of the hack and let the stone go. Eddie swept furiously, but the rock slid wide, missing the mark. It left a very sloppy set of rocks. Lennox caught Cutter's eye with an *I told you so* expression. Cutter shot back with *up yours, compadre*.

But Yount's reaction – a barely perceptible raising of the chin and brow – demonstrated his approval.

"Gentlemen," said Alexander Yount to his teammates. "I loathe a disorderly house. Let's get to work, shall we?"

Like sharpshooters, Yount and his rink fired their stones, tapping and shoving the guards out of the way, accumulating nothing but Juggernaut granite in the house. Eddie covered his face with his hands and peeked through his fingers.

"Jesus, these guys are good," he said to Lennox.

When the ice dust cleared after four ends, the score was Butte 4 and Long Bay 0, and the entire arena lay silent as a morgue. But Greg the Sportsco Guy still shouted into his mike, while signaling the hapless broadcast gofer to bring him another beer.

"Ohhh, that is some kind of killer granite!" Greg the Sportsco Guy whinnied. "After four ends, I'm getting the feeling Cutter is really struggling out there. The Juggernaut is very much in control. Everything they throw out, the man from Butt, Montana, seems to have the answer for."

"Uh, that's *Butte*, Greg," Paul the Color Guy offered.

"Butt, Butte – it doesn't matter. Cutter has dug himself into one hell of a deep hole and there doesn't seem to be a rope ladder anywhere in sight."

The crowd seemed to agree. They were clucking like hens in a barnyard. Gordon Cutter shook his head sadly. "Lambs to the slaughter," he said.

"There's nothing they can do?" This from Joanne, who sat beside him with her fluffy-mittened fingers looped, as always, through his arm.

"Not without Neil Bucyk," said Gordon. "They need their lead."

Joanne cocked her head at him, waiting for him to explain more, but Gordon just sighed heavily and turned his mind back to the game. Joanne wasn't a bright girl, and she knew it. All her life people had told her that she wasn't very smart, and placed her in special classes, and encouraged her to concentrate on her looks and not her brains. So she never really put much stock into her ability to solve problems. But every now and then it became apparent to her that the smart people were missing out on the easiest way to fix things. They couldn't see the obvious. They were all running around wailing about how something couldn't be fixed, when in fact they were just making things so very complicated.

Like now. Gordon said they needed Neil. Neil had

gone away to go do something he didn't want to do. Everyone said there was nothing to be done, like he was dead or something. But Neil Bucyk wasn't dead. Was he?

No, he was not. Everyone else might think he was, but she knew that Neil was just *playing* dead. Even though she was just an ordinary girl – a preacher's daughter kidding herself about the legitimacy of her profession, struggling to keep up with astronauts and curlers – she knew that Neil Bucyk just needed his moment. He needed someone who loved him, to call him from his cave, to summon him to greatness.

She was the one who loved him.

Excusing herself, she squeezed along the bleacher-rows, through the crowd of spectators, and started out on her mission.

The Long Bay Golf and Country Club brunch was well underway, oblivious to the pitched battle unfolding on the ice of the Long Bay Arena. Centerpieces of fresh-cut gardenias graced the middle of each well-appointed table, surrounded by candlesticks, flute glasses of champagne-and-orange juice, baskets of croissants, mixed fruits, and the hopefuls who had gathered to hear their names read into the roster. The waiters circulated languidly, delivering bowls of a fresh *salade Niçoise*, full of bits of green bean and crumbled walnut. Neil Bucyk sighed and picked up his fork (at least, one of the forks – he hoped he'd grabbed the right one, or boy would he hear about it later).

Neil didn't want salad for breakfast. He focused on

the deep green of the lettuce, impaling it on the tines of his fork, imagining a bowl of shredded wheat or a plate of scrambled eggs and back bacon. Out of the corners of his vision, he could see the elbow of the senior investment counselor to his left, and the vice-president of marketing operations to his right, because apparently it was not appropriate to sit spouses together. He hadn't known that, nor had he known to look at the place-cards before he sat, so he had been obliged to stand up and change seats, overturning a water glass with all its ice onto his right leg. It still felt cold.

But he hardly noticed it through the frost that blasted his way from his wife, from her seat across the table. Sure, she was smiling at him, and to a layperson one would think she was a benign and loving spouse: an elegantly dressed, well-bred, gracious woman. It was just like when mourners walked over to the dead in their coffins, Neil thought, and commented about how lifelike they were. How they looked just like they would if they were alive.

Linda Bucyk looked just like a nice human being.

Neil shuddered violently and closed his eyes tight. His fork in his right hand shook, spilling a fragment of walnut onto his plate. The sound of its tiny click seemed louder than the club president's voice, which droned out the names of the inductees, reciting them with the same emotionless inflection, name after faceless name. A roll of the dead.

He opened his eyes to find his wife still looking at him, and still smiling. She cocked her head in what anyone else would think was a quizzical fashion – a secret, affectionate gesture indicating concern. What the motion in fact meant was, *straighten up, worm – you're slouching and you're spilling – so help me Neil Jason Bucyk if you so much as say one word to embarrass me I will make your life so miserable that Hell itself would be a welcome relief*…

As he watched her, listening to the imaginary sermon of her voice in his head, he thought he noticed something about her makeup – how it seemed unnaturally thick, like the undertaker's pasty stuff that he used to cover burns or injuries. He frowned, trying to process this anomaly, for Linda was meticulous in "making up her face," and she never did anything so tasteless as to overapply her foundation.

But as he watched, he saw a crack appear at her temple, as the dried paste peeled away, and he saw exposed a patch of Linda's skin. That skin was the grey of the long-dead. He had, in his life, had to tend to bodies that were not fresh, and he knew this color. Surprised, but somehow not shocked, he put his fork down and gripped the table's edge, anticipating the disintegration he knew would come next.

Sure enough, when Linda moved her lips in a soundless question – *What are you staring at, dear?* – he saw aged, brown teeth, emerging from black and receding gums. Linda's hair, still bound in its tight bun, pulled free at the roots, so that the bun dangled from a few tenacious strands that still found purchase in her dead scalp. Her blue eyes sank back in their sockets. It was

like a time-lapse sequence of a decaying mouse, except
it was Linda, and it did not feel like a hallucination.

He glanced around the room. They all seemed dead.
The room was full of corpses, applauding softly with
rotting hands. He was in a roomful of dead people. He
was having a nice brunch in preparation for being
inducted into the Long Bay Club Of The Damned.

Neil began to pray. *If there is anything good waiting for
me after I've shuffled off this mortal coil,* Neil asked his
God, *could you please let me know?*

"YO!"

Neil, who had closed his eyes to gather his wits,
nearly fell off his chair. He didn't know God's voice was
female (although he'd often suspected God was a
woman). He opened one eye cautiously, and the room
was back to normal, the grim fantasy having passed.

But the woman who had yelled *YO!* was standing in
the broad doorway of the dining hall, fully half-a-dozen
tables away, and the president of the club had placed his
hands firmly on his hips, registering disapproval of her
interruption, her presence, and her appearance. For
Joanne also-known-as-Andrea was not country club
material. She was barely bowling league material, but
she looked like the best and most alive thing that Neil
Bucyk had ever seen in his entire life. Standing there in
her tiger-stripe stretch-polyester cut-to-the-crotch mini,
and her blue tights, and her spangly bugle-beaded top,
and her laced-up white ankle boots…she might as well
have been Venus herself.

"Yo, *Gasket*," she called, having seen that she'd

caught his eye. They shared a grin that sailed between them like a radio signal, like a laser beam. He couldn't believe his heart could feel so full.

"What's up?" he said.

"They need you." Joanne jerked her head in a come-on-now signal. Her ponytail, thrusting from the side of her head from a big purple scrunchie, bobbed invitingly.

He laughed. "Did the guys pay you to do this?"

She laughed, too, then purred back at him: "I pride myself on knowing what someone needs before they know it themselves."

By now, the shocked silence that had fallen over the assembled was crumbling into mutters and even loud voices of questioning censure: who was this woman, and who was that man? Was *that* Neil Bucyk? Who had recommended him? Obviously a mistake had been made...

But Joanne crooked her finger at Neil, and still grinning, he began to rise to his feet, as if she were pulling his string. He could feel, in fact, a definite tug. It came from his heart, which so very recently, had felt as cold and hard as a lump of frozen hamburger.

"Neil Jason Bucyk?" This from Linda.

He turned to her. She was back to being perfection, her hair back in its bun, and her teeth all cosmetic-dentistry white-and-polished. She smiled her rictus smile at him, trying to figure out how to frame this disorder into making it look like they had a perfect marriage. Somehow, she had to salvage this, because any second now the president was going to red-pencil The Bucyks from the membership roll.

"Neil Jason Bucyk, if you stand up from this table– "

But she didn't get to finish. If anything, as impossible as it seems, her warning seemed to *propel* Neil to his feet. He practically snapped to attention, doing exactly what she had forbidden him to do.

Even Linda now realized that all was lost. The gig was up. She could practically hear the red line being dragged through their names, the paper ripping beneath the pressure. And her face fell. It fell into the haglike truth of who and what she really was.

"Well, you stood up," she said. "Okay. I think the time has come for me to tell you certain things. About your children– "

But Neil just shook his head sadly, and interrupted her. She was so shocked she actually stopped talking, for the first time in her life at a loss for words. The whole well-appointed dining hall heard what he had to say.

"Linda, look at my hair. It's brown. Your hair is blond. Our boys have red hair. The only person we know with red hair is Ronnie. But you want to know something? They still call *me* Dad. Me." He looked around the room, and declared himself with full and quiet force.

"Me. Neil Jason Bucyk."

He ran to Joanne, who seized him by the arm in her big bunny-fluff mittens, bouncing up and down on the spot as she planted a kiss on him. He slipped his arm around her trim waist, and together they bounded out of the dining hall and into the clear, bright, Northern Ontario day.

When Linda Bucyk came out of the club minutes later, her princess demeanor in tatters around her, she found that they'd taken the car.

14

Nobody was chatting it up in the stands of the Long Bay Arena. The silence fell like an unnatural blanket, a muffling cloud of anxiety and unhappiness. For clearly, Long Bay was not going to overcome. They were simply, sadly, outmatched. They had tried, and it had been a good try indeed, and everyone was grateful for these men, for their incredible effort. For a while there had been a ghost of a chance – a ghost that visited every house in town. But now the ghost was checking its watch. It was time to give up and go.

The Cutter Rink had two guards in place, and the prospect of finally putting some points on the scoreboard. But the Juggernaut was stretching its limbs and sharpening its claws, in preparation to fire. Alexander Yount pushed out of the hack, balancing like a Russian gymnast, swaying neither left nor right as he slipped down the ice and released his stone. The crowd held what little breath it had left. In the empty air the sound of the Juggernaut brooms, whisking and whistling on the ice, was like a mighty wind foretelling disaster.

The Yount stone collided with another, slamming into both of Cutter's counters, driving them off the target. No points for Long Bay. A groan of disappointment rose from the crowd, followed by a smattering of encouraging applause and Little League–inspired calls of "never mind boys" and "you can still do it." The kind of noise that parents make when their kids' team is down eighteen to nothing, and people start talking about it all being about how you play the game, and not about winning or losing.

Curling is about honor, and it's about playing the game honorably. But it's also about winning, when an entire town is tied up in that win, when its heart believes in you and you believe in its heart. For towns do have hearts; they do move together as one. Cutter sighed beneath the burden of potential loss, and of knowing that honor and good play would be all they could offer the town. The ultimate consolation prize.

"Holy jumping," said Greg the Sportsco Guy. "This game may well be out of reach for Long Bay. Six to nothing for the Juggernaut! You can sense the crowd's disappointment. Can't you, Paul?"

"That's right, Paul. It's like a morgue in here," said Paul balefully. "All they need is the undertaker."

Down on the ice, Lennox thwapped the frozen surface beneath his feet with his broom, shaking his head in shock and dismay. "I can't believe this," he said. "They're waltzing over us. I don't know what to say."

"How about 'we're not doing so good'?" offered Cutter.

"Maybe it's our approach?" said Eddie.

"Or," said Neil, appearing beside them like he'd never left in the first place, "maybe you're short a broom."

Even though the other boys' mouths fell open, the crowd was less dumbfounded. At the word "undertaker" from Paul the Color Guy, Neil had been entering the arena, and a susurrus of rumor-driven mutters began to swell. It only took moments for Neil to reach his buddies, and apprise them of his presence, but in those moments the penny dropped for every man, woman and child in the audience. As Lennox and Eddie and Cutter welcomed their prodigal back to the fold – punching him in the arm and slapping his long-jawed face – the crowd rose to its feet in unison. The entire town of Long Bay threw its faith into the air like hats, and around the Cutter Rink that faith fell like gentle snow.

"How about we bury these guys?" Neil said.

Cutter found his voice, which was a little higher pitched than normal, owing from the strain of holding back all that sticky emotional stuff, like hope and joy and potential. "Sounds good," he said.

"Let's go," said Eddie.

"I'm in," said Lennox.

"I love it," said Gordon, as Joanne nestled against him from the bleacher seat beside him.

Greg the Sportsco Guy remarked gratuitously that the town's undertaker had returned from the dead to breathe life into the proceedings, an observation that went largely unnoticed as everyone tried to muzzle their excitement enough to focus on the game. But it was short-lived. As soon as the announcement *ladies and gentlemen, we are curling* sounded over the loud-speakers, the crowd lost its thin veneer of focus. It exploded in one fulsome, sustained cheer that made even the arrogant Alexander Yount frown. For he knew not one accolade was directed his way. Here, all his stardom meant nothing. Not one fan did he have. His frown deepened. He was not accustomed to being the one outside the spotlight.

When Neil pushed out of the hack, throwing his first rock of his new life, he felt all the warm blood and nerve impulses and lymph and breath in him coming togeth-er, operating him, moving his arm in a flawless swing, balancing him on his solidly muscled legs, focusing his eyes with eaglelike accuracy, firing his mental synapses in a lightning-fast calculation of rock speed and trajec-tory. Strategy, cunning, power, speed, balance, surprise, communication, teamwork, honor. All rolled into the poetry, into the game, into the rocks that bore down on the target: rocks that flew like they were winged, that smashed like they were titans. Lennox threw, and Eddie threw, and Cutter threw. A double raised takeout for the Long Bay side. A nestful of Cutter rocks in the house.

"Now they're cooking," said Gordon.

"With a nuclear oven," said Joanne.

On it went. Yount, for his part, could not shake entirely the vague unease that accompanied the realiza-tion that nobody wanted him to do well. He was,

despite his attitude of entitlement, well aware of his status as a crowd-pleaser. To have every shot of his greeted
with silence, and followed by more silence (and displeased silence) when he met his marks, made him feel
as if he were playing a game he knew nothing about, in
front of strangers who didn't know his name. It was
only a slight reduction in his confidence – this tiny scur-
rying idea that he was *not*, in this place, Number One –
but perhaps it had its effect. For with the Cutter Rink
lying three, Alexander Yount threw a bad rock. He
watched its flawed progress into the house with his jaw
set and his eyes as hard as flint. From the bleachers came
the delighted screams of the people who should be wor-
shipping him. He bit the inside of his cheek, a habit he
once had, as a talented upstart in the American curling
circuit – he had dealt with the pain of loss by distracting
himself with a simpler pain. He had not felt loss in
years.

Nor would he now. He released the skin of his cheek,
swallowed hard, and went on with the game.

In the stands, Eva Foley noticed two small, red-haired
heads – belonging to Neil Bucyk's children – trying to
squeeze into the row ahead of them, and not having
much success. They were both in their pyjamas, and Eva
could only assume the little beggars had snuck out past
their Sunday-morning babysitter, having been forbidden to come on their own. Poor wee blighters – and now
they couldn't get seats to see their own dad play.

She signalled to them, and the boys brightened and

made their way up to the Foley-Cutter-Strombeck contingent.

"Hi," said the older boy.

"Hi yerself. Come up onto my lap and watch with us."

One boy cuddled onto Eva's lap, and Lily offered her own for the second kid, because Brandon was sitting on his mother's. As soon as he popped up into the comfortable seat her body made, Lily felt two things: the first was an amorphous but powerful surge of motherly desire – of wanting a kid so bad, so she could sit with her arms around the wriggly little body, and show off the world to him – and that surge made her bury her nose into the velvety nape of the kid's neck, just above the collar of his pyjamas, and inhale the smell of boy, of baby shampoo and tinned spaghetti and yes, even hockey cards. Snips and snails and puppy dogs' tails – that's what this boy was made of. How she could hardly stand to hold him, and how she could hardly think of letting him go.

The second thing she felt was a desperate need to pee. As soon as that bony little-boy butt thwumped into her lap, it pressed on her bladder like a big fat thumb on a plump grape. Her period was due that afternoon, and it always made her more likely to pee a lot. But this! This was agony.

She made a strangled little noise and moved the kid down her thighs a little, sighing from the relief of the pressure. Damn, but she wasn't sure she'd make it all the way to the game's finish. One good cheer and she was likely to make one hell of a puddle.

She took a deep breath, tried not to think of her bladder, and returned her attention to the game.

In the seventh end, the Cutter Rink was lying two, but the Juggernaut had the hammer. "This is curling as intense as these eyes have ever witnessed," said Greg the Sportsco Guy, who had run out of beer early, and was filling the gap before the arrival of refills by downing a series of miniature bottles of rye that he'd filched from the airliner on Friday. It didn't matter. The crowd had long ago stopped paying too much attention to Greg the Sportsco Guy's hyperbolic observations. For unreal things were happening on the curling sheet.

Every eye watched intently as Alexander Yount threw a rock on a shot that he could make blindfolded, and somehow, inexplicably, missed. It wasn't a bad shot. It wasn't a flawed takeout. It was a complete *miss*.

The crowd went wild. "He has missed – the Juggernaut has missed!" screeched the allegedly disinterested Sportsco Guy, the announcement getting lost in the unbelievable roar that shook the building. Paul watched nonplussed as Greg's chair went ass-over-teakettle, causing a tremendous crash to be transmitted over the network's wires. Paul was amazed, too, but he wasn't about to throw the furniture around over it.

What had just happened – well, it was outright thievery – the Cutter Rink had stolen two points, right from under the Juggernaut's upturned nose. The score now? An incredible 7 to 6. The Juggernaut had only a single point's leeway, going into the eighth.

The four men of the Cutter Rink joined their hands and shook hard, then looked to Gordon Cutter in the stands. He raised his fist in salute.

Into the eighth end they went, still down a point, but otherwise as up as they could possibly be.

15

O fficer Frances Darte and every cop on- or off-duty, Belle, Milt from the Brake Shop, his special-ed son Hi, Primrose and Yolanda and Derwin the Taxi Driver, the men from the docks, the seventeen-year-old cook who'd wanted Julie Foley's autograph, the folks from AA, Marvin Fleiger and his long-suffering secretary, the high school teachers, the boy scouts, girl guides, the street sweeper and the laid-off miners, the housewives, the health-care aides at the old age home, all the old folks with their walkers and wheelchairs, all the wounded from the physio center, the town doctor and the orthodontist and the guys from produce at the Safeway, the kids from behind the counter at the Tim Hortons, the fire brigade and the book club, the United Church minister and the Catholic priest, Marvin Fleiger's rabbi from the temple sixty-two miles away, and his wife, and his kids, and the librarian, and the elementary school custodian, and the florist, and the guy from the Department of Transport office and the two judges and their court clerk from the District

Courthouse, and the telephone repair guy and the hydro lineman and the old Englishwoman who sold budgies at the Pet Purr-ee on Main Street North, all leaned forward in united anticipation as the eighth end's opening rock was thrown.

It whistled from Neil's hand with regal confidence, knowing exactly where it was going and getting there as planned. Everyone leaned back as it slid into place, sighing with satisfaction. Perfect.

But Alexander "The Juggernaut" Yount had spent some time thinking about things. His rise to the top of the curling world was not anomalous. It was no fluke. He was a strategist – the sort of man who also played a fine game of chess. His ice-cool personality, and his ice-smooth expression, were mirrors to his abilities to analyze. He could apply that sharp and unheated precision to self-analysis, as well. He recognized that he had been spooked. That vanity had caused his mind to wander off the point. Perhaps it had only been a tiny fraction of attention that had been paid to the disturbing notion that he was villain of the piece. That all the fireworks in the world wouldn't make anyone in this arena cheer Alexander Yount. Having recognized, coolly, that this was the case, he recognized as well that it had hurt him. He had felt…*hurt*. The cheek-biting distraction had not centered him. Therefore, he would have to deal with that annoying fruit fly of *hurt*.

He would freeze it dead.

So when the Juggernaut Rink threw, they threw cool because their skip had thrown cool, and they saw and sensed (like herd animals do) that their Alpha was back on his game. His commands were crisp and confident, plump with the implication of *fait accompli*. It did not make things simple, but it ended the rout that had caused the upstarts from Long Bay to come up with six points from nothing at all, and left Yount's merciless lead a mere shadow. A mere point.

But at the end of the ninth, Butte was still ahead by one. Yount's skin was misted over with a fine perspiration. Cutter gathered his rink for consultation.

"Into the final end," Cutter said. "Okay, guys. We can do this. Keep your eyes on the poetry."

"Whatever you say, Skipper," said Eddie.

Barnhart of the Butte Rink was in the hack. His stone ended where he wanted it, as did Neil's. The team members' talents were so closely matched that it seemed as if they were synchronized. It was up to the skips – shooting last – to upset the apple cart.

By the time Yount was preparing to throw his final stone, things had turned solidly to his advantage. The lay of the stones in the house favored the Juggernaut, and it would take only one stone, well placed, to shut Cutter's Rink right out of the picture, no questions asked. A skilled stone, that would stopper the house like a blocked toilet. End of the Long Bay dream.

The layout was thus: between the house and the hack, four rocks: three Cutter and one Yount. The Cutter stones lay in a slightly off-kilter line about twelve feet long, with large and passable gaps between them, leaving a clean path to the button. The only Yount stone in the quartet lay in front of one of the Cutter rocks, impotent and pointless. This guard was ineffective, since between the two Cutter rocks that stood in the trajectory for the button there was an easily broached gate, with lots of room for a Cutter rock to slide through.

It was in this gate that Yount must place his stone, for beyond the guard, on the eight-foot circle, Yount had two more stones, flanking the button beyond them and with another gap between them, and to cinch the question, beyond that he had four more stones. This ominous foursome stood like bodyguards behind a throne, looking over it. Their presence would make no difference if a Cutter rock could reach the button, which it could, *if* Yount didn't close that gap in the guard standing outside the house. Close it, with this final stone.

Yount could have chosen to throw his final rock so it would slide onto the button, between the Cutter stones and his own stones on the eight-foot circle. But then Cutter, shooting last, would simply knock him out of the house, and gain that one precious point that would tie the game and force an extra end. So Yount would not be doing any such thing. There was no reason to. That one stone – that stone in the hole – would seal Long Bay's fate like a tomb.

However, he had to place the stone perfectly on that tomb. This last stone – the last pearl on the string – would require skill tantamount to rolling a marble along a forty-foot slab of wood, and having it stop on a dime.

Nevertheless, in curling, these things are done, and

Alexander Yount limbered briefly before stepping into the hack and taking up his stone.

Out he slid, and his body stretched over the ice as he threw his rock toward its destiny. He sought to leave the house a veritable viper's nest of potential counters – too many for anyone to ever clear away – guarded by a Cerberus of stone.

"Off, off," said Yount, as his stone slid toward its goal. His voice did not need to be raised, not when he was so confident, and not when the arena was so silent. His sweepers lifted their brooms, and pushed themselves out of the rock's way. It was a confident rock, a rock with a purpose. It had been sent out like a messenger, and with its destination in mind it proceeded. Closer, and closer, approaching the gateway that was Long Bay's only hope, it whispered along the ice. At ten feet distant, it began to slow. Slower and slower it went, approaching the spot it belonged, like a raptor landing on a solitary, isolated, perch.

Into place slid the Butte Rink rock. Long Bay was shut out…cold.

"Oh, Momma," cried Greg the Sportsco Guy, "get a dictionary! Find the words 'touch' and 'precision.' The definition will read: *Alexander Yount.* Look at that, ladies and gentlemen. This man is monstrous."

When somewhere in the stands, one of the old ladies from the Legion Auxiliary dropped her hatpin, everybody jumped.

16

Stuckmore needed a rest. He had to take a whizz, for one thing. Five minutes, he decided, and that was it. He had reached the town's greeting sign – WELCOME TO LONG BAY, BIRTHPLACE OF JULIE FOLEY – and that was far enough for the next few moments. He unzipped and let fly into the roadside ditch.

Relieved, he sat down heavily, legs stretched out in front of him. He placed his battery to one side of him and the TV on his knees. He played with the antennae, trying to rid the screen of the gnatlike swarm of static. But he just made it worse. The image dissolved into grey snow.

Stuckmore moaned and cursed. He picked up the TV and shook it like a maraca. It crackled in meek outrage, scraping the skies for a vestige of signal. Then Stuckmore heard Greg the Sportsco Guy's voice:

"…a time out has been called, and the Cutter Rink discusses strategy…"

"Urgh," Stuckmore grunted, settling the TV back onto his lap. But his bulk must have been blocking, rather than aiding, the signal. It all disappeared again.

"You **** son of **** bent over a **** I'll eat your ****
on toast, you ****," he told the TV and the Sportsco Guy
too. His rest over too soon, he clambered to his feet,
retrieved the battery and the TV, and recommenced his
marathon.

The signal cut back in as soon as he started to walk.
An overhead shot of the house revealed the layout of the
stones. The convex arc of four Juggernaut stones lay
behind the button, two cheek-by-jowl just inside the
twelve-foot circle, and another two just to the rear of the
button, cuddled up close to one another as well.
Another four Yount stones formed the stalwart guard
that Yount had so carefully built, and completed, with
his last stone. Yount stood to gain, in the worst case, six
points.

Of course, they didn't *need* six points. They were
ahead by one, and this was the Cutter Rink's last stone
– the last stone of the game. Yount had only been
required to keep the Cutter Rink from scoring. By this
layout, he had done just that. He had won the game.

Greg the Sportsco Guy issued paroxysms of over-
statement, expounding bug-eyed on the particular
spread of stones involved, how cleverly and effectively
the Juggernaut had seized Long Bay by the throat, and
how tight and fatal was the squeeze. No matter what the
Cutter Rink threw, it made no difference. The technician
drew electronic scribbles – thick colored lines – all over
the overhead shot of the house, while Greg the Sportsco
Guy blustered about how this wouldn't work and

neither would that, and Paul the Color Guy just tried to say the occasional intelligent thing. Soon the entire image was covered with red-and-yellow-and-green doodles and arrows and circles and curlicues, and the stones and sheet were no longer visible. At which point, Greg the Sportsco Guy crowed, "It's hopeless! Just *hopeless!*" and the broadcast switched back to the four Long Bay men, engaged in their time-out discussion.

"I don't know why they're bothering with the time out," Greg the Sportsco Guy said. "I don't know what they have to discuss. I wouldn't want to be a fly on the bum of that conversation, because from where we sit, Long Bay doesn't have a shot."

Stuckmore growled deep in his throat, watching the powwow the Cutter crew was holding, trying to discern what they might be saying. But the Sportsco Guy did not shut up. Yap yap yap went the Sportsco Guy. Stuckmore no longer wished to hear the Sportsco Guy. The Sportsco Guy was making him angry enough to smash something. But he did not wish to smash his TV. He wanted to watch the show. But he was going to smash if the Sportsco Guy didn't shut up. How could he both watch the game and not have to listen to the Sportsco Guy? Was there an alternative to smashing?

A thin trickle of fresh blood emerged from the gash in Stuckmore's temple, where the triangle of glass was still lodged. The pressure of problem-solving was enormous, but eventually the light dawned. The solution came to him. He did not have to smash. Smashing was not necessary.

Sighing with relief, Stuckmore turned down the volume. No more Sportsco Guy. Just the pictures. He continued along the highway, his TV before him, and his battery beside.

The men of the Cutter Rink were not so fortunate. Cutter felt like it was Custer's Last Stand and he was Ol' Yellowhair calling 'Wait a second! I'll think of something!' while the Sioux Nation massed on the horizon.

Gordon Cutter came gingerly down from the stands to join them. His head was propped up by the sausage-like whiplash collar, and his motions were stiff and painful. The arrival of their god and mentor didn't make the Long Bay squadron feel much better, for it turned out he had little to say, but merely stood grimacing at the rocks at their feet. No one spoke. The crowd grew more and more silent, eavesdropping like nosy neighbors pressing their ears to a thin common wall. But their team just stood in a cluster, their heads together, looking from stone to stone as if what they were facing weren't real.

At last, Gordon gestured with his broom. The crowd drew in its breath. The boys primed themselves for instructions.

Gordon Cutter lowered his broom again; clicked his teeth; shook his head. "Doesn't look good at all," he said.

"Damn," said Eddie. He looked into the bleachers, finding Lily, who sat there with one of Neil's kids on her lap, waving and grinning with that I-love-you-even-though-we're-losers look on her face. He loved her for that look, but it wasn't what he wanted today.

"I just wanted to know what it feels like to win," Eddie said. "Just once. Come on, you guys. There's gotta be a shot?"

Lennox wiped his face roughly with the back of his hand. "In some *other* game, maybe. But not here."

Gordon Cutter's voice was almost inaudible, as if he were only thinking and the silent words had just slipped out like phantoms. "There is one shot," he murmured.

They all looked up at him. "What shot?" said Cutter.

"I propose 'around the clock,' four stone takeout. Go up the outside between our two stones here, hit the pair of Yount rocks on the back twelve, bounce over to the other pair and take them out, spin our rock back upsheet to the button. Tie the game. Force an extra end. Around the clock."

"You," said Cutter, "are completely stoned."

"True. But I've seen it. Swedes."

"Swedes?" Cutter said. "What Swedes?"

"Nineteen seventy-three World Championship."

"If a Swede can do it," said Eddie, seizing Cutter by the elbow, "you can do it."

"You overestimate me."

"No," said Neil. "I don't think we do. I don't think we ever did. Any of us." He and Eddie and Lennox exchanged nods of agreement.

Cutter processed this. They knew him. They knew he was human. They also knew that he was, despite everything, one of the most capable curlers in the whole country, if not North America. If not the world. It wasn't hubris to think this, nor was it flattery for the guys to think it of him. He knew he had a gift, and he had their blessing. It was his duty to try.

Cutter nodded to himself, as he thought things through. He thought of their high-as-the-sky debate the night before, out on the slag heaps, when they'd sorted out the difference between the world's Mozarts and its Salieris. It had all seemed so easy to describe – to separate – when they were just four old buddies partying it up, when there wasn't anything serious on the line, when no one could get hurt. The difference between Jesus and Yuri Geller? Cold sober now, Cutter could see the difference plain as day. It had nothing to do with being the Son of God versus being a magician who bent spoons with his mind. It had to do with honesty, heart, and human spirit.

And the difference between Christopher Cutter and Alexander Yount?

It couldn't be will, he thought. Not will, alone. Both he and Yount had plenty of will. But he knew he had something else, that surely Yount did not have. He had the heart – not so much his heart, but everyone's. The heart of a town.

The difference between him and Yount was not in the level of skill. It went far beyond that. Cutter, and his rink, were going for this – not on the promise of money and mink coats and fireworks, not for tour buses and cheerleaders and the desire to be the best in the world just so one could say, "I'm the best in the world." None of that entered into it. They were going for this because of something inaccessible, intangible, indescribable.

They were going because of the purity of the heart.

Coach Foley's voice came to him from the stones, and the ice, and the uniform breathing of the people in the stands. *The purity of the heart is to will one thing*, Coach Foley said. What did that mean?

It meant: *will THIS!*

Cutter spread his arms out, a rallying gesture. He did not speak. He did not need to.

"All right then!" Lennox cried. "Get on the brooms, boys!"

They slid into their positions. The crowd, which had been silent as spies during the time out, now muttered and mumbled, buzzing like a giant beehive as it adjusted to the newfound energy of purpose. Every face turned to watch Cutter. The cameras all swept their gaze to him too, as he leaned over his rock and looked out to Jim Lennox, holding the target broom.

But then it was noticed that Lennox was not so much in the house, but in the boonies. He stood way off to the left edge of the sheet, where the portal lay between the Cutter stones, heralding the path to the rearmost Yount rocks. The cameras swung to record this bizarre development.

"What's Lennox doing way out there in the weeds?" said Eva.

Amy frowned. She couldn't figure it out either – not for a moment, anyway. Then she remembered her father trying something crazy, just for fun, when they were mucking around – a one-in-a-million shot that involved giving such a spin on the stone, and which involved the most expert aim and the most furious broomsmanship – an inside-of-a-circle sweeping series of blows, that would serve to take out three, four, even five stones, and still land your own rock on the button. A shot that meant the stone would go one direction, hit the opponent's stone on its inside edge, take it out, bounce to the next (heading along that inner curve), leapfrogging from stone to stone and taking each out, but staying in play itself, until it ended up going *the other way* – an impossibility, really, a shot for a billiards trickster, not a curler – even her dad had never done it, and he'd laughed at himself for trying – but he'd said, he'd said it could be done, somehow–

"Oh my God," Amy said. "Cutter's going to try going around the clock."

The term was self-explanatory for Eva and Lily and the kids, but Joanne did need a moment's explanation. Amy did the honors, and Joanne's brow darkened as it occurred to her just how tough it was.

"But that's impossible," she said, imagining a stone circling inside the row of rocks that lurked around the button. "How can they make it do that?"

"They will it," said Amy.

"Hush and pray now, girls, hush, boys," said Eva.

They all leaned forward to watch Cutter ready himself. It was taking him longer than usual to prep for the shot. Lennox stood faithful, with his broom set. There was no sound even from the Sportsco booth. Cutter took a huge breath, pulling together everything he'd ever known and learned and done that was curling. Joanne was wrong: the physics were not impossible. But it was as close to impossible as *damn* is to swearing.

Cutter threw. The rock's trajectory was wide, bizarrely wide, as if Cutter hadn't even been aiming for the house. Which, of course, he hadn't been – Lennox's target was hardly central. But now the curl started. And the men with brooms – all three of them, for Lennox had fallen in almost at once to sweep too – fell on it, as Cutter screamed instructions, his voice the bay of a demon. *HARD HARD GET ON IT, HARD!*

The bristles slapped the ice, two hard strong brooms in four hard strong arms. The curling continued, and the stone approached the house at a slowly improving angle. But it was not quite enough yet. The stone had to curl, and it had to curl soon.

HARD HARD HARD HURRY HARD…

And it curled. The rock curled so quick, it was like a top, twisting around on itself. But even so, it was touch-and-go. The curl did not seem to be quite enough. It still had to shoot through that gap, before going on to the crucial elimination of the other four stones. Its aim was infinitesimally off, not by more than a sixteenth-of-an-inch, but Cutter could see that flaw. It would take a miracle to correct it now.

HARD HARD HAAAAAAARD…

And then, the miracle. The rock's trajectory shifted, imperceptibly, but clearly, just enough to make that impossible twist. "*CLEAN!*" screamed Cutter, but it was from reflex, because it didn't matter what the stone did now. He rose to his feet as his heart sank, and the impossible stone made the impossible shot. It charged through the gate. It hit the two left stones, and pushed them out of the house; glided laterally across to the other pair, sending them away as well. Pop, pop, pop, pop. Finally, exactly as planned, the stone slid happily upsheet, and landed just off the button. The closest stone to the house, and it was a Cutter stone. Tie score. Extra ends. The game was *not* over.

Angels and trumpets and fanfare and bedlam broke loose. Cutter stood numb, the only still and silent thing in the arena. Around him, riotous joy: hats were flung and veterans blew their whistles and kids squealed and jumped on the seats. Yount's men tossed their brooms aside, their faces tight as drums, and Yount himself scowled and paced small circles.

But Cutter didn't move. Not even when his men came running up, bounding and leaping and punching the air, did Cutter move.

"Around the clock!" Greg the Sportsco Guy was bawling. "He has done it, he has gone mano-to-mano with the Juggernaut and he has tied the game! This is the greatest, I don't know what you'd call that shot, it shouldn't have happened– "

"Hang on there, Greg," said Paul the Color Guy. "Something's wrong."

Lennox had been the first to feel the change when he slid up to his skip. Neil and Eddie took a second to absorb that Cutter wasn't celebrating. Then, the crowd caught on. An awed and dreadful hush began to spread.

"What's wrong?" said Lennox, his hand on Cutter's elbow.

"It was…" Cutter could hardly speak. He gritted his teeth, and went on. "It was a burned rock. Neil. Neil, I'm sorry, you touched."

The official slid over to them. His name was Bernie Myers. Bernie Myers was well-known as a fair man – curling being a game of honor, though, he rarely had to intervene. This situation looked grim. Was the game still on, or not?"

"Something up, Chris?" he asked Cutter.

Cutter looked long and hard at Neil. Neil dropped his head. The words he had to speak came out heavy as stones themselves, but without the poetry.

"I burned the rock," he said.

Bernie's face went blank. He drew his lips in over his teeth, thoughtful for a moment. Then he covered the mouthpiece of his headset, pulling it away from his lips so he could speak to the team unheard.

"Guys, this is no time for sportsmanship," he said. "The town needs this."

A single look swept around the circle of the men of the Long Bay Rink. They were not that surprised, that even someone like Bernie would think it foolish to throw away the town's joy – and the miracle of that shot – over a technicality. Except it wasn't *just* a technicality. It was a foul; it was unfair. It was exactly what had caught them out ten years ago, and now they had the chance to make good. To clean house, Gordon had said. The call was Cutter's.

Cutter said, "It was a foul, Bernie, and I'd like you to call it."

Groans and mutters everywhere, as Bernie headed back across the sheets to the scoring table. The scoreboard flipped back, erasing the miracle. Long Bay was no longer tied. What's more, they lay with their throats exposed to the monstrous Alexander Yount.

But to everyone's surprise, Yount – as magnificent as Louis XIV – waved Bernie away. "Reset," he said, imperiously. "Let them shoot again."

"What!" said Barnhart, as Bernie pulled a shocked face and headed off to reset the stones. "Why are you giving them such a break?"

"Do you want to win that way?" said Yount. "With everyone here thinking that we won on what was just the slightest little brush of an ill-placed foot? Everyone here will go away believing that I won by a fluke. I will not have that. These people do not want the Juggernaut to succeed. I will not tarnish myself, Barnhart. I will succeed as the Juggernaut, or not at all."

Barnhart cocked a somewhat snide eyebrow at his skip. "I have seen you win on fouls before, Alex."

Yount snorted: a chuckle of agreement. "Yes, yes," he said. "But besides all that sportsmanship stuff, Barnhart, we both know the man could never make that shot *twice*."

Knowing he was about to win clean, Yount turned back to the game – to Cutter placing himself once again in the hack. Cutter seemed to be readying himself exactly the way he had before, and Lennox was once again far off to the edge of the sheet. Yount confidently folded his arms. He was looking at a dead man curling.

But then, the dead man did something unexpected. First of all, he bent over to the stone he was about to throw, and he put his cheek to it. His cheek? No, his ear. As if he were listening. A strange smile crossed his face. At the sight of that smile, Yount felt a twinge of concern. It was as if he were seeing a spell being cast. A line from *Hamlet* came to mind, about there being more things in heaven and earth…

Alexander Yount shivered.

Suddenly, Cutter rose upright. "Time out!" he called.

"This is unorthodox," said Yount, watching his rival head to the stands. What on earth was this delay? Yount would really rather have this tidied away, now that Cutter's goose was so effectively cooked. What the devil was the man doing?

The *man* was approaching a woman – a woman in the stands. A pretty woman with a child on her lap. Yount shook his head in disgust. Women just interfered with one's game and life. They were a sign of weakness.

Cutter leaned into his weakness, Amy Foley. Amy, his strength. Brandon wriggled off her lap. Cutter's face came half an inch from hers.

"They're all staring at us," she said, smiling nervously.

"Yeah, I know. I just wanted to finish that conversation we started in your truck."

"We didn't say anything," she replied softly.

He grinned. "Look into my eyes," he said, "and tell me that."

She looked. But she couldn't tell him any such thing. His grin became her grin, too.

"You're going to go for it, aren't you?" she said.

"Yeah."

Greg the Sportsco Guy, who had been struck dumb by this event (which, having nothing to do with either sports, liquor or himself, he did not fully understand) suddenly brayed his feelings into the broadcast system.

"I think bewilderment pretty well sums up the mood out there, and yours truly is fairly mystified!"

"I think the man's in love, Greg," said Paul the Color Guy.

Cutter touched the back of Amy's hand, then backed away, watching her eyes for as long as possible before turning and sliding back out onto the ice. He grabbed the Copernicus stone containing Coach Foley's ashes, and fixed himself firmly in the hack.

Lennox once again set the target broom. Cutter crouched with his stone, and his will, gathering himself like a storm cloud. This would take all the strength he had.

Suddenly, Lily Strombeck yelped. "Holy SHIT, I have to PEE," she squealed. She wasn't kidding – it was not just a matter of *having* to pee, it was a matter of she *was* peeing. Neil's kid's bony ass had plopped on her particularly hard, and a little bit of moisture spread in her panties. Damn, but her period had started on top of everything else. What rotten stinking luck, but if she didn't get up right this second, she was going to not only piss her drawers, but she'd also end with a big red blotch on the back of her pretty yellow skirt. That hadn't happened to her since high school. Great. What fun being a woman. And not even a *whole* woman – she couldn't even have a baby.

"Lily, for gosh sakes, not *now*," said Eva, but Lily ignored her and clambered her way out of the bleachers. She wasn't missing anything but heartbreak anyway. She'd seen the way Eddie had looked at her. She'd seen that he was sick and tired of nothing but failure. For the first time, she could not stand by and watch another thing collapse for him. Not when her bladder and her privates were all whining for attention.

Eddie didn't notice that his wife's seat was empty. He was too busy trying to figure out what the hell his skip was doing. Why was he taking so long? And what the hell was *this*?

For Cutter had changed the target. He was ignoring his vice-skip's broom. Lennox, suddenly catching on, stepped off the sheet, putting his broom aside. Yount – bewildered, his famous cool slipping ever-so-slightly – quizzed him.

"What is this?" Yount asked. "What *is he doing*?"

"He's making poetry, baby," Lennox replied, his heart in his throat, tears in his eyes, and his cigarette in his lips.

Cutter's heart said: *I will this.*

Cutter's arm extended behind him in a mighty, power-gathering swing, and all at once, he burst out of the hack. And, he threw. He threw the most perfect of stones. Down the sparkling ice screamed the Copernicus stone, formerly of the bottom of Trout Lake, formerly of an octet of rocks that had been instrumental to the downfall of a curling team ten years ago, now the final resting place of a man who loved curling and who loved his town and his children and his wife. That stone picked up mass, momentum and menace. Onto it fell the men with brooms, as Cutter roared an unending chant of sweeping commands. "GET ON IT!" he bellowed. "ON IT, HARD, HARD, HARD, HAAAAR-RRRRD!"

Hurryhurryhurryhurryhurry went the bristles of the brooms on the ice before the rock that was more bullet than granite sphere, that was more deadly than a missile. Not a sound rose from the audience, and the cries of Cutter and the whispering of the brooms were all the noise there was.

Not eighteen inches from the Yount wall, Cutter called off his boys: *CLEAN!*

Up went their brooms, and they leaped aside just in time to avoid touching the rocks. But they had to leap farther than that. For as they leapt, the Copernicus stone slammed into Yount's guard stone with such force that both stones exploded. The Foley rock split, and the key stone of the Yount battalion shattered into quarters as well. Shards of granite spun across the ice, sending the players scattering. All of Yount's stones, disturbed by the violence of the impact and struck by flying shards, slid away in terror, just far enough to be out of play.

Here it was: all coming down, in the end, to bits and pieces. A large chunk of granite, of Copernicus stone granite, sprung ceilingward, rising in a graceful arc from the point of impact. The crowd held its breath as it finished its ascent, and then began to plummet. Its fall seemed to take hours, but it was only a second's worth of time before it landed where it belonged. Where it had been willed to go, by powers so much more awesome than anything the Juggernaut – with all his entourage, and all his fame – could ever have conjured.

Coach Foley's stone – a mighty single piece of it – landed on the button.

It was the closest chunk of curling rock to the button. A point. They'd scored a point. Long Bay was back in the game.

But there was no cheering. Amazement smothered joy. Not a soul in the Long Bay Arena breathed. For not only had a chunk of Copernicus stone landed on the button, but so had chunks of Donald Foley. Gentle snow, barely discernible in the bright lights of the arena, fell in a fine dust around the house. Larger bits of ash – solider, weightier pieces – fell, too.

The crowd was as silent as death itself. Everyone knew the rule, now, about broken stones, after the Geriatrics had wiped the butts of their heroes just a few scant weeks ago. But no one knew what the rule was about tampered stones. Coach Foley's granite urn was not regulation. "There's Long Bay stone, and Juggernaut stone, and what looks like ashes or cinders or something… " stammered Greg the Sportsco Guy, looking to Paul for assistance. But Paul had nothing to offer. He didn't know the rule either. The officials drew their rule books from their pockets, fingers flying nervously over the pages. No one dared speak. Sportsco broadcast silence. Warm breath misted in the cold air.

Then – breaking the silence, from within its center itself – there came the sound of a broom tapping against the ice. A sound of salute. Shaken from their reverie, everyone – the crowd, the media, the men with brooms, and the officials – turned to the source of this sound, answering it like a summons.

It was coming, of all places, from Alexander Yount.

He lifted his broom off the ice and pointed it, in a gesture of great respect, toward Chris Cutter. Alexander Yount was honorably, graciously, *honestly* admitting defeat.

There was no longer any question. The score was no longer tied. The skip of the Butte Rink had conceded. It was over.

Cutter swallowed hard. He lifted his own broom in return salute. For a moment, he thought he saw Yount smile.

The Golden Broom was theirs.

17

ily sat on the pot in the Ladies' loo in the Long
Bay Arena's basement, waiting the one minute for
her test strip to produce the single lonely line that
meant she wasn't pregnant. Since she snuck out to "go,"
the stands above her had fallen completely silent. The
deathly quiet told her that poor Eddie had once again
been handed one of life's big disappointments.
Everybody up there on the stands was too disappointed,
she thought, to even groan.

Poor Eddie. And here she was about to hand him
another disappointment. Even though she'd been mis-
taken about her monthly starting (the little bit of damp
she'd felt had turned out to be from the piddle-dribble
when Neil's kid pushed her chock-full bladder into
overflow mode), something in her heart told her this
was the last time she was going to be using these stupid
sticks. Call it a premonition, call it coming to her senses.
She wasn't going to do this stupid testing anymore, not
when there was only a chance in ten thousand that she
was preggers. She had no more chance of being preg-

gers than those boys did of winning that Golden Broom. Which they hadn't done now, had they?

It was all a joke, a bad joke, this curling thing. And this trying-for-a-baby thing, too. Lily shuddered as she finished counting to sixty. She didn't like this ritual anymore. Her faith was teetering and sickly. She didn't like *that* feeling either. So she prayed a little, because not having faith and hope and stuff made her feel like she was letting God down. Which wasn't nice to poor God. He had enough things to look out for without her crabbing at Him all the time about a curling game and not being able to have a baby. She had Eddie, and things were fine, really. They had each other. So what if there wasn't going to be any baby?

Still, she couldn't help haranguing God a little bit. "It's not like I want a reward or something, God," she told Him, trying to sound polite and not naggy. "It's not like I think you're a mail-order catalogue or something. But like, I'm hanging on here for dear life, and for Eddie, and hey, God? Can I maybe have a sign or something? Just a little one?"

There wasn't so much as a beat of breath before she got her answer. As if an earthquake had struck, or an explosion in the mine, the floor beneath her sneakered feet vibrated and the walls of the stall shook. The exposed copper pipes that ran across the ceiling buzzed, and a drip of condensation fell at her feet. At the same time, a deep roar sounded, sweeping through the room in a huge wave, cresting and then subsiding into a continuous reverberating cry.

After "earthquake" and "explosion" and "flood" – all explanations that raced through her head in a mere two seconds' time – the truth hit her like a slap in the face with a wet tea towel. The noise was not of disaster. It was the sound of hundreds of people leaping to their feet, stomping their heavy boots, and it was the sound of hundreds of voices screaming with joy. It was the sound of real success. Of victory. Somehow, Eddie had won – Eddie's *team* had won – and here she was on the gosh-darned *toidy* with her knickers around her knees and a pee-stick in her fist? What the heck was she doing, still sitting here, when Eddie would be looking for her? How would he feel when he looked for his Lily-dilly, to celebrate his at-long-last *success*, and she wasn't there in the crowd?

"Holy jumping catfish, holy doodle, thundering bald-headed elephants, *shit*," she muttered, as she struggled back into her underpants and her tights and pulled down the hem of her skirt, making sure ever-so-quickly that it wasn't stuck into the waistband of her pants, which Lord knows had happened to her once, and she'd ended up walking all over the Safeway with her rump in its floral-print cotton panties hanging out like some toddler peeking out from under the living-room drapes, before Cissie Tudhope had come over and enlightened her as to why her bum had felt so cold.

"Geez Louise, Geezus Murphy, I'm coming Eddie!" she cried.

The pee-stick clattered to the ground, falling neglected from her fingers. "Aw, shit, forget it," she said, starting out of the bathroom stall, because the roar had moved into the passageway and Lily was missing the party! But the dang pee-stick had cost money and she might as well look at it, so she almost grudgingly bent down to pick it up from the not-necessarily-very-clean floor of the Long Bay Arena Ladies' privy. She moved to shove it into the metal sanitary napkin bin, useless thing that it was. She flipped up the lid to the napkin disposal. She stuffed the stick inside. The little window, with its two little lines, lay briefly revealed before she snapped the lid shut.

And snapped it right open again. *What the hell was that? TWO lines?*

She grabbed the stick from the bin, the roar in her ears no longer the sound of the crowd cheering and stomping and running up and down the halls, but the sound instead of her pulse thumping in her temples. It was the boomboomboom of a big bass drum leading a parade, it was the Hallelujah of heavenly trumpets, it was her heart waving flags of victory and throwing ticker tape from tall buildings. It was a second heartbeat in her own body, the sound of her baby, of Eddie's baby, alive and inside her, a miracle that wasn't supposed to happen.

"Lily, Lily!" As she stood shaking she heard her name called, and called again, from the hallways. Eddie's voice. Eddie was looking for her.

"Lily, honey, you in there? The girls said you was in there. Lily baby we did it, we– "

He never got to finish. Lily, who was not a small

woman, hit Eddie, who was not a big man, in a flying tackle, knocking him backward a few steps and up against the opposite wall of the corridor. People were slapping Eddie on the arm and ruffling his hair, congratulating him, but he was carried away by his wife, who squashed him up against the tiles while smothering his confused but not displeased face with kisses. He thought it was all because of the Golden Broom, and he hugged her in return, lifting her up off the ground, using his legs for leverage and balancing her on his belly.

"We did it, we did it!" Lily shouted, grinning ear-to-ear. He nodded like a trained seal, hugged her tighter, spun her around.

"Yeah!" he responded. "We won the Golden Broom!"

"No!" she declared, squeezing one hand up between their bodies, so that the stick she held by its one end was right under Eddie's nose. He looked at it, cross-eyed, bewildered.

"Look!" Lily cried, waving it under his crossed eyes like a conductor's baton. "We did it – we're pregnant!"

Eddie fell down. Lily went with him. Onto his knees, then onto his hands and knees, and then onto his face. Well-wishers lifted them back up, and propped Eddie against the wall. "I'm pregnant," he told the passers-by who shook his hand and fake-sucker-punched him in his gut. "Hey, guess what? I'm pregnant. Hey! Me! Pregnant!"

Lily slipped herself under his arm, so he could hold onto her for support as they headed back into the arena to rejoin the other men with brooms. Eddie put one hand on Lily's tummy as they walked.

"Betcha he's got a curling broom in his little hand already," he said.

"Whaddya mean, 'he'?"

So intent were they on their progress through the celebrating crowd, and so busy were they gazing into each other's eyes, that they didn't even notice the leather-jacketed, sweat-smelly Sasquatch come fighting its way through the crowd, down the corridor on its way into the arena.

Stuckmore no longer carried his battery and his television. But he still had a chunk of glass sticking out of his head, and his hands were clenched tight. He'd come a long way for this satisfying moment. He'd wait until they were all lined up – all four of them – and then, he'd let them have what he'd come here to say.

18

The crowd had to be shoveled off the ice by the officials and the Sportsco wranglers, clearing a way for the customary handshake between the teams, which had been delayed by the riot that broke out upon Long Bay's victory. Eddie, still quivering and unfocused, managed to tag himself onto the end of the team lineup in time to shake hands with the Butte Rink. The mood in the arena was too contagiously euphoric for the Butte men to be bad-humored about it losing. They knew that the formality of the concession was irrelevant. They'd lost – they'd lost absolutely. Two miraculous shots, one after the other…when there is divine intervention, one does not keep score using numbers. The winner, fair and square, was Long Bay.

The Juggernaut skip, the princely and pompous Alexander Yount, shook hands with genuine good grace, even though it did seem that his smile was something he'd had to create on short notice, owing to his inexperience at being a Good Sport, and his unfamiliarity with playing the game with honor. It had been a long time since he'd felt the honor of his own game, and he couldn't say that he disliked the feeling. It was, somehow, better than winning.

But so estranged had he been from the world, for so long, that he had lost the knack of ordinary conversation.

"I've played on a lot of ice, on this planet we call home," he announced to Cutter, accustomed to his every word being marked down for posterity, "and I don't believe I've ever seen a better shot."

"Thank you," said Cutter, shaking his hand firmly.

"It was a pleasure."

Yount wheeled and paraded off, as if he were as centerstage as he'd been at the start of the event, almost three days ago. His sparkly suit was as sparkly as ever. Alexander Yount was still, in his mind, the *man*. But he would never forget the day he lost to Long Bay. It would be, oddly enough, one of his proudest recollections.

None of the Cutter crew saw any of that, though. Lennox leaned into Cutter's ear and said, "'On this planet we call home'?"

Cutter snickered. "Like I said, the guy is creepy…*Hey!*"

He ducked back just in time to avoid being kneecapped as two red-haired midgets – Neil's kids – came charging across the ice, wearing their bedroom slippers and pyjamas, and hurled themselves at their father. Neil scooped them both up, one in each lanky arm, so that he had the younger one dangling laterally off his hip and the other clambering monkeylike onto his shoulders.

"Dad, Dad!" they crowed.

Neil snuzzled his face into the younger one's stomach and gave him a belly raspberry. When he pulled his face clear of the kid, and let the boy hang over his shoulder, he found himself face-to-face with Joanne. She landed a big cherry-flavored kiss right on his open mouth, her lip gloss as fruity as an orchard, and her cologne as fresh as cut flowers. His garden-girl.

She cocked her head in mild befuddlement, and cracked her gum. "Whatcha looking at?"

"You." He lowered his head, trying to hold onto both squirming kids while saying something totally important. Figuring out how to say it. "You…I…" he stammered.

She kissed him again, his one boy's flannelette-covered bum brushing her ear as she did so. She didn't mind. She'd always kinda liked kids. And Neil. She'd always liked Neil.

Lennox saw them kissing and stuffed his hands in his pockets. He'd stopped paying Joanne a couple of weeks back, because "fitness instructor" wasn't part of the deal they'd made, and she'd said she'd be happy to work gratis, owing that she was having such fun. That arrangement, he'd figured, had made her stop doing her rent-a-girlfriend duties in the bedroom area, if you catch the drift. Now he could see where her mind had really been at.

His male pride was hurt for about point-zero-five seconds. Joanne was actually a pretty cool dame, in her way, and she'd done a lot for the team with her jogging and her sit-ups in Eddie's Retro Gym. But the world was full of pretty cool little dames. There was that chick, Available, for instance. Neil was welcome to the settling-down routine. He mentally wished them luck and turned back to Cutter.

Cutter, though, was in full embrace with his father. "You did it, son," Gordon said, slapping Cutter on the back with both hands, despite the pain moving his arms caused in his own back. "You cleaned house."

The cameramen slowly circled father-and-son, recording it all. The Sportsco guys had come down from the broadcast booth and were now interviewing spectators, as well as trying to get comments from the men with brooms themselves. Lennox waved them off (he was not about to light up a spliff on-camera), and Neil was too busy playing helicopter with his kids and enjoying the effusive attentions of Joanne. They tried Eddie, but all he said was the incongruous, "I'm pregnant."

Paul the Sportsco Guy found Eva Foley in the crowd, and asked her how she felt.

"How do I feel?" she said. "That's my Donald out there on the button! Good God at the Saturday Races, son, how do you think I feel? I feel wonderful!"

The wranglers and the folks from the Curling Association set up the team photo quickly, herding the four men into a line, hurriedly pinning up the red-blue-and-gold silky banner reading WINNERS OF THE GOLDEN BROOM behind them, and the two-foot-high copper-and-silver trophy before them, and handing them an oversized cardboard sheet made to look like a cheque for twenty thousand dollars.

"You with the cigarette – take off your hat!" called a photographer.

"Kiss my– " Lennox began.

"The hat stays," Cutter interrupted.

They posed, and posed again, as the professionals took shot after shot, and the crowd came forward, pointing little dollar-store disposable cameras, and expensive SLRs, and old Instamatics and Polaroids. The flash of bulbs and the whirr of film advancing went on long enough that the boys began to see stars – white spots in their vision, obliterating the press of people that swarmed before them, chattering and waving cameras and tape recorders.

But through the blur of flashing lights, Jim Lennox thought he saw something – something gruesome but familiar; something he'd thought he'd done away with. He'd forgotten about it, entirely, and it couldn't (he thought) be true, that it would be popping up at this moment. How…where…*what* was *that* doing here?

"Shit," said Lennox, just as the thing spoke his name. From the back ranks of the crowd, emerging from the entrance portal into the arena and onto the ice surface, its massive arms swaying like something vaguely simian and definitely sinister. Its face was streaked with dried blood and motor oil, and its hands were clenching and unclenching, the fingers black and burned. From its forehead poked a glittering horn of glass.

"JIM LENNOX," it bayed.

"Shit shit *shit*," said Jim Lennox.

The crowd turned, and seeing what stood behind it,

split like a dried pea, forming a path as clear as a sidewalk, covered in red carpet. Like a bizarre and gigantic Bride of Sasquatch, Stuckmore strode along that red carpet, up the aisle that had formed. After a moment's respite the cameras began to whirr and click again. Some people will film anything. Even a maiming.

Jim Lennox began to stammer in terror. His friends stiffened and clenched their fists, ready to defend him, but pretty sure they'd just be smushed like ladybugs in the process. Neil cocked his fists like a boy in a private-school boxing class. Eddie thought *but I'm pregnant!* before putting up his own dukes in a considerably less formal manner. Cutter tightened his hand on his broom and turned it upside down, wondering if its butt end could be inserted somewhere debilitating before Stuckmore had a chance to snap his neck like a candy cane. Where were the cops? The last he'd seen of Frances Darte, she'd been slipping out the back way with Belle, the waitress-*cum*-bookie at the greasy spoon. They'd been holding hands. So much for police protection.

"Okay, okay," said Lennox, lifting his hands up in a futile self-defensive gesture. "Before all the violence starts up, Stuckmore, now listen big guy – the money's not a problem, because look!" He grabbed the trophy, and looked around for the cardboard prop cheque. "Look, we just got this big-ass trophy– "

Stuckmore drew a large breath, expanding his ample chest so greatly that for a moment the boys winced in preparation for the blast of fire they half-expected to pour from this dragon's mouth. But instead, Stuckmore raised one hand upward, pointing his finger to the heavens like a Bible-thumping born-again preacher, and he spoke.

"I am Lloyd Stuckmore," he said. "of the Kingston Stuckmores, formerly of the Stuckmores of Aberdeen. I can trace my family back twelve generations of curling men. We are all curling men, we Stuckmores. And we believe that Alexander Yount is the physical manifestation of everything corrupt in God's greatest game. James Lennox, on behalf of all curlers, I thank you."

He stepped forward and shook the quivering hand of Jim Lennox, who managed not to fall over from relief only because his friends were holding him up. No one on the Long Bay Rink, or in the crowd, was about to argue that they didn't actually feel quite the same way as Stuckmore did about Alexander Yount – that Yount had actually redeemed himself at the end. They figured that this fine big fella Stuckmore, from twelve generations of curling men, had a right to his own opinion about Alexander Yount, or anybody he cared to venture an opinion about. Fair was fair.

Perhaps he'd like to join them all at McTeague's for a beer?

Stuckmore allowed that he most certainly would like that, and – wrapping his arm around Jim Lennox like it was a python and Lennox was a bushbuck – he headed off to join his new friends at their local watering hole.

"O Canada," off-key but well meant, shook the rafters. The men with brooms had triumphed.

19

Lined up on the bar in McTeague's Tavern, squat and gleaming and proud of themselves, sat seven intact Copernicus stones and one injured one. The injured one – which had been brought back from the dead, reassembled through the use of that wonder substance, duct tape – was particularly proud of itself. It wore its silvery bandage like a sash of honor, and every time one of the bar's patrons came over to touch it for luck, it hummed happily beneath the stroking fingers. A very honored stone indeed.

Jim Lennox pushed his way over to the bar, shoving his friends and neighbors aside in a most friendly way, and gestured to Nug with a fistful of twenties. It hadn't taken him long to hit the bank machine to withdraw an advance on his $5,000 share of the prize money.

"I want a round of Rigor Mortis," he instructed Nug, "for all my friends!"

A cheer went up behind him.

"I don't know that drink," said Nug, somewhat embarrassed, for he knew every drink there was to know, and he didn't like being caught out.

Lennox pointed to the upper shelf, with its glittering phalanx of Scotch and vodka bottles, of rye and gin and crème-de-menthe. "See that shelf?"

Nug frowned. "Uh-huh."

Lennox slapped the twenties down on the bar. "Put all of it in a bucket."

Nug gathered up the money. "Get serious, you hoser," he said cheerfully. "I'm not pouring all that good booze in a pail." He seized the Golden Broom trophy cup, from where it sat on informal display at the far corner of the bar. "*This* is the proper receptacle for such a high-class libation, wouldn't you say, Jimbo? – Hey, Eddie – Lily! Get a friggin' room."

Lily and Eddie were collapsed upon each other, barely managing to stay standing upright. Lily, who was approaching three sheets to the wind, had her fulsome leg wrapped around Eddie's back while balancing (just barely) on the other. He had one hand on her gorgeously rounded butt and the other up the back of her sweater. They were also playing a rousing game of tonsil hockey.

"Mmmph," said Eddie, disengaging his mouth. "Hey, Lily, you know, we don't *have* to do this – we done it already– "

Lily landed both her feet on the floor and began to drag him off to the keg storage room. "Yeah, I know, but I got addicted. Come on!"

Neil and Joanne watched them go, not without some jealousy. But they weren't interested in their first time being in a storeroom among the beer kegs. That was for married folks. Picking up their flutes of champagne (that Neil does have a *touch* about these things, don't he just?), they clinked glasses and sipped, staring into each other's eyes.

"So, like I was saying," Neil said dreamily, "I always wanted to own a nursery. Be a gardener. That's all I really wanted."

"Really?" sighed Joanne. She reached out and encircled his hand in her own, while the other slipped along his thigh, up and down, in a very appealing way. "You're kidding, because I love plants and – and – you know, making things grow."

He wriggled a bit, because only a few feet away were his two boys, downing chocolate milk "shooters" with Lloyd Stuckmore. But the boys were far more interested in playing pretend drinking games with Bigfoot than they were in watching a pretty lady fondle their father's leg. Kids, eh? Go figure.

Cutter had to laugh at the kids and Stuckmore. He himself had practically wet himself when he'd heard the bugger yelling for Lennox. Now here Stuckmore was, tame as a pussycat, and all because of curling. He caught Amy's eye from across the crowd, and winked. She winked back, her arm around her mother. Eva caught the winks flying through the air, and smiled a big denture-exposing smile. She waved Cutter over to her, and over he came, greeting her with a large but tidy kiss on her softly powdered cheek.

"Good God in His high chair, Christopher, I do thank

you. And I know Donald thanks you. Although I don't know why I say that. I have no idea if dead men are grateful. But I am. So I thank you. Now you go ahead and dance with Amy, you hear? You spend way too much time curling and far too little with my daughter. Go on now. Dance."

Amy threaded her hand through Cutter's arm, and shook her head at her mother – too much time curling, indeed. As if there was such a thing. She looked up at Cutter, who was looking right back down at her, as if he'd been waiting for her to turn his way.

"Go on now, shoo," said Eva. "I'll look after Brandon for you, dear."

"This riff-raff giving you trouble?" said Gordon Cutter, who had drunk enough Rigor Mortis to cease feeling the pain of his back. He was wearing his neck brace on his head, like a cotton-and-kapok crown. "Eva, my darling, would you like to dance with the King of Curling?"

"Lord almighty, the hubris of the man!" she cackled becomingly, and folded herself into his arms. He swept her out onto the ten square feet of carpet that had been designated as the dance floor by all the revelers present. There, they cut a rug like they hadn't cut in years – and both felt something beginning, as others had come to an end.

"Look at those two," said Amy, as she led Cutter none-too-gently toward the door.

"Hey, quit pulling!" Cutter protested. "You're tugging on a Champion Athlete, you know."

"You're as bad as your dad – whine, whine, whine." She pushed the door open and they burst out into the fresh, cold, evening. The stars were out and the street was as deserted as it had been those weeks ago, when they had walked alone the day of Donald Foley's funeral, and everything had seemed so glum and hopeless. Now they knew that no matter how glum things seemed, hopeless they never were.

They walked not five paces before Amy stopped in her tracks. She turned to Cutter and peered up at him, with mock severity.

"What?!" he protested. "What did I do?"

"It's what you didn't do," she said, taking him by his lapels, and drawing herself up onto her toes. "Are you going to kiss me, or do I have to do *everything?*"

"I like a woman with initiative," he said, and drew her to him.

A big kiss, it was. Through the tinted windows of McTeague's, a denizen of locals pressed their noses against the glass and watched as Cutter and Amy wrapped themselves up in each other.

"That's more like it," said one fella to another.

"Never thought that thing he had for Julie would work out," said one of the ladies.

"Nice to have the boy back," said another.

"Oh, look," said still another citizen of Long Bay, as a golden cup was passed his way, "here's our trophy. And it's full of liquor. Ain't we just the luckiest souls on all the planet? Eh, everyone? Aren't we just the god-damndest luckiest people ever to throw a rock?"

The hurrah that rose in response to this salute so shook the room that the curling rocks on the bar all shimmied, vibrating with a barely perceptible buzz that surely to God was just because of the force of the sound waves. Surely it was just the impact of the voices and the stomping feet that caused those curling stones to dance. Surely it wasn't the spirit of Donald Foley, running through them all, and through the men with brooms, who had brought so much to the Town of Long Bay, and so much more to themselves.

EPILOGUE

On a grey afternoon, out on Trout Lake, a small metal boat puttered along peacefully. The sun was breaking through, here and there, piercing the cloud cover, which looked like it might clear away if it put some effort into moving. A solitary hawk circled and wheeled high above. It whistled sharply.

The men in the boat – five of them – looked up at the hawk and smiled. It seemed to them all that a spirit was watching, on this the final chapter of their quest.

In the boat were eight curling stones. One of them was wrapped with duct tape. The boat came to a halt, its engine grumbling as it cut out. The silence of the afternoon lay unbroken around them. The hawk cried out once more, and then disappeared. Beneath the boat lay a hundred feet of cold, pure, Canadian water.

"Gentlemen," said the tall, white-haired man, who was obviously their mentor. "Begin."

The first man stood. He bore a close resemblance to the white-haired man, except his hair was dark and his eyes were blue. He picked up the rock wrapped in silver tape, and flung it over the side. It kicked up a spray, and sank deep into the depths.

"Rest in peace, Donald," said the dark-haired man.

Then, each of them rose, careful to balance the boat.

They each took a stone, and the grey-haired man and his son took two apiece. One at a time, they threw their stones overboard. The grey-haired man nodded to himself, and sat. His son smiled grimly, with satisfaction, and sat as well. The gaunt man with the contented face wiped his hands together, and he too sat. The short man with the scruffy beard and the innocent, awestruck eyes waved goodbye to his stone, and – like the others – sat.

And the angular, suspicious-looking, cigarette-smoking, scruffy guy in the squashed hat forgot to let go of his stone's handle as he threw it, so into the lake he went. He was about fifteen feet down before it occurred to him, through the sticky haze clogging his brain, that perhaps he ought to let go.

He rose sputtering to the surface. The other men were all still sitting down. The white-haired man had started up the engine.

"Finished swimming?" Gordon Cutter asked.

"Jesus H. Christ, that's cold!" Lennox replied. "Here, assholes, help me in."

Cutter reached over the side and grabbed his friend's arm. "Come on, Jimbo," he said. "Breakfast's at Eddie's. Right, Eddie?"

"Right."

Gordon Cutter started up the engine, and off they puttered again, leaving the Copernicus stones at the bottom of Trout Lake, where their legend would grow, alongside the legend of the Men of Long Bay, the wonderful, miraculous Men With Brooms.